A Russi Rendezvous

By

A. Machin-Taylor

RB
Rossendale Books

Dr Machin-Taylor's first novel *'The Female of the Species'*
(ISBN 978-1-326-03355-2)
was published in paperback in 2014

Published by Lulu Enterprises Inc.
3101 Hillsborough Street
Suite 210
Raleigh, NC 27607-5436
United States of America

Published in paperback 2015
Category: Fiction
Copyright A. Machin-Taylor © 2015
ISBN : 978-1-326-25364-6

Dedication

To The Washington Post

Acknowledgements

Donna Moore, my editor, whose advice and encouragement has been invaluable

Jess Duncan for advice and comments

Marian and Alistair Forsythe - friends for fifty years.

The Washington Post. A great newspaper with a reputation for clear and accurate reporting. The involvement of that newspaper and its employees in this story is complete fiction.

My wife Janet for continued support and encouragement.

Prologue

Several Weeks Earlier...

Normally on a Sunday morning the top floor of MI6 would be totally deserted. However, on this day three members of staff were waiting outside the chief's office.

"What's the panic?"

"I've no idea. I got a message at half six telling me to get to the chief's office by ten o'clock. I don't have an operation running so I can't guess why he wants me."

They heard the lift doors shut on the ground floor and the buzz of the lift as it came up to the sixth floor. As the doors opened, three of their colleagues emerged.

"Morning all. What's the panic? Has Germany invaded Poland again?"

"On a Sunday? Not likely; in Germany you're not even allowed to cut the lawn on a Sunday."

The lift disappeared back to the ground floor and the assembled men waited in anticipation. When it reappeared, a tall distinguished man wearing a Guard's tie stepped out, grunted good morning and walked into the chief's office without knocking.

"Who the hell is that?"

"That's Benson; he's JIC."

"Christ, it's not Poland; the Germans have invaded *us*."

The chief's door opened and C stood and looked them over. Having determined that all his section heads had arrived, he said, "Sorry to get you out of bed on a Sunday morning." He turned, walked back into his office and took his seat at the head of table, gesturing them all to sit.

"At six this morning I received information that the Russians have arrested Penkovsky and his handler, Greville Wynne." C paused as a collective sharp intake of breath went around the room. "As some of you know, Penkovsky was one of our best sources in Moscow; over the last two years his material has been invaluable. There are bound to be some serious repercussions."

"Do we know how the Reds got on to them?"

"We know next to nothing at this stage. Very few people here knew their identities; maybe one or both of them have been careless."

"Who is Wynne? Which section is he in? I don't think I've come across him before."

C frowned. "He's not a member of *any* section. He used to work for us many years ago but left the service and has an engineering business now. When we found out that he was paying regular visits to Moscow on business, we invited him back to be a courier. After that he became Penkovsky's handler."

"Well, if he's a freelance, is he deniable?"

"That depends. If they know what Penkovsky has been supplying, it will be obvious that he's an important member of our service. I don't think Wynne's deniable. My feeling is, we should admit that he was a straight business man who we asked to deliver the odd message for us."

"OK, but how does this affect my operations in South America?"

C narrowed his eyes and gave a slow nod. "It will affect us all. We all use couriers; we need to ensure that they are properly trained. One sloppy mistake and we lose a courier and a valuable intelligence asset. We also need to ensure that knowledge of the names of couriers is limited only to those who need to know."

Benson chipped in. "This will be general knowledge within a few days. The Reds will play it as the UK abusing the friendship and trust of Russia, and that it will harm Anglo-Russian trade. Then our left wing MPs and newspapers will accuse us of incompetence and right wing plots to destabilise Anglo-Russian friendship."

"So what's new?"

C frowned at the man who had spoken. "What's new is that I agree with everything Sir Oliver has just said. I don't want any more bad press until this has died down. Also, Penkovsky was our prize asset as far as our Washington cousins are concerned. I don't want this to damage that relationship, so if they ask us for info or help do your best for them."

He stood up. They had obviously been dismissed and left the office in a sombre mood. They knew that it was the firing squad for Penkovsky and, probably, Wynne as well.

****

A few weeks later, reassembled at the same table for their monthly full meeting - which also included the deputy section heads and Sir Robert Holdsworth sitting in for Oliver Benson of the JIC - they looked at C expectantly.

"Now, gentlemen, we come to Item Five on the agenda: the aftermath of the Penkovsky affair. We have received information that the Reds got on to them from information they received from the West. Therefore, I have been looking at the way we use couriers to service our overseas agents. I find that it's a fairly open secret as to who does what - to the extent that they have informal meetings in the Travellers Club." He looked over his glasses at the assembled group. "I believe there is even a group who meet regularly and who call themselves the *China Spy Club*. This has to stop. Immediately!" He paused and looked at each of them in turn. "You are to weed out any that you find have made themselves public knowledge or that have been in the role for more than five years. In addition, we have had three resignations after the fallout from the trial of Greville Wynne. The upshot is that we need some new couriers. These are to be recruited with the greatest discretion, and their identity is to be known only to their handler and his section head. Any training sessions will be individual and not in groups. No team building exercises, no contacts with other agents. And *definitely* no informal drinking sessions in the Travellers."

One of the section heads spoke up. "That's all going to be easier said than done; it's not easy to find good reliable people who go to the East on a regular basis."

C nodded. "I appreciate that. But it's a lot easier than finding a treasure like Penkovsky. If we don't have a safe communication system, we shut down the agent until we do."

There was a general murmuring and talking other than through the chair. C rapped the table. "Right, item six on the agenda is Central Asia. Our sources in the region are becoming somewhat dated."

"Aren't we all?" As the meeting ended, C looked at the silver haired man sitting at the end of the table.

"John, can you hang on for a minute." After the others had left the room and the door closed, he said, "You've lost two couriers to Eastern Europe; we need to replace them as quickly as possible. The main problem is your man Todorov; the information he's been providing is priceless. I get a call from our friends in the Ministry of Aviation every week, asking if anything new has arrived."

The head of the East Europe section squirmed, frowned, but didn't reply.

"We need to get back to Todorov fast; do you have anyone in mind?"

"To be truthful C, we don't. We are casting our net far and wide to find someone."

Chapter 1

"David, your apparatus is making a funny noise."

"So what? It's giving funny results."

"Well, the needle's on red!"

"It doesn't matter if it's just over."

"It's a lot over; it might blow up."

"Leave it. If it blows up I'll go climbing for a week."

The fly on the ceiling looked down on a laboratory full of complicated equipment. The sign on the door said: *Min. of Aviation Rocket Materials Laboratory*. Inside, three young men were working. One was doing the crossword in the newspaper, another was writing a report on which his pen hadn't moved for twenty minutes. The third - David Hopkins - sat at his desk, one eye on the report that he was trying to read and the other on his apparatus to make sure it was running OK. Once in a while, he would get up and walk across the lab to take readings from one of the instruments.

They were supposed to be developing novel materials for use in rockets and rocket motors, which had sounded exciting when they started, but their enthusiasm had soon deteriorated to the usual Ministry of Aviation boredom level.

To most people, rockets would appear to be an exciting field of research, but the fact that they had still never seen a rocket - even after two years of work - plus the lack of urgency, drive and ambition in the laboratory was demotivating. Most of Monday was taken up with the solution to the Sunday Times brainteaser. The Times crossword took an hour or so most days and the early part of each afternoon was spent debating the problems that arose in the lunchtime bridge game. David spent the remainder of his working day gazing through the window, thinking that it was time that he looked for a new stimulus elsewhere.

And now, the time had come. He'd seen an advert in one of the scientific journals; an American multinational wanted a chemist with biological knowledge to work with a new research group based in London. For David, the advantage of his joint honours degree was that, like a chameleon, he could change his colour and become a chemist with a strong background in biology.

After two interviews he was offered the job and had the daunting task of finding somewhere to live in London. He was talking mainly to himself when he said, "I'm wondering what to do about finding accommodation." His mother interrupted him, "Miss Robson has a son, Giles Morris, who lives in London. He's said he'll help you to find a place to live."

He asked her, "How can a Miss Robson have a son called Morris?"

"Miss Robson used to be a professional foster mother. She's spent all her life raising foster children who were either orphans with wealthy relatives or illegitimate children of wealthy parents. Giles was one of those children."

Apparently, Giles had been educated at Dartmouth Naval College and then had served as an officer in the Royal Navy for quite a number of years. After leaving the Navy, he had developed a career in business in the City. Although his Miss Robson lived in Cheshire and he was now in London, he had continued to have a caring relationship with his elderly foster mother.

When the day came to leave for London, David thought that it was like going up to university for the first time, not really knowing what to expect. All he took with him was a small

13

suitcase with sufficient clothes to last a week while he found somewhere to live, his plan being that - once settled - he would drive down with all his stuff in his car. In his wallet was a business card for Giles Morris, with his home address and phone number:

24 Bentinck Mansions, Bentinck Terrace, Westminster.
Home Tate 7111   Office Monarch 8125

David had booked into a relatively cheap commercial hotel in Kensington and, once in his room, he called Giles at his office. A rather cultured voice answered the phone. "Hello David, I've been looking forward to hearing from you. I suggest that you come over here about half nine tomorrow morning;   I've arranged to take the day off and will spend some time with you looking at available flats that are being offered by the various letting agents."

The following morning, David took the tube to Victoria and - using the A to Z - found Bentinck Terrace, which was quite close to the Westminster Cathedral. Bentinck Mansions were more or less the whole of one side of the street, a very impressive row of buildings some six storeys high. David found number twenty-four and went inside. He was surprised to be met by a porter. "I'm looking for Giles Morris but he didn't give me his flat number."

"If you take the lift to the fourth floor, Mr Morris will meet you there, sir."

The lift was a rather antiquated affair with a sliding grille door with brass hinges and handles. David pressed the little white button marked 4 and the lift slowly and sedately rose with no noise, apart from a *clank* when it reached the fourth floor. Waiting by the lift was a very smart man. Not old, David guessed his age to be between thirty-five and forty.

14

"I'm Giles. It's a pleasure to meet you at last. Miss Robson has often talked about you." Giles led the way and showed David into his flat. In reality it was an enormous apartment, beautifully decorated with what looked like antique furniture, together with heavy silk drapes and two large oil paintings on the wall. David's curiosity must have been obvious.

Giles explained, "The whole apartment has six bedrooms, with four on the floor above. It's owned by Colonel Collis. I have a part of the apartment comprising two bedrooms and a sitting room as a separate flat. We share the entrance hall and this drawing room."

"I've spoken to a few agents and have obtained a list of available flats from two of them." They went through the list, looking at the rents compared to David's budget and their proximity to where his new job was based. As his new employer was in west London, it made sense to think of flats in that area. They were cheaper than those in central London and it would be much easier to find parking for his car.

They went to the first flat agency and arranged to look at some of the more central apartments before lunch and then others further west after lunch. The flats that David could afford in inner London were terribly small and not that nice, and the agency explained that all the nice flats were much larger and usually taken by four to six people sharing. "You know David, I think that you are much more likely to get something suitable further west."

Over lunch, Giles asked all sorts of questions about what David had been doing at the Ministry of Aviation and what was he going to be doing in his new job. It was rather embarrassing, in that all David knew was that the company was setting up a new research facility which would cover technical problems arising from anywhere in Europe. "The division I'll be working for is called D&A Products; it sells chemicals and polymers that are used in food, food packaging and food processing. I have no idea of what problems might arise. It's going to be a very different world from the rockets of the Ministry of Aviation."

After lunch David went alone to look at three flats in West London. The first was cheap but rather dingy but the second seemed perfect. It was in a Victorian house in a quiet avenue in Ealing. The flat was a very large bed-sit with a double bed, a dining kitchen and bathroom. There was easy on-street parking available and it was close to the North Circular road, which would make it easier to drive to the office and not far to get to the M1, to drive north to Cheshire. It had the added bonus that the owners of the house were a young couple with similar interests to David; they needed to let the flat to help pay their mortgage on the house.

That evening, David rang Giles, "I've found a really comfortable place in Ealing and not that far from my new office. So now I'm looking forward to starting my new job on the first of the month, which is the day after tomorrow."

Giles replied, "That is good news, why don't we have dinner together on the evening of the first? You'll then be able to tell me about your new office and more about the company and we can talk about what the job involves."

So on Wednesday evening David was once more in Bentinck Mansions. On the second visit he had more confidence to look around and absorb his surroundings. He was amazed that anyone could live in such opulence, particularly in London. Before going out to the restaurant, Giles poured out two whisky and sodas for them. David had never seen such large whisky glasses and so much whisky in each. As he sat there sipping his drink, his eyes were scanning the large room. One cabinet in particular caught his attention. It contained a display of around thirty or forty carved ivories. Giles noticed his interest and walked over to the case. "If you're interested, come and have a close look; the workmanship is stunning."

"I've never seen so many altogether before. My grandfather had two ivories. One of them was a ball inside a ball with another inside that. When I was little I was fascinated to think how such a thing could have been made."

Giles went on to explain, "In the latter part of the nineteenth century and up to the start of the war in 1939, the Collis Family had business interests in Hong Kong and Macau. As a result, they had accumulated the collection over many years at their house in Hong Kong and then brought it back to the UK."

Over dinner Giles told David that his foster mother had asked him to help David to settle in London. "I'm very fond of her but I don't get to see her as often as I would like. Your mother has really helped her over the years, you know, so I'm delighted to be able to help now."

"Actually, I *didn't* know. My mother doesn't really talk about that."

Giles nodded. "Yes, especially since she's got older. I'm very grateful to your mother for her kindness."

They talked about life in general, about his ambitions and about his family, but whenever David asked Giles similar questions, he only received vague answers.

"How did you come to meet Colonel Collis? Were you related?"

"No. My father had known the Collis family for many years."

"And what about your father? What was he--?"

"I lost my father many years ago. So, David, what are you doing on Saturday? I'm going to a party at a house in Wimpole Street and you would be very welcome to come along; they are always keen to meet new faces".

David noted the abrupt change of subject but went with it. "I'll look forward to that; I don't know anyone in London as yet."

As the time was getting on for ten o'clock and David had to get to Ealing Common tube station, they finished the meal, paid the bill and walked to the tube station. "So, I'll see you about seven o'clock on Saturday, then."

David nodded. "I've just thought; I'll have run out of shirts by then. Is it a posh party? I'll need to buy a new one."

Giles laughed. "Don't worry, it's not that posh."

When David started his new job it seemed to be much more interesting than had been described to him at the interview. The new research group was staffed entirely by newcomers; he was the last and the youngest of seven senior managers, all of whom had started in the last three months. Apart from the two senior managers from the USA, they were all learning the business. It became obvious, though it hadn't been mentioned at the interview, that David's experience in translating German and French scientific papers had been regarded as significant. They had, apparently, assumed that he had good spoken languages because it was explained that he would be visiting customers with technical problems anywhere in Europe. "All my experience has been in translating scientific German which is very much easier than speaking it."

"Well you'll have to get some tuition or practice to improve your spoken German."

The following Saturday, despite Giles' reassurance, he bought a couple of new shirts and got ready for the party in Wimpole

Street. As Giles and he were in the cab heading to the party, David realised that he didn't know anything about whose party they were going to.

Giles filled him in, "Our host tonight is Arthur Whiting-Prior. His family own an estate and a paint factory in Essex. Arthur is a lovely person but a bit of a waste of space: affable, but doesn't do very much."

When they arrived, David was introduced to lots of people whose names he promptly forgot, but everyone was very welcoming. The young and not so young ladies all wanted to chat to him. He didn't think they had met many northerners before. He didn't know if it was because of his accent, or their curiosity at meeting a new face in the party. He could understand why they were asking questions about him and how long had he known Giles, but it seemed strange that they were just as curious about Giles.

"What does Giles do for a living?"

All David could say was that he knew that Giles had been in the Royal Navy for some time and now had an import business. "How long have you known Giles?"

The young woman he was speaking to shrugged and looked at her friend. "I don't know...a few years, I suppose."

"Oh, I see." David was taken aback. "I thought you knew him well?"

Another young woman laughed "Oh, we all know Giles, but nobody really *knows* him."

"How long have *you* known Giles, David?"

"Not long. His mother and mine are neighbours and good friends in Cheshire."

Once they knew he was from Cheshire, they asked if he hunted and knew so-and-so; it seemed that although everyone appeared to be a Londoner they knew a lot about Cheshire and its people. Some couldn't believe that he had his own horse but didn't hunt. All in all, they were very friendly and welcoming to the new boy from the north.

David eventually took the half past eleven tube to Ealing Common, wondering if it was the last tube. He made a mental note to find out: if he was to party in London he needed to know when the tubes stopped running at night.

****

The first few weeks in his new job flew by; it was a hectic life for everyone in the group. They were establishing new departments, hiring people, writing up procedures; in effect planning how the group would be run in the future. Because his job was very specific, it did not need a large group. However, he had to find a secretary and an assistant who would be coordinating his work with other departments when he was away from the office. Because at the beginning David's job was straightforward, he became a general support for the other departmental managers. This was a big advantage to him because he became familiar with the work and the people in the other groups as well as his own. It became apparent that, in some ways, his job was more responsible than he had originally thought: he was to be the main technical interface between the various sales groups and their customers anywhere in Europe.

Although nobody raised the subject, David was worried that his linguistic abilities would be inadequate. Since French was the better of his two foreign languages, he started to take Le Monde as his only newspaper and listen to Radio Allouis when he was at home in the flat. It was his spoken German that would let him down, he felt; so he persuaded his boss to pay for him to go on a month's intensive German course at the Berlitz School.

The following Saturday, Giles and he were having dinner at Carlo's in the Brompton Road, and he told Giles that he would be away for a month at Berlitz to brush up his spoken German. Giles immediately came out with a torrent of German, then, in English, said, "We will start the tuition as from now."

David was taken aback. "I never knew you were a linguist. How did your German become so fluent?"

Giles hesitated a moment. "It's one of my better foreign languages."

"But how come you speak it so well?"

"Oh, I speak other languages, too. I've picked up some Japanese because of our business interests in the Far East, but by far my most fluent language is Russian."

"Really?"

"Yes. When I was in the Navy we were encouraged to learn Russian; it was then that I discovered my flair for languages. It was strange really, because I wasn't very good at Latin at school."

"I've never really known exactly what you do, Giles. What *does* your business involve?"

Giles waved his hand, vaguely. "Oh, you know: import-export."

David asked, "Do you work for the Collis Bank?"

"No I don't work *for* them, I work *with* them. They provide finance for the import business. In other words, they provide the guarantees to the overseas suppliers until I get paid by the UK customers. Also, Collis have overseas customers who would like to export their products to the UK. I help to find the UK buyers."

It became apparent that David's assumption that Giles' business was London based was not strictly accurate; Giles told him that he spent at least six months every year travelling

21

overseas. When David asked him which countries he visited, he was - once again - rather vague.

"My last trip was to Japan, but on the way back I stopped off in Poland; some of the Japanese office equipment was destined for Polish customers."

It seemed to David a rather strange business to be in. David thought of business as where a company made something and then sold it to its customers, whereas Giles seemed to be living by his wits, wheeling and dealing with different customers in different countries every month. He left that evening determined to find out more about Giles and his mysterious import-export business.

Chapter 2

David arrived at the Berlitz language school in Holborn with absolutely no idea of what to expect. He had been instructed that the German course would start at nine o'clock prompt and that he should report to reception on arrival. The first day would finish at six. On the Tuesday they were to report to Holborn with their luggage - sufficient for the first two weeks of the residential course - which was to be held at Wakeham Hall near Berkhamsted.

On arrival, David checked in at reception, where he was surprised that the receptionist couldn't speak English. His very rusty schoolboy German was just about sufficient to make sure that he was in the right place at the right time. There were a few others hanging around in reception, all looking equally confused. When another two had arrived, they learned that altogether there were twelve of them on the four week course.

They were then herded into a meeting room and were asked to introduce themselves and state what level they were at with their knowledge of German. Or, at least, that was what David *thought* the instructor had said. He was already confused because there were twelve of them on the course but only ten in the room. As they went round the table – six men and four women – they learned that three had A level German but had not used it for years, three had O level German, one was born in France but had gone to school in Germany until she was ten, and one man David didn't understand at all. He had a very strange accent and David gathered that he was originally from somewhere overseas.

When it came to his turn, David explained – in a mix of German and English – that he hadn't studied German at school but that he had had a German governess while his parents were abroad and that she had started teaching him to speak German. "She was a German lady from Bremen who had married an English soldier called Oakley, who now works for my father. When my parents returned, my father wanted me to continue learning German, so I would be sent to visit Mrs Oakley every weekend and spend a day with her speaking German." David went on to explain that he had continued to use his knowledge of German after he had graduated, by translating and abstracting scientific papers from French and German for the Journal of Physics. "It was a nice side line; I got ten shillings for a German paper and seven shilling and sixpence for a French paper. It meant, however, that while my vocabulary and written German aren't bad – my spoken German is rubbish."

The first morning at the school was hell, with no coffee break. It was German grammar all morning, with a recommendation that they should try to speak German over lunch.

When they went into the canteen for the buffet lunch, eight of them sat together at one table so David had to sit by himself. The last to come in was a young lady with long dark hair. He hadn't really noticed her before, because she had sat behind him in the classroom. She came and sat opposite him at the table, then leaned forward and said in a quiet voice, *"Je m'appelle Nicole. Parlez-vous Francais?"* David was taken aback. He hadn't realised that she was French; when speaking German her pronunciation had been as bad as his. She continued. "They said we are not allowed to speak English. They didn't say anything about our speaking French." She smiled, conspiratorially.

They continued chatting in French over lunch. No instructors were in the room and the others were all making so much noise trying to converse in German that no one realised. Over lunch, Nicole and he came to an agreement: when they wanted a break from German, she would speak to him in English and he would speak to her in French. That was a good deal for both of them; since he needed to improve his spoken French and Nicole wanted to improve her English. She told him that she had joined a major Swiss pharmaceutical company based in Basle. In her job she needed to speak to customers in French or English but had to use German when talking to her employers.

The following morning the ten of them all gathered in reception, with their collection of rucksacks and suitcases. The one or two that had been smartly dressed on the first day were today, as scruffy as the rest. At half past nine a minibus arrived to take them to Berkhamsted.

They found Wakeham Hall, which was to be their home for the next two weeks, to be a large redbrick Victorian house set back in its own grounds. They were shown to their rooms and asked to be back downstairs for coffee at 11a.m. The accommodation was basic but comfortable. David noted that the only magazines in the room were German and that the radio would only tune to a German station. He had no doubt that, if he were to use the telephone in the room, it would only connect to a German speaking operator.

The first three days were torture for all of them. For David, it was harder than anything that he ever had to do at university, and everyone was complaining about a continual headache. After classes finished at five o'clock they were supposed to have an hour's relaxation before dinner but most went straight to their room and fell asleep. The tedium was relieved on the

25

Thursday morning by the arrival of the final two students; both middle aged ladies, both civil servants. One worked in London; the other was based in Cheltenham. It appeared that they were both modern language graduates who had studied German at university but who wished to refresh their spoken German.

As the course progressed, the group started to fragment into smaller social units. It was assumed that, as Nicole and David spent a lot of time together, they were starting a relationship. Nicole and he agreed that this was a good idea because it meant that they were left alone to have their escape from German into French without anyone realising what they were really up to. The added benefit for David was that he was improving his spoken French free of charge and that, when he ran into difficulties in German he started to think in French. As for Nicole, her English was very good - apart from a lovely French accent - and she was quite happy to escape from German into French.

In this way, the first three weeks passed quickly and there was no doubt that everyone's spoken German had made a dramatic improvement, with the debates and discussions becoming quite lively. However, going into the last week there was a feeling that the end couldn't come soon enough, to the extent that one or two of the group started to skip a lesson or not bother completing the written assignments. They had been told that at the end they would have an oral examination and that a pass would earn them a diploma. Most of the students had disclosed that a pass or a diploma wouldn't give them a promotion or an increase in salary so they weren't that bothered about the diploma. That included Nicole and David, who both had good jobs and saw no great benefit in having a diploma to put on the office wall. One night they walked into the village and spent the evening chatting about themselves and their families.

Nicole told him, "My full name is Nicole Marie Derencourt and I grew up in Bordeaux."

"Do you still live there?"

"No. My parents do but after leaving the Sorbonne, I stayed in Paris. What about you, David?"

"My mother's family were originally from Normandy and had been called de Meschines but at some point in time they dropped the de."

They discussed their ambitions and the course, and talked about their new jobs and their new lives. Their conversation flowed freely, mostly in German, but switching to French, when either of them got into difficulties.

"I suppose it proves that this course has been successful, even though we've slightly gone our own way."

David smiled. "I'm glad we did. You've been an additional bonus, Nicole. I hope we can keep in touch afterwards?"

****

On the penultimate day each member of the group had their individual oral examinations comprising an hour of conversation, after which each of them was given a different four or five page document which they had to read for twenty minutes and then discuss for an hour with one of the examiners. Both Nicole and David received their diplomas, but only four of the others passed as well as them. David whispered to Nicole, "Do you think that our French interludes removed some of the stress created by the intensity of the course, and therefore enabled our brains to function better?"

Nicole grinned at him. "No, the real reason is clear: it's because we are both extremely talented." They both struggled

27

to hold back their giggles as the serious ceremony of handing over the diplomas continued.

As the group said their goodbyes and exchanged addresses and telephone numbers, promising to keep in touch, David knew that the only address and contact number he would keep would be Nicole's. She gave him both the address of her parents in Bordeaux and her apartment in Basle, promising that she would keep in touch.

When David got back to his flat in Ealing he tossed his case into the corner and lay on the bed. It was strange. His mind was confused. On the bookshelf all his books had titles in English but his brain was thinking, in German, that he was French, and that he should go to Basle to marry Nicole. He fell asleep and awoke, still fully dressed, eight hours later and very hungry. He looked at the clock and realised that, although it was half past ten, the Chinese takeaway at the bottom of the road would still be open. As he tucked into Satay chicken and egg fried rice, he remembered that the following Monday he would be back at work, speaking English and wondering how he was going to keep his German and French up to their current high standard.

Chapter 3

O nce back at his desk David was pleasantly surprised that his colleagues had rallied around while he was away and taken care of most of his routine workload. All that remained were a few things that only he could handle; one of these concerned the proposed food packaging regulations in Poland. The D&A Sales office had been informed that the Polish equivalent to the UK Ministry of Health required them to carry out some specific analytical work on food packaging films. As he walked into his boss's office, he could hear the speaker phone. "They want to determine if any chemicals in the films are being extracted into the food." His boss looked at him, "I suggest that you get over to Warsaw to find out exactly what they want. We don't want any arguments about the validity of the results afterwards. There isn't a panic, but I would like to get it sorted within the next three or four weeks."

Giles had told David about his recent trip to Warsaw, so David called him to get advice on where to stay, what it was like travelling behind the Iron Curtain, and to find out how he obtained the necessary visa. When he called Giles' office he was out, but David was told that they could get a message to him so that he could call him back when he returned. Just after lunch he received a call from Giles' office to say that he would call him at home after six o'clock.

David hadn't been in for more than a few minutes when the phone rang.

"Hello, David!"

"Giles, hello. You're sounding very cheery."

"I am, indeed. Just concluded a business deal I've been working on for six months."

"Great. What sort of deal was that?"

"A very satisfactory one. Very satisfactory, indeed."

Typical Giles. David could tell that was all the information that he was going to get.

When David told Giles about the pending trip to Warsaw he suggested that they had dinner together the following night, which seemed like a good idea. David had so much to tell him about the Berlitz course and he knew that Giles usually had some interesting stories of his own.

When he arrived at Bentinck Mansions, Giles was waiting for him in the hall; apparently Colonel Collis had some important visitors in the drawing room. David could hear muffled voices through the closed door, as Giles put on his coat.

They went out and walked past the cathedral into Victoria. Giles told David that they were going to his favourite Italian restaurant. As they talked, David lost all sense of direction other than that they were somewhere in Victoria. When they reached the restaurant they ordered a carafe of Chianti while they browsed the menu. After a brief discussion on what were their favourites, they ordered and then Giles asked for a full report on how the job was going. Did it live up to David's expectations? What were the other people like? Did he get on with them? Then, when it appeared that he had satisfied his curiosity about the job, he switched to asking how David had got on at the Berlitz School. Giles raised his glass and looked at the wine inside. "And this bit you have to tell me in German." He switched to the language himself, flawlessly. "What are the merits of the total immersion method of teaching a language? Did it work for you?"

David found the transition to German was almost natural now. "My feelings are that it's great, but only for people who have the mental capacity to handle such a concentrated and demanding course."

"And what about the rest of your class? Did they have that mental capacity?"

David shrugged. "Some were OK, but others lost it, even though they had done German at school."

"And whereabouts are you going to in Warsaw?"

"Apart from it being at the Ministry of Health, I have no idea of the address. I'm being met at the hotel by someone from the Ministry."

Giles nodded. "It's bound to be in the centre somewhere, probably together with all the other government buildings." When David asked about hotels, Giles told him that, whilst he could recommend some, the usual procedure was that the Ministry would make the hotel booking for him.

"It's better that way because government departments have the first call on all the best hotels."

"Ah, OK. I didn't realise that. At least I know they'll put me up in a good hotel!"

"Indeed." They stood up to get their coats and Giles continued. "Actually, I was wondering if you could do me a small favour."

"Of course; if I can. You've been so helpful to me that I would be glad to repay the favour."

Giles shrugged into his coat and brushed some invisible dust off the shoulder. "It's not a big thing. Once you know the dates of your trip, could you give me a call? I may have a Polish import licence that needs to go to an office in Warsaw. It would be helpful if you could take it with you and mail it when you get to Warsaw."

"Of course. Happy to help. I'll give you a ring once I know the dates."

"Excellent. Thank you. Oh, and I'll lend you a good street map of Warsaw that has the street names in both Polish and English."

A week later it was all fixed. David was flying out to Warsaw on the 10 a.m. BEA flight from Heathrow on Monday the twenty-eighth, his meeting at the Ministry was at 9 a.m. on the thirtieth and his return flight departed Warsaw 4 p.m. on the thirty-first. The Ministry had booked him into the Excelsis Hotel and a Mr Jozef Wozniak would meet him at the reception desk at 08.45 on the thirtieth. That evening, David called Giles at home and gave him the details of his trip.

"They seem to have everything timed to perfection. I'm sure if I asked, they'd even tell me the exact times I need to clean my teeth."

Giles laughed. "I don't doubt it. Anyway, that will fit in well."

"Great."

"Now, why don't we have dinner together on either the twenty-sixth or twenty-seventh and I'll give you an envelope with the forms in and the directions of where to meet my friend Kamil, so that you can give him the envelope."

"Oh. I thought that all I had to do was to post the envelope once I got to Warsaw?"

"It just so happens that Kamil lives close by your hotel. It will be easier for him to pick them up, rather than for you to go to all the bother of getting Polish stamps and putting the envelope in the mail."

"Ah, I see. OK, that seems a better plan."

As the twenty-sixth was a Friday Giles booked a table for the two of them in Manzi's fish restaurant in Soho. Until then, David had never realised that there was a famous fish restaurant in London. Over dinner, Giles explained that the plans had changed a little bit.

"Not far from the hotel you'll find Okopowa St." He handed David a map. "See? I've marked it here. Halfway along is the old Jewish cemetery, Cmentarz Zydowski. It's a beautiful, quiet oasis in the middle of Warsaw. I thought you might like to see it. You'll find the big main gate, here." He pointed the location out on the map. "Now, the gate might be locked." David looked at him, puzzled. "Oh, don't worry; it's not illegal to go there, but they don't exactly encourage Jewish people to go looking for their ancestors. If it's locked continue round to the other side of the cemetery, Mlynarska St. Here." He tapped the map again. "You'll find the old Christian cemetery. Go through the gate and head north and you'll come to a huge mausoleum like the front of a chapel, built in brick and stone with a cross on top; that's the tomb of Archdeacon Hermana Junga."

"Hang on, hang on. I think I need to write this down."

"Not at all, it's quite straightforward. And, remember, this is just in case the gate's locked. Round the back of the tomb there's a hole in the wall to get into the old Jewish cemetery. Head towards the main gate and you'll see a large drinking fountain with four lion heads on it. If the lion head on the north side has a chalk circle on it, it means that Kamil has a packet for you to bring back to me. Go back towards the gap in the wall, walk in about fifty metres to where there is a cross path and turn right. That's East. After two hundred metres or so, you'll come to an area of really old graves; one of these is quite conspicuous; the tomb has three large black boulders one on top

33

of the other. That one's the tomb of Henryk Wohl. Between the middle boulder and the top one is a deep crevice in which you will find the packet for me from Kamil if there is one. Take that and leave the envelope for Kamil in the crevice. It's quite dry and rainproof; just push it in so that it can't be easily seen."

"Bloody hell, Giles, I thought that you just wanted it posted. I don't have that much spare time and I wanted to see something of Warsaw. Can't I just nip round to Kamil's and post it through his door if he lives so close to my hotel?"

Giles shrugged. "I know, I know. Some sort of trouble with his wife. Means he's not using his apartment at the moment. I was hoping he'd be able to just come to your hotel, but he's fully booked, so this was the best we could come up with at short notice. And don't worry, the cemetery is right in the middle of a lovely part of the city and it's not a large place; it will take you no more than twenty-five minutes, walking slowly. I thought we'd choose somewhere which meant you get to do a little bit of sightseeing that visitors don't normally get to see. Don't forget to take a camera; parts of Warsaw weren't damaged during the war and some parts have been restored to their former beauty."

****

David spent a fairly lazy weekend, during which he checked his tickets and passport about five times. It was all new to him - he hadn't travelled abroad that much - and it was his first time behind the Iron Curtain. His colleague, Willi, who was based in Copenhagen, had given him some ideas of what to expect. Willi was responsible for the company's sales in the Eastern bloc countries and his summary was illuminating. "They're all disorganised and inefficient; always more concerned about watching their back than getting anything done. Make sure they

34

know you're English and not American and don't speak German unless you have to. In fact, it's probably better not to admit to speaking it at all. Don't change much currency into Zlotys; all they want are dollars or Sterling."

With that advice ringing in his ears, David boarded the BEA Trident flying to Warsaw. He had thought that, with the present political East-West climate, there would only be a few on the flight, whereas to his surprise it was nearly full. The chap in the next seat asked if this was his first trip to Warsaw. "Whatever you do, don't take a cab from the airport; they'll rip you off. Take the city centre bus; it's only a dollar. If you need a cab from the bus station they're more or less honest."

David got his street map out of his briefcase and his fellow passenger showed him where the Excelsis was. "It's easy walking distance unless you have a heavy case; no more than seven hundred metres or so from the bus station."

David followed the man's instructions and arrived at his hotel without either being ripped off or getting lost. When he checked into the hotel, he found it to be clean, but somewhat sparsely furnished compared to a similar city centre hotel in London. His room, likewise, was spotlessly clean but with only the essential furniture: a bed, one chest of drawers and a small cupboard that he supposed was meant to be a wardrobe. The room was on the fifth floor facing north. He had a look at the street map and worked out that he could see Okopowa St, which didn't look that far away. David had a look around on the ground floor and found the dining room. The menu on the wall was in Polish and English. It looked OK so he decided to eat in the hotel, rather than wander around Warsaw looking for somewhere else to eat.

After lunch, he set off to explore the city centre, taking his camera with him. It was only then that he realised what a pounding Warsaw had received during the war. Very few buildings had escaped unscathed; in the twenty years since the end of the war those which had been badly damaged had been demolished, but the sites had then been left untouched. There were some new buildings and some in the process of being repaired, but it was obvious that Warsaw had a long way to go to regain its pre-war glory.

David returned to the hotel and found a week old copy of the English version of Iszvestia, which kept him amused until it was time for dinner. The best thing that could be said about the meal was that it was wholesome, though the bowl of cherries and cream that he had for dessert was delicious. After dinner he sat at the bar. Although it stocked Scotch whisky, bourbon, London Gin and a French brandy, the prices in dollars were eye watering. A shot of whisky was four times the price it would be in a London bar. Polish vodka was cheap but he had heard about that and wasn't prepared to take the risk, so he settled for a Polish beer.

David had noticed that there were two rather beautiful young ladies - he guessed them to be about twenty or twenty-one years old - sitting at a table in the bar. One got up to leave, saying something in Polish to the barman, who smiled as she walked out. The other one - a drop dead gorgeous blonde - came and sat next to him at the bar. For a while nothing was said and he continued sipping his beer. She then turned and looked at him, saying in good English, "No fucking for Zlotys." David didn't think that he had heard right, so he turned and faced her as she repeated, "I only fuck for dollars." He didn't know what to say, so he ignored her and went back to his beer. The barman gave him a smile and said something to the girl in Polish, after which she got up and left the bar. The barman came over to David with another beer and said slowly, "University student. She needs money to study."

As David went back to his room he thought what a shitty world it was, where it was necessary for women to sell their bodies in order to get an education.

Chapter 4

Next morning, David was waiting in reception when Mr Wozniak arrived in a taxi which then took them to the Ministry. David really didn't know what to expect. Three others were waiting for them in the meeting room and were introduced as Mr Kazmarek, Mr Dudek and Mrs Zawadska. Mr Kazmarek thanked David for coming and welcomed him to Warsaw, telling him about the others around the table. Mr Wozniak and Mrs Zawadska were scientists, while Kazmarek was responsible for Food Safety within the Ministry. He never explained what Mr Dudek did and David never asked. They asked him to explain what they were doing about food safety standards in the UK and why.

"We're only a little way ahead of Poland and, until we have a fully formulated Food Safety legislation, we're following the procedures and legislation laid down by the FDA in Washington."

"Are D&A prepared to give us the results of their analyses on foodstuffs that have been packaged in plastics?"

"Absolutely. If necessary, I'll bring them myself, so I can answer any questions you may have."

This was exactly what they wanted to hear and there were smiles all around the table. Mrs Zawadska asked if the company could let them have details of the analytical methods that D&A used and David promised that he would do this as soon as he returned to the UK. He suggested that they repeated some of the D&A tests to ensure that they obtained the same results. He told them that if they had any problems he would come over with one of the analysts to help them. This produced another round of smiles and thanks, whereupon Mr Kazmarek came round the table and shook his hand. The meeting was all over by half past eleven. They invited him to stay for lunch but he declined and said that he would like to explore Warsaw a little as he only had that afternoon before returning to the UK the following day.

David went back to the hotel and stretched out on the bed. He had been very apprehensive before the meeting, as he had no idea what to expect. He certainly didn't think that they would have reached an understanding so quickly. He decided on a quick lunch before he set off on his explorations of Warsaw's cemeteries.

He had no intention of wearing out his shoes walking across Warsaw, so after looking at the street map, he took a cab to the Radoslav Circus which was at one end of Okopowa Street. He thought that - as he had no idea of where the entrance gate was - if he started at one end of the street he couldn't miss it. It was a lovely afternoon and David had loads of time so he walked slowly, taking in the sights, but there was nothing he thought worth photographing. Superficially, all big cities appear the same but, underneath the skin, each has its own character. He was part way down the street trying to imagine what it had looked like before the war, when he realised that he was walking alongside the cemetery wall. About two hundred metres further he could see a police car, parked on the right hand side of the road. As he got nearer he could see that it was parked at the entrance to the cemetery and that the large gates to the cemetery were closed. David had no idea if they were locked, but he wasn't going to try them right under the noses of the police. As Giles had said, it might not be illegal to go into the cemetery, but they might get curious.

He continued his slow walk alongside the wall then around the corner into Mlynarska Street, where, after a few hundred yards, he found the entrance to the Christian cemetery. It had an improvised notice in Polish and underneath in English saying *Evangelical Christian Cemetery*. David followed the directions given by Giles. It was impossible to miss the Hermana Junga mausoleum; it was huge, and as Giles had said, it looked like the gable end of a chapel. Sure enough there was a gap in the wall behind, obstructed only by some brambles and nettles. He could see that someone had passed through recently, because the nettles had been trodden down. Once inside the Zydowski cemetery, he wondered about the instruction to find the water fountain. He thought he might as well just go straight to the Henryk Wohl grave, instead of all that messing around looking for the drinking fountain. Being inside the Zydowska Jewish cemetery was like being in a birch forest; there were hundreds and hundreds of mature birch trees. In the newer part, all the graves were aligned in orderly rows but, in the old part where he was heading, all the gravestones were arranged in a haphazard manner and were covered in green moss. What was noticeable was the peace and quiet; the traffic noise had disappeared. Silenced by the trees, it was no more than the buzz of a bumblebee.

He soon found the pile of three great black basalt boulders. He stood there surveying it for a few moments, wondering why Henryk Wohl, 1836-1907, had such an unusual grave. Was he, perhaps, a mountaineer or a geologist? As Giles had described, at the back of the grave there was quite a deep crevice between the middle and top boulders. He couldn't see anything so he put his arm in up to his elbow and pulled out a little box about three inches long, two inches wide and an inch or so deep. It was well sealed and he stuffed it into his pocket, taking out Giles' A4 manila envelope which he folded in half and stuffed in to the crevice as far as he could.

That was simple. He was struck by how strange he must look, rummaging about amongst the graves, and wondered if there was anyone else there who might have seen him. More importantly, he worried if it were possible for the police at the gate to see him wandering around in there? He looked around a little sheepishly. He couldn't even see the top of the entrance gate because of the trees in the old part of the cemetery. It was more like a jungle than anything else, so it was unlikely that the police would be able to see him.

He retraced his route, past the Archdeacon's mausoleum and back to Mlynarska Street. Then, after consulting the map, he made his way slowly back to the hotel, taking in the architecture and sights as he passed. Passing the hotel bar he decided to reward himself with a drink. He couldn't contemplate the price of the Scotch so he settled for a shot of Polish vodka. He had no idea of the alcohol content; suffice to say he regretted drinking it. As he drank the vodka he took the little box out of his pocket and turned it over and over in his hands, wondering about its contents. He had no doubt that Giles wouldn't ask him to bring back anything illegal but had a real urge to open it and see what was inside. He shook it gently. It didn't rattle and he couldn't feel anything moving about inside and it was very light. Back in his room, he tucked the box into his case and forgot all about it. In the end, the return to the UK was totally uneventful; customs didn't even look at him as he went through the 'Nothing to Declare' channel. He arrived at Chatsworth Gardens somewhat exhausted, but he soon perked up when he found a lovely long letter from Nicole waiting for him.

****

When David arrived at the office on Thursday morning there was a message from Giles waiting for him, inviting him for dinner at Bentinck Mansions at half past six.

When David arrived, he followed Giles into the drawing room. Colonel Collis was sitting reading the Times. As David entered, he looked up. "Did you have a good trip?" David was surprised that Giles had told him about something as insignificant as his trip to Poland.

Giles handed him a large whisky. "Successful meeting, David?"

"Yes, I had a very amicable meeting with the Ministry and satisfied all their concerns; it was most successful."

"Excellent." Giles motioned him over to a chair.

"By the way I left your envelope in between the two boulders as instructed. In there I found this little box; it doesn't have your name on it, but I assumed it was for you."

As he gave it to him, Giles asked if he had rubbed out the chalk mark.

"What chalk mark?"

"The one on the lion's head."

The drinking fountain. David had forgotten that part of the instructions.

"No, I didn't, you never told me to rub it out."

"Ah well, it doesn't matter. It was just a question of not leaving graffiti about the place."

David experienced a slight feeling of guilt and was glad that Giles couldn't know that he hadn't actually *been* to the water fountain. Or did he?

The colonel looked at his watch. "When are you two going out to dinner? I'm getting hungry, and Doris will have my dinner ready soon."

Giles and David left for dinner and during their meal, David asked if Doris was Mrs Collis.

Giles laughed. "No, no. Doris is our housekeeper; she sometimes cooks for the colonel if he's dining alone."

"Ah, I see. So, what was in the little box I brought back?"

"Oh, that. Nothing really."

"Nothing? You mean I put myself out for nothing?" David tried to pass it off as a joke, but inside he was pissed off.

"Not nothing, exactly, but nothing of importance."

"Giles that's not good enough. I want to know, because if I'd been stopped by Customs, what could I have said?"

"And were you?"

"No, of course I wasn't, but it didn't strike me until too late that if it was something illegal, they wouldn't believe that it was for you - it didn't have your address on it, so you could always deny it."

"Really, David. Do you think I would ask you to do something illegal?"

"Well, no, but--"

"It was just a favour for Kamil. The box contained two rolls of film – Kamil's holiday snaps. In Eastern Europe the film processing is absolutely crap, and all photographs tend to be scanned by security. If there is anything dodgy or politically incorrect on them they go to Communist party headquarters. Then you get a visit from the police... or worse. There, I hope you're not disappointed that it wasn't anything more exciting."

"And was there?"

Giles looked puzzled. "Was there what?"

43

"Anything dodgy on the films?"

Giles laughed, "How the hell would I know, you've only just given the films to me. But I very much doubt it. Possibly a semi-naked woman on the beach, if you consider that dodgy. Who knows! Now, shall we have some dessert?"

Chapter 5

David's secretary found him having a cup of tea in the canteen. "I've been looking everywhere for you; Willi Jansen has called twice this morning asking for you."

Willi was based in Copenhagen and handled the sales and marketing for all the Eastern Bloc countries with the exception of East Germany, which was covered by the sales office in Hamburg. When David returned his call, Willi wanted to discuss their business in the CSSR. Over the previous five years it had grown by a significant amount to over three million pounds in sales, all manufactured in the London factory. Apparently, the Czechs now wanted to set up a taste test panel to ensure that the packaging was not tainting the food. Willi knew that the company had set up such a panel in the London labs. He asked if David could get over to Prague to explain what they did and how they selected the panel.

David thought for a moment. "If they're going to interpret the results properly they'll have to understand the statistics we use, otherwise the results will be meaningless."

"You know that and I know that, but you'll have to convince them to use the same methods as we do. Then you'll have to teach them the correct methods to use."

"But they've got good statisticians in Czechoslovakia; they don't need *me* to teach them statistics, Willi."

"It's not really a question of teaching them statistics; it's more about convincing the government people to believe what the statistics tell them. I could do it but they won't believe me. Because you're a scientist they'll accept what you say. I'm not sure when they'll want the meeting - probably in a few months' time. I'm due to be there the week after next, so I'll try to find out when and where they want the meeting, so that you can get it into your diary."

****

A few weeks later, Giles and David were having one of their regular dinners out. David had told him about a small, but rather good, Indian restaurant that he had found in Acton. Giles said that the Indian restaurants in the West End weren't very authentic, so he was keen to try David's recommendation. Over dinner, Giles asked him how the job was going and David told him what he had been doing and that they were currently involved in some work with the CSSR.

"Ah! That sounds like an interesting change for you. Are you likely to be needed in Prague, in the near future?"

"Why do you ask?"

"Oh, just some export permits and financial guarantees we need to move to our distributor in Prague. Whilst they're not urgent, I would prefer it if they could be delivered by hand, because it would be very inconvenient if they were lost. The permits might have expired before they could obtain new ones."

"Sorry, Giles. I can't help you there. I've no plans to visit Prague and, as far as I know, there are no technical problems with our business in the CSSR."

"Ah well, never mind. It was just a thought. You're right about this restaurant by the way."

"Good, isn't it?" The talk turned to plans for the weekend.

****

It was barely three weeks later that David found himself at the Czech Embassy, with an official giving him a multiple entry visa valid for five years. On the visa under 'Reason for visit' he stamped 'Official Business'. According to the company's MD,

Jock Johnston, the Czechs were now raising all sorts of safety questions.

"I think all the publicity in the USA on food safety issues has galvanised the East Europeans' concern on the safety issues involved," he had said. "None of the Eastern bloc countries want to be seen lagging behind the USA. They want us to send an expert to Prague as soon as possible to help them sort out the problems. The Ministry in Prague has telexed the embassy in London authorising the issue of a visa." So here David was.

David thought of Giles' export permits and wondered if he still needed his help, so he called him at the office. "Good morning Giles. I'm off to Prague on Tuesday; do you still need to get those documents over to your customer? I could do it providing it's simple, because I won't have a lot of time to wander around Prague. So no convoluted trips to cemeteries this time."

Giles laughed. "That will work perfectly. I'll call them this morning to arrange where you can meet. Whatever you do, though, don't rush Prague - it's too beautiful. There's so much to see and I really suggest that you take a day's holiday just to wander around and see everything. I'll give you a call at home tonight to arrange to get the papers to you."

True to his word, Giles had called that evening. "The original papers have been sent by courier but we now have a problem, in that there are some others that need to be there within a few days, so I'm really pleased that you're going to Prague and can do me this favour."

"No problem – I'm happy to. Where do you want me to drop the papers off?"

Giles paused. "Ah, how about the Holocaust Memorial at the Pinchas synagogue? It's nice and central and will be a good place for you to visit."

"Giles, you are the oddest tour arranger I've ever come across."

Chapter 6

The following Monday, David was on the 10.30 flight from Heathrow to Prague, but, after an uneventful flight he became concerned when they appeared to be landing in a ploughed field. For whatever reason, they had descended to landing height a good half mile before the runway and David was relieved when he saw the tarmac underneath them. Prague seemed to be a very small airport compared to London. As soon as he entered the arrivals hall he could see his colleague Willi Jansen waiting for him.

They drove into Prague to the hotel that had been arranged by the Ministry. What a dump; it was a cross between a youth hostel and an army barracks. Willi explained that, in the eighteen years since the end of the war, all building resources had been put into rebuilding ruined factories and providing houses for the workers. Hotels were seen as nonessential and the workers would not like to see luxurious accommodation being provided for foreigners, or senior managers, when they had only basic living facilities themselves. In a very quiet voice he said, "Mind you, you should see some of the places where the top Communist Party members live."

After checking in, Willi suggested that they found somewhere to eat, explaining that, although the hotels were rubbish, Prague had quite a good selection of traditional restaurants. Over dinner, Willi explained the problems that they were having. While the Czech customers wanted to use their products, there was always someone in the Ministry who wanted to make his name by making life difficult for any Western company. Apparently, in Communist countries such as Poland and

Czechoslovakia, one's career was advanced not on merit, ability or hard work but on ability to creep up the Party ladder by saying all the party slogans to the right people. The company's difficulties stemmed from two individuals who wanted to make their name in the Ministry of Health by condemning all products imported from the West on safety grounds. Willi had argued that all the products were exactly the same composition as those in the USA and had been approved by the FDA in Washington, but this argument was like a red rag to a bull.

David laughed "I thought, being commies, they would like a red rag."

His job was to discuss the composition and to present the scientific data proving the safety of the individual components. This was something that he could readily do, even though it seemed a total waste of time.

Their meeting was scheduled for 9.00 a.m. at the Ministry the following day. After a somewhat uncomfortable and sleepless night and a not very appetising breakfast of black rye bread and ham, they made their way to the Ministry. The meeting was supposed to be with a Mr Svobodik and a Mr Jelinek, who were responsible for the approval of food additives and food packaging used in the CSSR. However, there was also a frosty faced individual with an unpronounceable name who just grunted when they were introduced. Willi leaned over to David. "Party official. He's here to see that the other two toe the party line."

The discussions involved Svobodik and Jelinek asking detailed questions on the toxicology of the additives and, when David answered these, they would ask the same questions again in a different way just to see if they could catch him out. David thought it was like having a university viva. They didn't want any

50

specific information; instead, they were trying to find out what he *didn't* know. This charade continued all morning until, at noon, it was agreed that they would break for lunch. They left the Ministry and were walking to the restaurant when Jelinek pulled David's sleeve indicating that they slow down. "Don't worry. Your products are all approved, but we have to do this to prove to the Party that we are doing our job."

Over lunch and a couple of drinks, East-West relations improved – with the exception of Frosty Face who never smiled and only grunted when necessary. David wondered if he had understood anything that had been said. Though, as the meeting was conducted in English and German depending on who was speaking, it might have been that he only spoke Czech.

They returned to the office just after two o'clock. The atmosphere was now most cordial and David was thanked profusely for all the help and information that he had given to them. Willi was told that the contract for the following year would be signed by the Minister the following day and he could either collect it, or it could be mailed to him in Copenhagen.

As they left the meeting into a lovely spring afternoon, Willi told him that he planned to drive to Bratislava to visit the factory where their products were used. He suggested that David went to the State Tourism Office because every hour they started a guided tour of the city which was very good and, apparently, visited certain parts of Hradcany Castle that weren't open to casual tourists. David thought this a great idea. His meeting with Giles' import agent wasn't until the following day and it might help him to find his way around Prague.

Willi was right; the tour was very interesting and included St Vitus Cathedral, Hradcany castle, the musical clock and a very old monastery with a beautiful library. David was the only

51

Westerner on the tour. All the others were from various parts of Eastern Europe - fortunately including four from East Germany, which meant that the tour guide gave her commentary in Russian and German, so he was able to understand most of it. The most useful part was when they paid a visit to the Old Jewish cemetery and the Pinchas synagogue. Adjoining the synagogue was the memorial to the victims of the Holocaust, which was where Giles had asked David to meet his contact the following afternoon.

When he walked into the memorial, the general colour of the walls was a light tan, but - on closer inspection - the colour was actually made up of a name in yellow, a date of death in red and the concentration camp in brown. David had no idea how many names were on the walls — it looked like thousands, maybe millions. He stayed for a short while but then needed air, leaving with tears running down his face. Until then, the Holocaust had only been a historical fact. But now, faced with such detail, it had an immediacy and reality that was numbing.

****

The following afternoon he set out again for the cemetery. Now he knew where he was going, David walked slowly from the Old Town across the King Charles Bridge, enjoying the beauty of Prague. Once across the river, it was a short step to the Pinchas synagogue and memorial. He saw a little notice on the wall by the gate, in Czech and German, stating that the cemetery was first used in 1439. In 1439 the Old Town would have been the whole of Prague, and David wondered whether the Jews had been segregated in a ghetto on the far bank of the Vltava.

Inside, there were few people and those that were there, were congregated around the memorial. None ventured into the old part of the cemetery. Here, it was other-worldly. It wasn't eerie but it left David feeling that the living weren't welcome. There were hundreds and hundreds of gravestones, most only separated by one or two feet, leaning in all directions. Most seemed very old, weathered and moss covered. David could believe that they were five hundred years old.

Giles had given him detailed instructions about what he was to do on reaching the cemetery and David had laughed at the intrigue and complexity. Halfway along the right hand wall of the memorial he was to look for Silberstein-Treblinka-1943 and remain staring at it. His contact would arrive at 3p.m. and ask if he was looking for Silberstadt. David's reply was to be "No, but I have a friend called Silberstadt." His reply would be "My father was Silberstadt." It all seemed very melodramatic, but it all went to plan and he handed over Giles' shipping documents or whatever they were. Silberstadt shook David's hand and thanked him and immediately left the memorial.

Giles had suggested that he had a good look around the old cemetery which he had described as hauntingly beautiful. Giles had been right; it really was a very special place, not sad or mournful, but somehow slightly surreal. A lot of the gravestones were falling and slanting in a random manner. The writing on the stones didn't look like Czech and David assumed it was Hebrew. Giles had suggested that he go to the really old part in the northwest corner and take photographs of one or two of the graves. David wondered if Giles was Jewish; he seemed to have a predilection for old Jewish cemeteries. He then thought of Henryk Wohl's grave and suspected that he was in reality looking for a similar hiding place in Prague.

David followed Giles' instructions and started to take a few photographs in the oldest part of the cemetery. As he did so he had the feeling that he was being watched, he looked around

53

but couldn't see anyone. He took his second photograph and, as he looked through the viewfinder he saw an old man leaning on a stick, apparently watching him. When he looked again he saw no one. He thought he must have been mistaken until a movement caught his eye. A very old gardener stood watching him, almost invisible against the background. David waved to him but the old man ignored him, turned away and started sweeping up leaves.

Chapter 7

Some months later, after dinner one night, Giles and David were talking about their experiences while travelling around Europe: who had had the longest delays and where, best meals eaten, experiences in rubbish hotels around the world. David told him about the dump that he had been put into the first time he went to Prague. "I'm off to Prague again on Tuesday but I've made sure that I'm in a decent hotel this time."

"Again? How long will you be there this time?"

"I'm due to arrive about four and my meeting at the Ministry of Food is at nine the next morning I'm never sure just what problems may arise so I've booked a return flight on Friday morning. I'm hoping to be able to do a bit more sightseeing; I thought it was such a beautiful and interesting place last time."

"Perfect timing. Any chance of you taking a letter to my business contact in Prague again?"

The last time it had been so easy that David couldn't really refuse, particularly as Giles always paid for dinner if David had run a little errand for him.

Giles took his silence for agreement. "The report's at home at Bentinck Mansions. We could go and have a nightcap there and it'll save me mailing it to you."

The report could not have been more than five or six pages because the envelope wasn't very fat and it would just fit into David's briefcase, which he knew would be bulging with all the paperwork that had to go the Ministry in Prague. The envelope was simply addressed to Pavel Vaclav, with no other address on it.

"How am I going to deliver it, if I don't know the address?"

"It's better if he meets you somewhere and you just give it to him. You'll recognise him; he's the one that you met the first time you went to Prague. Where do you want to meet him? Where was it you met him the last time?"

"We met up at the Holocaust Memorial at the old Jewish Cemetery."

"Ah yes. I suggest that you meet Vaclav at the side entrance to St. Vitus."

****

On Tuesday the plane arrived in Prague, on time. David took a cab to the President Hotel and checked in. The room was a vast improvement on the People's Barracks that he had been in the first time. As it was a lovely sunny afternoon, he wandered around the Old Town, taking in the sights. Willi, who would be with him at the Ministry the following day, was due to arrive about half past five. David thought that they could have a further explore while looking for somewhere for dinner.

By the time they had finished dinner, plus a few Pilsners, he was ready for bed. Willi and he discussed the form for the meeting at the Ministry. David was the lead but, if they started raising commercial issues, they agreed that Willi would take over from him.

The next day the meeting followed the usual form: the Czechs raised all sorts of problems which David countered with the correct technical details, with the Czechs then becoming quite adversarial. Willi and he countered with quiet replies to their objections. This thrust and parry was followed by lunch, with the Czechs - as before - taking them to a nice restaurant for a prolonged lunch, which Willi paid for in dollars.

Once they were back around the negotiating table, all the Czech objections faded away; the atmosphere became very cordial and they accepted David's report with two minor face-saving amendments. The overall result was a further five million pounds of business, secure for another twelve months.

All the business was finished and David wished he had a contact number for Vaclav so that he could deliver the report and get home a day early. He tried unsuccessfully to find him in the phone book, and wondered if Vaclav actually lived in Prague. When he asked in reception if one could ring directory enquiries, the man in charge of the switchboard told him that the telephone directories were incomplete and, lowering his voice, said that the only way to get an entry was to be an active member of the Communist Party. There was nothing else he could do, so Willi and he went to find a peaceful bar until it was time for dinner.

The next morning, Willi was driving to Budapest to visit their Hungarian customers. David didn't envy him; his job meant that he could be away from home for up to ten days each trip and, because of the uncertainties of disorganised East European hotels, he carried a sleeping bag in case he had to spend a night sleeping in his car.

Giles had given David two possible times to meet Vaclav at St. Vitus. The first was at ten thirty and, if Vaclav didn't show up, David was to wait in the same place again at three. David got to St Vitus early, hoping that Vaclav would be there so that he could get a cab to the airport and see if he could get a flight that day. Rather than stand waiting, David wandered around the square until he saw Vaclav walking up to their meeting point. David hurried to catch him and called out to him. However, when Vaclav saw David, he carried on walking and went through the little door into the dark interior of the cathedral. David followed him and, as soon as he was inside, the door closed.

Vaclav immediately took out from underneath his coat a large package wrapped in brown paper and said, "Please take this to Giles; it will cost a fortune to send it in the mail."

David wasn't happy. Giles had said nothing about collecting a package, particularly a large heavy one that certainly wouldn't fit into his briefcase. He forced the package into his coat pocket then gave Vaclav the envelope from Giles.

Vaclav stood. "Thanks a lot," he said, and scuttled off into the main nave and headed for the big entrance door. David turned round and went back out of the little side door, shaking his head.

As he walked back to the hotel, David decided that he would put all his papers into his suitcase and the package for Giles into his briefcase. After this rearrangement he paid his bill and took a cab to the airport, hopeful that he could change his reservation to an earlier flight. However, when he checked with BA they told him that all the flights that day were full and that he should try CSSR which he did, but they also had no seats available. David then saw an Air France desk and thought that, if he could get to Paris, there were so many flights to London from there that he was bound to get on one of them. Air France were most helpful; David thought the lady on the desk probably welcomed the opportunity to speak French. She rerouted his ticket and he was on the flight to Paris leaving in forty-five minutes, which connected with AF734 from Paris to London, with only a one hour wait in Paris.

David was quite surprised when Air France provided a really good lunch on the flight. He thought that they must have brought it with them from Paris. When he commented to the steward the reply was, "No Frenchman would be flying over lunchtime without being fed." Once the flight had landed at

Orly, he had plenty of time to get to the gate for London. As he was walking through the main concourse he recognised Roland Porter, the technical manager from the French office, walking towards him. Roland saw David at the same time and gave a wave and a big smile; they stopped for a chat, neither of them in any hurry, and then David had the brainwave of asking Roland to take the package for Giles into the office in Paris and have it sent over to London in the company mail.

"Since I'll be a day early getting back to London, I thought I might drive north and have a long weekend with my parents in Cheshire. I don't want to carry the package around all weekend."

"Of course! I'll send it over and it will be on your desk by Tuesday when you're due back in the office."

When David arrived at Heathrow, he collected his suitcase and was walking through the customs 'Nothing to Declare' channel when one of the officers stopped him.

"Excuse me, sir. We'd like to examine your case."

David couldn't object but, as he had nothing to declare, he wasn't worried. "Of course." He opened his suitcase and stood back.

After they had looked through his case and briefcase they searched his pockets. "When you were in Prague did you buy, or were you given, anything to bring back to the UK?"

David wondered how they had known that he had come from Prague. "I've just arrived from Paris, actually."

"Yes sir, but we know you started your journey in Prague."

"All I have is in this case and my briefcase. I have nothing else to declare."

As he repacked his suitcase the officer walked across to a telephone, spoke to someone and then disappeared through a door.

As he was driving North up the M1, all David could think about was what it might mean. He wondered idly whether Giles had set him up to smuggle something into the UK, but he couldn't think what they could have in Czechoslovakia that would be worth smuggling into the UK. The opposite way round he could understand. He dismissed the thought as an idle notion once he had joined the new M6 and forgot all about Giles and his parcel. Instead, he considered his plans for the next few days and which of his friends in Cheshire he should visit.

****

When David got into the office on Tuesday morning he found a note on his desk saying that Giles had phoned on Friday afternoon. When Mary came in just on nine o'clock she told him that he had called three times the day before. "He was very insistent and asked when you would be in and if I had a number where he could reach you."

"If he calls this morning, tell him that I am in the office but have had to go into a meeting with the MD."

He had just finished reading through the previous week's mail when the parcel arrived from Paris. Roland hadn't repacked it, all he had done was scrawl David's name across the front and put it into the samples bag as it was. The result was that the brown paper wrapping had torn across from one corner, where it had been damaged. It wasn't difficult for David to extend the tear so that he could examine what was so important in the parcel. It looked like a great sheaf of A4 paper, but the top few sheets were blank, so he looked at a few sheets from the middle. They, too, were blank.

David looked again at the torn wrapping. It was only a sheet of brown paper with Giles' name written in black ball point. He could easily rewrap it and scribble 'Giles' on it. He tore open the parcel. Curious, he leafed through the papers inside. Every sheet was blank. The package contained about two hundred sheets of blank, white paper. What was so special about this paper that Giles was so desperate to get his hands on it?

David was rather annoyed, to say the least, that he had carried a fair weight of blank copy paper all the way from Prague, but he couldn't help wondering if there was something special about it. Was there a reason why the customs people would be looking for two hundred sheets of blank, white paper? The copier room was only down one flight of stairs. David fetched about the same amount of blank Xerox paper and had Mary wrap it in brown paper and then write 'Giles' on it.

"Can you copy the handwriting on the original packaging?

Mary looked at him curiously. "Yes, I think so."

"Thanks. I am going out for an hour or so. If Giles calls, tell him that his parcel is here if he wishes to collect it, otherwise I will deliver it tonight and he can buy me dinner."

"I'll let him know."

"And don't say anything about our repacking it."

David picked up the packet of CSSR paper and walked over to the analytical lab to see his pal Mike, who was the chief analyst.

"Mike, I brought this paper back from Prague. The Czechs tell me that it's very special but they didn't tell me why. What can we find out without destroying it? Can we see if it's the paper that's special or if it has some coating on it?"

Mike donned his white coat and gave David one to wear, "We have to make you look like a serious chemist, even if you aren't one."

"OK, so, what are we going to do?"

Mike took one of the sheets of paper over to a bench and switched on a light, putting the paper underneath it and peering closely at it. "This is a UV light. I'm just checking for writing."

"Secret writing?" David peered over Mike's shoulder. "I don't see anything. It just looks normal."

Mike pulled out random samples and scanned each one under the UV light in turn. "No, there's nothing that looks like writing on any of these sheets." He then took one of the sheets, wiped it with a wet cloth and squeezed out the water into a beaker. He then repeated the test doing the same thing with another liquid.

"What's that you're using?"

Mike lifted the container. "Hexane. It will dissolve any organic ink that isn't soluble in water."

He then put a small tube containing the liquid into an instrument. "We'll see if this will tell us anything."

Mike shook his head, "The water sample tells us nothing and the hexane signal is too weak to be useful." "What does that mean?" asked David.

"It's too weak to identify anything. I'll evaporate some of the solvent and try again."

This time the signal was stronger but the spectrum wasn't clear and didn't tell them anything. However, when Mike then looked at the samples in another instrument, as he saw the result he said, "OK that's a better signal. This indicates the presence of an aromatic compound which might be phenolic. Now, we will look to see if we can detect any metals in the coating." After a few minutes the machine printed out the result, Mike frowned and pursed his lips. "This tells us that there's something containing Cobalt on the paper, but I'm damned if I know why or what it is. I suggest we look at a piece of the paper using reflectance Infra-red."

Mike pulled over more equipment and did some more tests. "Yep. Here's a similar spectrum to the one we saw in the hexane sample. But look," he moved out of the way so that David could see. "See that?"

David nodded. "Yes, it looks different – as though the strength is varying over the surface of the paper."

"Exactly. I think this paper has some writing or print or drawings on it in invisible ink."

"Really? Can we see what it says?"

"Unfortunately not. Unless we know exactly what it is, we can't find out how to make it visible."

"Damn"

"Don't worry. I'll keep trying. Leave it with me."

When David returned to his office, Mary told him that Giles had called and picked up the parcel, leaving a message that he was very grateful to him and would give him a call later in the day.

Chapter 8

The next morning, David had a meeting with a client in Bedfordshire. He set off early and was at Sharnbrook by ten o'clock. The meeting finished just after twelve and, after a snack lunch at a café on the A1, he was back at the office just after two o'clock. There were two police cars in the car park, one of which left as he pulled into the car park. As he passed reception, he was told that there were two police with Mary, waiting for him to get back.

David bounded up the stairs, two at a time. He was greeted by an agitated Mary who introduced him to the policemen who were both from CID.

"We've been burgled!"

"When?"

"Last night. I came in this morning and all the drawers were open. I know I closed them last night before I left, so I called the police."

"The whole building?"

Mary shook her head. "No, just this floor. Can you believe it? And they forced open the only locked door – the one where we keep our tea and biscuits."

"Have they taken anything? Apart from the digestives that is?"

One of the policemen cleared his throat. "They don't appear to have taken anything. However, we'd like you to take a look through all your desk drawers and filing cabinets to see if anything is missing."

David went over to his desk. "We don't lock anything at night, because there's nothing of value or confidential kept in the office." He rummaged in the desk drawers. "No, as far as I can see, nothing's been taken."

The detectives shrugged and thanked them for their time. "They either found what they were looking for, or they didn't find anything and gave up looking."

David thought that it wasn't surprising that Sherlock Holmes was so successful if that was the best conclusion the police could come to. After they had gone it was back to the normal business of securing the permits and permissions to use D&A chemicals in food products. David had just finished a cup of tea when reception called to say that there was a Mr Giles Morris and another gentleman in reception, who would like to see him urgently.

Mary met them at the lift and brought them to the office. Giles introduced his companion as Brian Forsythe and, when Mary had closed the door, Giles told David that Mr Forsythe was from Special Branch. "We need to ask you some questions about the parcel from Pavel Vaclav." David prepared himself for an interesting conversation.

"Before we start, I just want to give Mary a brief instruction so that she can be getting on with her work." He went out to Mary's office and told her that he would put the intercom on. "I want you to listen to everything that is said and get as much down in shorthand as possible." He then went back into his office.

"After Vaclav had given the package to you, what did you do with it? Did it ever leave your hand?"

David shook his head. "I took the package back to my room, took all my papers out of my briefcase and packed them into my suitcase, so that I could fit your package into my briefcase. I then took a cab straight to the airport to get a flight back to the UK."

Forsythe butted in. "What flight did you get? We know you arrived from Paris. Why was that?"

David stared at him a moment, then turned to Giles. "Giles, before we go any farther, I want to know why we have a Special Branch detective asking these questions?"

"The papers in that package are of vital importance to the government."

"Maybe so, but which government, I wonder? Is that British or Czechoslovakian?"

Giles bridled. "British of course."

"Well, I'm pleased to hear that, but before I answer I'd like to see your friend's warrant card or ID."

Forsythe produced something that was an ID, but it looked nothing like a police warrant card and it didn't mention Special Branch. David excused himself and went back to Mary in the outer office. "Call Scotland Yard on Whitehall 1212 and ask for Special Branch."

Mary's eyes widened. "What do you want me to say?"

"Tell them we have a Brian Forsythe here who says he's from Special Branch, but we think his ID is false and it doesn't seem to be a police warrant card. Ask them if he's genuine and, if not, whether they have any idea who he is."

He went back into the office and explained. "I had returned a day early and, as all direct flights to London were full, I changed my ticket to Air France and flew back via Orly."

"How did the Vaclav package get to the UK?"

"Well, it certainly didn't fly back on its own. How do you think it got back?"

David was beginning to think that the Customs search at Heathrow hadn't exactly been a random check and that these two knew the package hadn't been with him when he arrived from Paris. He also concluded that these weren't some trivial commercial papers that 'would cost a fortune to mail', as Giles had so neatly explained it away.

"What's the problem? Giles collected the package while I was away." Mary put her head round the door and asked if she could see David for a minute. He closed the door behind him and she whispered, "He's not Special Branch. They transferred me to a senior officer who asked what he looked like. They think he works for something called Department 14 in the Ministry of Defence."

David went back into his office and looked at Giles. The cocky bastard had been using him. David determined to show him who the smartest one was.

"Gentlemen, we have a problem. Last night we had a burglary here in our office, but, as far as we can tell, nothing was stolen. Apparently, the thief didn't find what he was looking for. Now you turn up and fraudulently impersonate an officer from Special Branch. I suspect the two events are related, so my secretary is about to call the police."

"But...I...It's--"

David held up a hand to silence him. "Giles, it might help if you tell me what's going on and what exactly it is that you do in Department 14."

Giles went pale. "After I'd collected the Vaclav package, I took it to my boss in Whitehall. When they opened it they found that it was just plain photocopy paper."

"And what was supposed to be in it?"

Giles didn't answer, but Forsythe said, "It was a very important report that was being sent to the Ministry in London."

"Well, while I was carting the package all over the place, the wrapping got torn on one corner, so when I returned to the office I had a look and decided to rewrap the report for you."

"Did you read it?"

"How could I read it? It was then that I found it was just two hundred sheets of plain photocopy paper. Your friend Vaclav didn't send your report. Instead, he tricked me into carrying a load of copy paper all the way back from Prague."

Giles sighed. "It wasn't ordinary copy paper."

"As far as I am aware copy paper is just copy paper unless there was some information on it. Was there any secret information on it?"

"No, it was plain paper."

"Well then, you can't blame me for not knowing it was special paper. It looked a bit grubby to me, what with the package splitting. I didn't want you to know that had happened, you might have thought I was careless with it - so I did you a favour by throwing it out and replacing it with some nice clean Xerox paper." David picked up the phone and called Mary on the intercom. "Mary, you can stop recording our conversation now and get on with something more useful."

Once the light on the intercom had gone out, David continued. "Giles, I thought that we were good friends but you and your colleague have done nothing but tell lies. You've treated me like a simpleton. I, in good faith, have done everything you've asked me to do. And now you've told me yet another lie. That package did contain a mass of secret information that had been printed using an invisible ink based on a cobalt aromatic compound, which we're working on deciphering. That report is so important that you had one of your people impersonate a customs officer at Heathrow in order to intercept it. Then, Giles, you were pestering Mary to find out where I was, and you had someone break into our office last night to find it here. In the meantime, I guessed that it wasn't ordinary plain paper so our Chief Analyst and I have had an interesting morning finding out just what is on that paper."

Giles and Forsythe exchanged worried looks.

"As for me doing little favours for you to save time or save on postage, you must think I'm stupid. What I have been doing is taking and bringing back intelligence information for your Department 14 or whoever. I now realise that, had I been caught on any of the previous occasions, I would have been arrested or shot. The reason you used me was not to save on costs, but because I was totally deniable; if I was caught you could say that I had absolutely nothing to do with British Intelligence."

Giles looked very embarrassed and apologised, admitting that everything David had said was true. Forsythe sat there, stone-faced, saying nothing. After a couple of minutes of silence he said, "It doesn't change the fact that the document contains some of the most important intelligence to come our way in years. We need to get hold of the report immediately."

David looked at him. He would twist this bastard's tail and teach Giles not to treat him like an idiot. "The report will be here, on my desk, tomorrow afternoon, providing you agree to the following. I am proud to have been able to serve my country and would have done so even if you had explained the risks that I was running. Therefore, you will come back tomorrow with an Official Secrets Act form. I've signed it once at the Ministry of Aviation but I'll sign it again - an updated version. You'll bring a contract of employment so that I become an official member of Department 14, MI5 or MI6, or whatever you call yourselves and I will be paid accordingly. Then, whenever I travel to the Warsaw

Pact region, you can use my services, providing you tell me exactly what I'm supposed to be doing. Oh, and while you're at it, you should also bring an Official Secrets form for Mike, our analyst, as he's also seen what you have on that copy paper."

Forsythe agreed that, in principle, they could do what he had asked, on condition that David would have to be vetted by security before being formally employed. He then asked for David's assurance that the report would be kept in a very secure place until the following afternoon. However, in order to be sure, he told David that he would put a twenty-four hour guard on the building.

David snorted. "If your burglar of last night couldn't find it, why would you think that someone could find it tonight?"

Forsythe said, "I am not taking any chances. It may interest you to know that we had no one at Heathrow, so I intend to find out just who else was taking so much interest in your bags."

****

Giles and Forsythe returned the following afternoon. Forsythe, as sociable as ever, asked David if he was going to keep his part of the bargain, because they had the necessary forms for him to complete which had required considerable effort on their part.

The Official Secrets Act form was identical to the ones David had signed before. He wondered whether one's security classification increased the more one signed it. A second, three page form confirmed his appointment as Senior Liaison Officer in the Foreign Office, subject to him passing the security vetting process.

"Why doesn't this say I'm employed by MI6 or Department 14?"

70

Giles smiled slightly. "No-one actually works for MI6; everyone's employed by either the Ministry of Defence or the Foreign Office. It's been decided that it's better if you are employed by the latter."

Forsythe added, "Department 14 is within the Foreign Office but it doesn't really exist. It's more a... state of mind, shall we say."

David had no idea what that actually meant, but, before he could ask, Giles asked if David was happy with the arrangements.

"So far, you've said nothing about salary or expenses."

Forsythe said, "We propose to pay you a retainer of three thousand pounds per annum, but when you're working for us in the UK, you will be paid at the rate of five thousand pounds, and overseas will be at a rate of ten thousand per annum. As for expenses, if you're travelling on company business we assume you will continue to claim expenses from the company."

"As I told you originally, money is of secondary importance to my being able to serve my country, therefore I can't argue over salary." David stood up. "I assume that you'd now like to see your precious report. Would you please follow me."

He led them down the corridor to the photocopy room. Giles and Forsythe looked around. Giles said, "I thought you said that it would be kept in a secure place."

"Well, it was sufficiently secure for your man not to find it."

"Anyone could come in here." Forsythe was aghast.

"Where's the last place you would expect to find a secret report, but the most obvious place for blank copy paper?" Neither one answered. David gestured to the photocopy machine.

"Where?"

71

"It's in the Xerox copier; if you remove the bottom two hundred and ten pages from the paper tray you'll have your report."

Giles asked, "How did you know that it wouldn't be used?"

"I told Mary to keep the paper tray full. It holds five hundred sheets and we only make about fifty to a hundred copies a day, so it was quite safe in there."

Giles picked up the paper and started to count the sheets. "Don't bother counting it. I've put a marker on the bottom sheet of the ordinary paper so I know exactly where your secret report starts. Here are the first two hundred and nine pages of the report, page two hundred and ten is in my desk; it's a bit dog eared and stained after we played with it in the lab."

When they returned to the office, David took the sheet from his desk and handed it to Giles, who looked at the stains and creases with concern but said nothing. He had a guilty look, knowing that he had not played fair with David.

Forsythe turned to David. "You may not realise it, but you've been of great service to your country and we in the department are extremely grateful. However, no matter what you've done, we have to go through established procedures before we can say that you're employed by the government."

"Positive vetting, you mean?"

"Yes. Here are all the forms to fill in with details of your parents, where you were born, education etc. Political affiliations, if any. The usual stuff. Then, when it's all been checked, you'll have to go to Denham for a day. That's where we do all our interviews; overlooking the fifth hole at Uxbridge golf course."

They got up to leave. "One moment." Giles and Forsythe looked at him, expectantly. "Will I ever get to know what's on that paper?"

It had been an interesting week and he sat down to write his weekly letter to Nicole, telling her all about it. In the end he tore it up and wrote the usual love letter with all the excitement removed.

Chapter 9

David heard nothing more, until - some two weeks later, Giles called and asked if there was any chance he could get to Poland the following week. Whilst it was highly unlikely that David could get away, he wasn't about to tell Giles that. Instead, David told him that he wasn't prepared to do any more for him until his position was approved and verified.

"Don't worry, David, your appointment has been cleared and you will be contacted in due course."

"Well then, I'll go to Poland in due course. If it's so urgent, tell the vetting people to get a move on and, what's more, I don't see how I can be cleared when I haven't even been interviewed as yet." David couldn't help wondering if Giles was still being obtuse. A great chap in some ways, but he had decided that he should treat him with caution and not believe everything that he said.

Later that afternoon, Mary found David in the lab. "There's a John Whiston on the phone. He says he needs to talk to you and it's urgent."

When David picked up the phone the caller said, "Can you come over to Park House, Denham, tomorrow afternoon or Thursday afternoon for the vetting interview?"

"It will have to be on Thursday because tomorrow I have a meeting with my boss and a customer that can't be changed." That wasn't true, of course, but David wasn't going to jump every time the Ministry said jump. When he arrived at the address given, he parked the car and wondered if he was in the right place. Park House was an enormous - but sadly dilapidated - Victorian pile. The gates to the drive were closed and very rusty and the gravel drive had more weeds than gravel and was overhung by trees. It looked more like a film set for The Spiral Staircase or some other spooky movie, rather than a government building.

After he had rung the bell three times, he heard someone coming to the door. It was opened by a rather old lady with white hair tied back in a bun. She was wearing metal rimmed spectacles and looked at David over the top of them, saying nothing. "I have an appointment with a Mr John Whiston."

"Oh yes, we've been expecting you. Mr Whiston is away; you'll be seeing Mr Sloane."

David was taken to an office on the first floor. As he looked out of the window, he could see that it really did overlook Uxbridge golf course and assumed that it was the fifth hole that he was looking at.

There were two men in the office. A miserable faced individual aged about fifty stood up saying, "My name is Sloane. This is Wilson, my number two." Wilson - obviously brought up without manners - didn't stand up, just nodded and grunted. David wondered in which of the eighteen holes the FO had found these two. It wasn't that they were adversarial, just brusque and ill-mannered. It crossed David's mind that they were waiting for him to rise to their bait and drop his guard. In front of Sloane there was a fairly thick folder which David assumed was made up of the reports they had obtained about him from school, university, the RAF and the Ministry of Aviation.

All the questions were fairly straightforward, "Why didn't you like working at the Ministry of Aviation?"

"I *did* like working there but my group was full of idle layabouts, and pay rises were given by age, rather than being based on ability or effort. Also, I couldn't see any prospects for the future."

"Why did you join the Young Conservatives?"

"The Y.C.'s are a great social group, with lots of interesting meetings and quite a few pretty girls."

"Do you vote Conservative?"

David tried to remain impassive, he realised that they were trying to get him riled.

"We have a secret ballot in this country, so you can never know how I vote."

"We'd like to know and we have ways of finding out."

"Well, that's an interesting thing to say. I had assumed that you had a role in protecting our democracy."

"Hopkins, do you want the job or not? Because you can't have it without our approval." Sloane growled.

"Is your lack of manners part of the interrogation technique? Because, if so Department 14 are going to lose an extremely valuable conduit into Eastern Europe. I'm not applying for any job; my role has come about by coercion, seduction, lies and deceit. The only reason I'm here is that I have volunteered to serve my country, in spite of all that deceit."

"I'm sorry, Mr Hopkins. I didn't mean to cause offence. We don't get any information about the job you might be doing, or what you might have done in the past. We have to decide whether or not you should be given a security classification. It's for others to decide if that classification is appropriate for the job you'll be doing."

At this point Wilson butted in, "I have one last question. Have you ever been a member of the Communist Party?"

"No."

"Have you ever applied to become a member of the Communist Party?"

"That's two questions."

He thought that if they'd done their homework properly, then they were trying to get him to tell a lie, as they could then use that to justify refusing a security clearance.

Sloane said, "I don't understand your answer."

"He said that he had one last question and then asked a second. If I've never been a member of the Communist Party, is it likely that I had applied to join?"

"No, I suppose you're right. Should I put 'never applied to join', then?"

"I can't guess how you know, but I *did* apply to join when I was 15. It was at the height of the Korean War and I thought that I would like to know what the bastards were up to in England. Anyway, I found an application form at school, filled it in and sent it off. When they replied, my father opened the letter and went ballistic. He then went to see the headmaster and told him off for allowing Communist Party leaflets to circulate in school."

Sloane and Wilson both stood up and thanked David for being so frank with them.

"Mr Whiston will send our report through to the Ministry tomorrow. Mr Wilson will show you out."

As he went through the front door Wilson said, "You did well in there; I'm sorry that he's such a miserable git but everyone respects his judgement."

Three days later, David received a letter from the Foreign Office confirming his appointment as Senior Liaison Officer at the Foreign Office, seconded to Department 14. He wondered if

77

Department 14 was a mythical entity and whether his pay cheque would also be mythical.

****

A couple of days later, Giles called and asked David to meet him at his office in Whitehall. When he arrived, Giles said, "I want to show you around the department and introduce you to some of the people that you may find useful."

They entered one office. All it had on the door, apart from 'Room 224', was a sign that read 'Please don't knock, we are probably asleep.' Inside were two scruffy individuals, one in a white coat. Giles said, "If you need another passport or any unusual documents come and see Rob; he can fix you up with anything, given a few days' notice."

Rob looked up. "Does he need a duplicate so he can keep visas in separate passports?"

"Probably not necessary, he's only working in the Eastern Bloc."

****

That night, Giles took David out to dinner to celebrate his being officially on the payroll. As they entered the restaurant, Giles steered David over to a table where a man was dining alone. "There's someone I want to introduce you to, he's a senior member of MI5." The man looked up from his soup. "Good evening Peter. I'd like to introduce you to David Hopkins. He's just joined our merry band and has been doing us great service in and out of Eastern Europe."

The diner half stood up, "Pleased to meet you, David. I've heard about your adventures, no doubt I'll see you around the office." He sat down and went back to enjoying his dinner.

When they were having coffee Giles explained, "Peter's started to write a book about his time in MI5. It will contain

78

some quite secret information so he'll be prosecuted under the Official Secrets Act."

"In that case, why let him write it?"

"Because, if we prosecute him, people will think that the information is true, especially the Reds."

"Well, isn't it?"

"No. The important stuff is a complete fabrication."

David shook his head. "That's a bit sneaky. Do you think they'll buy it?"

"Oh Yes. It's Sidney Reilly all over again."

"Who's Sidney Reilly?"

Giles signalled for the bill. "Sidney Reilly was our best spy in 1920's post Revolution Russia. In 1925 he was diagnosed with terminal lung cancer and given only a few months to live. He went back to Russia knowing that he had been betrayed and would be arrested. Under torture he disclosed two very secret pieces of information, both completely false. He screwed up the Reds for years."

David was starting to realise just how devious his new employers were.

****

Over the course of the week David thought that a duplicate passport might be useful in Eastern Europe after all. It might come in handy if someone over there took exception to his comings and goings. He called Rob to ask his advice. Rob explained that, if David had six passport photos taken, he could provide the new passport within two hours. When David presented the photos Rob explained that, while he could have another authentic British passport, it would still be on record at the Passport Office and registered in his name. "If you want to change your ID completely, it's better to have a foreign passport then no one knows who you are, although if anyone were to check with the country concerned you'd be in trouble."

Rob's assistant intervened, "Though not if you're French."

Rob explained. "We have a little deal with our opposite numbers in Paris; they give us a dozen passport blanks, and in return we give them British passport blanks. These are recorded, so if we issue a French passport it will be registered in your name - I mean, your French name - at the passport office in Paris." David thought for a few seconds.

"Well, that's what I want, then; a French passport in the name of Meschines, with a Paris address."

"First name? How about... Pierre?"

"No, that sounds corny. I'll go for... Alain."

Rob said, "Why do you want a French passport anyway? What's so special about having a French ID?"

"For one very good sentimental reason, my mother's name was Meschines before she married my Dad."

"I'll have it ready for you by the end of the week. It'll cost you. I'd like some duty free tobacco whenever you go somewhere where it's cheap."

Chapter 10

A few weeks later over dinner, David explained to Giles that he had booked a holiday in Bulgaria with the added bonus of a few days in Istanbul. He had been asked to give a presentation to the Ministry in Sofia and then he was travelling to a new resort on the Black Sea called Slunchev Bryag, which he thought translated into Sunny Beach. After a week of sea and sun, he was taking a Russian boat from Burgas to Istanbul and then, after four nights in Istanbul, back to Burgas.

"Which hotel are you staying at in Istanbul? The only one that's any good is the Hilton."

"We're not staying in a hotel - we sleep on the boat but eat onshore at some restaurant. I think it's a different one each night."

"When will you be there?"

"My meeting in Sofia is on the eighteenth and then I fly to Varna. Then eight nights in Sunny Beach, four in Istanbul, then back to Burgas on the thirty-first and a flight back home on the third of July. The great thing is that the company are paying my airfare, and I get cash equal to one night in a hotel, as spending money."

"It's possible we might have a little job for you, but it depends on your dates. I'll call you tomorrow to see if we can arrange something."

The following afternoon he received a call from Giles at the office. "Can you be in Sofia on the twenty-second?"

"No, that's right in the middle of my holiday, I'd have to get to Varna airport and fly to Sofia and back in a day. Sorry, I don't want to do that."

"OK, could you get to Varna on the twenty-fourth? I'm told that there's a bus from Slunchev to Varna four times every day, so it shouldn't be a problem."

"What am I taking this time and to whom am I supposed to deliver it?"

"You're not taking anything; you'll collect a fairly thick report from one of our people, Bogdan Todorov."

"Is that his real name?"

"Yes."

"Poor bugger!"

"Now, Bulgaria isn't like Poland or Czechoslovakia; they're suspicious about all contacts with Westerners, other than through the Tourist Travel Office. So Bogdan has given us detailed instructions on where he'll meet you. We'll get it typed up and a street map of Varna for you before you leave."

****

A couple of days before he was due to fly out, Giles called and invited him to have dinner with himself and Colonel Collis at Bentinck Mansions. Before they sat down for dinner, Giles produced a large envelope and a bunch of papers.

"We've put together some useful information for you." He pulled out a schedule. "Here you have the bus timetable for buses from Slunchev to Varna. I've no idea how punctual they are, but it does confirm that there are two in the morning and two in the afternoon. Here's the address of the office block and a description of where you're to meet Bogdan. The building is only part occupied so there shouldn't be many people about. The meeting is on the fourth floor which is unoccupied. No one will see you there. This is a street map of central Varna. I've marked the office block on it. It's on Nikola Kanov Street, not far from the cathedral. Apparently, it's in a nice part of Varna, so if you're early you can wander around and look like a tourist."

David took the folder from him and gave the map a cursory glance. It seemed a fairly straightforward pickup.

Over dinner Colonel Collis started asking questions about his background: was his father in the army? Which school had David gone to? The questions continued and David wondered if he was been interviewed for a job at the bank. By the time he had to leave for the last train to Ealing, all three of them had had too much to drink. Tomorrow was David's last day in the office and he didn't need a hangover. He had a lot to do before leaving for his holiday.

****

The BEA flight was about thirty minutes late leaving Heathrow and, by the time they arrived in Sofia, they were almost an hour behind schedule. When they left the plane, they were taken to what turned out to be Customs inbound. What they were looking for David never knew, but everybody's bag was opened and inspected. Someone said that they were fanatical about banned books coming in from the West; others said it was to check on Western propaganda. When his bag was opened they looked but said nothing, then they searched his briefcase. They didn't speak any English or German, so it was a question of using sign language. One of the customs officials pointed to one of the reports. When David showed him the letter from the Ministry of Food, bearing the Bulgarian government crest, the official lost interest.

Then another character appeared. "How much Sterling are you bringing into the country?"

"Thirty pounds." This was true, but what he didn't tell the official was that he had four hundred dollars in twenty dollar

83

bills in his money belt. He had been warned by Willi that an emergency fund in dollars was essential when travelling in the Eastern bloc.

On leaving Arrivals, David saw an elderly lady holding up a notice with his name on it. She said in broken English, "I will take you to your hotel, you will stay in your hotel, do not go out after I have departed. I will meet you at half past eight in the morning and we go to the Ministry building. Afterwards I will take you to the airport for your flight to Varna."

David thought, '*Welcome to sunny Bulgaria. Have a nice day.*' He hoped that the people at the hotel in Slunchev were a bit friendlier.

The presentation and discussion at the Ministry went well, but, unlike Prague, there was no friendly invitation to lunch afterwards. His Ice Maiden chauffeur came to the meeting room and escorted him to the car. On arrival at the airport, she pulled up outside of the departures door, pointed at it and said, "You go in there."

When David saw the plane, an old Ilyushin 14, it looked like a load of scrap. It had dirty soot marks all over the engines and one of the wings had a patch painted a different colour to the rest of the wing. Inside the cabin it looked worse - two of the overhead lockers had no doors, and one locker looked loose. The back of his seat was fixed and couldn't be adjusted, but the main problem was the noise from the engines; it was deafening and with a lot of vibration. David wondered if the propellers were synchronised correctly.

An hour later they arrived - deafened - at Varna and it was raining. So much for a Black Sea sunshine holiday. However, things started to improve when he saw a big *Balkantourist* sign with his name on it. Balkantourist had told the London travel agent that he would be met at the airport but David wasn't really expecting them to turn up.

Everything in Slunchev looked brand new. All the hotel gardens were immaculate and the hotels were shining white, cream and pastel colours. The tour guide shook his hand. "Welcome to Slunchev. There are two other guests from the UK staying in the hotel, I have told them to expect you later in the day." Most of the other people were speaking German. David assumed they were from East Germany but he found later that a lot were from the CSSR and Hungary, German being the only common language in East Europe other than Russian.

He hadn't been in his room ten minutes when there was a knock on the door. It was his British countrymen, a young married couple from Ware in Hertfordshire. "Hi David. I'm Don Janes and this is my wife Nina. We arrived yesterday and they told us that you were due today. What kept you? We flew BalkanAir from Ostend to Varna. How did you get here?"

"I've been in Sofia on business and I didn't find the people there very friendly. What's this place like?"

"We've started to explore the place. We've tried two restaurants so far, they were both serving good food. One was mainly local dishes and one more international food."

The three of them then went down to the beach and tried the sea, which was clear and warm, ideal for swimming. Afterwards they then walked up to the beach bar and, over a cold beer, Don told him that he was an electrical engineer and Nina, his wife, was a teacher. David told them that he was a chemist. He didn't want to get into why he was in Bulgaria other than that he was looking forward to the trip to Istanbul.

They spent some pleasant days together on the beach and in various bars but, unfortunately, David was uptight about the trip to Varna and couldn't really relax. A couple of times Don asked, "Dave, are you worried about something? You look as if you are thinking about some problem. Is it trouble back home?" Of course, David said no, but he assumed that they thought he had left a big problem behind in England. The only time David relaxed was when he wrote his letter to Nicole, in which he enclosed a postcard of Nesseber - a beauty spot near to Slunchev. He then remembered that he should send a postcard to his parents as well.

He was up early on the twenty-fourth, had breakfast and went for a walk. He didn't want to have to explain to anyone that he was going to Varna in case they asked why. The bus arrived more or less on time and he arrived in Varna just before noon. It was a very pleasant day, not too hot, so David became a tourist wandering around the cathedral area. At the back of the cathedral he discovered a 'Peoples' Bistro' where they served superb pastries with strong black Turkish coffee.

David found the office block without any difficulty and took the lift to the sixth floor. It was deserted. He waited there until just before two o'clock and then walked down to the fourth floor. Todorov was waiting by the lifts, wearing the designated yellow tie. He was holding a fat A4 file. As soon as he saw David, he thrust the file into his hands. In very broken English he said, "Take good care; it is very important." He then called the lift and said, "Wait ten minutes after me; it is good if we are not seen leaving together."

David gave him the thumbs up. "OK."

He went over to the window to watch for Todorov leaving the building. After a couple of minutes he saw him leave and start crossing the square. David was about to turn away from the window and leave the building himself, when he saw three men, two walking towards Todorov from the side and one behind him. Todorov turned and looked back towards the building where David was as the three men grabbed him by both arms. It appeared as if he was being arrested.

Alarm bells rang in David's head. He needed to be out of there quickly. Before he could move, he heard two shots and looked back through the window. Todorov was lying face down on the ground, not moving.

David ran to the back of the building; there must be some back stairs or fire escape. He opened a door and found an unlit concrete staircase. He considered losing the file somewhere but didn't want to stop, so he kept on down the stairs. At ground level a small window gave enough light for him to recognise some fire doors. The doors didn't look alarmed so he pushed. They didn't move so he shoulder charged them and they opened just enough for him to squeeze through.

David pushed the doors closed and looked around him. He was in a dirty, littered back alley, covered in scrap paper and broken bottles. As he got to the end of the alley, he poked his head out. One of the three men who had accosted Todarov was hurrying by on the other side of the road. David ducked back into the alleyway and pressed himself up against the wall. He counted to ten, then poked his head out once more. The road was clear, although, in the distance, he could hear shouting and running. Had Todorov's body been found? Or were they looking for him?

He exited the alleyway and walked as slowly as he could in the general direction of the bus station, avoiding the most direct route. He tried to appear as casual as possible, although he was certain that he must stand out from everyone else. The report was stuffed inside his jacket but it showed, so he put it inside his shirt and buttoned his jacket. When he could see the bus station he speeded up a little, still trying to look casual, simply someone who was late for a bus. He would catch the first bus that would get him out of Varna, wherever it was going. He approached the buses and saw one with its engine running. It appeared to be ready to leave. On the front it said *Bucaresti*.

David had been asked to go to Bucarest on three previous occasions. Each time the meeting had been cancelled but his passport contained a multiple entry visa for Rumania. At the ticket desk he paid for the ticket in dollars and flashed his Rumanian visa at the man behind the counter. The man didn't ask for his name, nor did he examine David's passport.

He sat near to the back of the bus and shut his eyes; he didn't want anyone to start a conversation. Within ten minutes they had pulled out of the station and were heading into the suburbs of Varna. In truth, David had no idea where they were heading. He thought they were going north but when he looked at the road signs he couldn't recognise any of the names. Eventually, the bus got onto a concrete motorway that bypassed all towns and villages. The only motorway signs were for Ruse and Bucarest.

After an hour or so they entered the outskirts of Razgrad but didn't stop and again appeared to bypass the centre. Time seemed to pass very slowly. There were only fifteen or so passengers on the bus. David dreaded the thought that one might start to talk to him. Was he as conspicuous as he imagined? All the other passengers had luggage, whereas he didn't even have a briefcase.

For most of the journey David pretended to be asleep, but he was developing a plan. It all depended on whether or not he could get into Rumania. After another hour they entered the town of Ruse, which seemed to be at least the size of Varna and quite industrialised, with factories right in the centre of the town.

The coach pulled into the centre of the town to where there seemed to be a service station and café. The driver shouted "Ruse" and held both his hands up to show all ten fingers, which David assumed meant a ten minute stop for refreshments. All fifteen passengers went to the café for coffee and cigarettes. While he was waiting in the queue, he saw that the shop also sold travel goods. He was particularly interested in a smart-looking back pack, a little more upmarket than a normal rucksack. David took it down from the shelf and went to get his coffee. At the cash desk he offered a twenty dollar bill. He had no idea of the actual price but was surprised at the amount of change that he received.

After ten minutes they were on their way again and then he saw it: the Danube. As they approached, David was stunned; it was amazing, so wide. He had never before seen such a huge river. It was difficult to guess, but it looked to be almost a mile wide and was crossed by a great bridge. When they were crossing the bridge they seemed to be over a hundred feet above the river.

Halfway across, they came to a sign saying *Rumania*, but there were no customs or passport control on the bridge itself. It seemed strange that a major border crossing had no control point. However, after about two miles into Rumania they arrived at a major checkpoint. There was a queue of trucks and cars at each of the four gates and the coach tagged on at the back of one of the queues. Progress seemed to be tediously slow. Several of the passengers got out to stretch their legs and David joined them to have a look around.

At the front of the queue officials in uniform, who - judging by their apparent preoccupation with paperwork - David guessed to be customs officers. His worry was not getting into Rumania; his visa meant that he couldn't be accused of illegal entry. Instead, his fear was that the Bulgarians might be watching for any Westerners trying to leave the country. David noted that when the customs officials were checking the trucks they seemed only to be concerned with cargo manifests and didn't seem to be asking the drivers for their passports. There were no refreshment facilities at the customs post but there were toilets. Several of the coach's passengers went to use the facilities and, when he joined them, it became obvious that these were borderless toilets: it was possible to enter on the Bulgarian side of the border and leave by the exit on the Rumanian side. So this is what he and three others did. They walked out on the Rumanian side and then walked back to the customs gates and waited for their coach to pass through. When the coach was at the checkpoint the driver, who was talking to the official, pointed to the four people waiting on the Rumanian side. As the border official looked at them, David gave them a casual wave, trying to look as natural as possible. In fact, he was scared witless. However, the coach was waved through by the officials, whereupon it pulled through the gate and stopped to pick them up.

Almost immediately, they left the main highway and drove into the centre of Giurgi. The plan that David had been concocting while travelling from Varna, was to get to Constanta and back to Bulgaria by sea. He knew that the boat for Istanbul started at Odessa, called at Constanta, then Burgas en route to Istanbul. As before, the driver indicated how long they would wait at Giurgi, this time pointing to the clock, and David understood him to mean that they had a thirty minute stay. He picked up his backpack and got off with some of the other passengers.

David could see that the main railway station was no more than two hundred metres away on the opposite side of the main road. In Varna someone might have seen him boarding the bus for Bucarest but if he changed to the train to Bucarest, no one looking for him could be sure where he'd gone. Just in case someone was curious at his not returning to the bus, he left the bus park on the opposite side to the station and then walked around the block.

The train station looked deserted. He looked into several offices, all were empty. When he returned to the platform, he noticed on the far side an old steam engine which was obviously still used because steam was venting from the valve on top of the boiler. It was connected to a long line of empty trucks and the engine itself also appeared to have been abandoned. David returned to the booking office in time to see a scruffy bearded man in uniform enter the station from the street. He took one look at David and went behind the desk in the booking office and then made it obvious he wanted him to buy a ticket. David asked if he spoke French. He at least understood the question, so David asked for a ticket to Bucarest. David thought if he booked to Constanta, the man might remember if someone started asking questions, whereas in Bucarest lots of people would be booking tickets to Constanta.

Within half an hour the Bucarest train arrived; a smart bright blue modern diesel electric. Giurgi being the end of the line, there was a loco at each end so the driver just swapped ends and, within twenty minutes, they were away.

As soon as they were out of the station they picked up speed and rattled along but not for long. At times the train was crawling, then it picked up speed for a while and then back to a crawl. The countryside was boring; very flat and monotonously cultivated in long, narrow fields. They then came to countryside that looked more like the prairies: extensive areas of open grassland. What seemed rather sad, were the number of ruined unoccupied villages; it was impossible to tell if these were the result of German and Russian battles in World War II or the product of collective farming. The train slowed to a final crawl on entering Bucarest some two and a half hours after leaving Giurgi.

David had no idea of the train times to Constanta but, as Bucarest was the main port of Rumania, he assumed that there would be a regular service. He started speaking French at the ticket office but the official behind the desk said nothing and walked out of the office. A few moments later he returned, together with a young lady who addressed David in pretty good French.

"I'm sorry, you have just missed the train to Constanta; the next one is at six p.m. and will get in to Constanta just after eight p.m. There is a good café on the station but outside there are shops and several cafés where you could wait."

He walked out of the main entrance into a large tree-lined square with no sign of shops or cafés. He turned left, passed what looked like the station hotel and came to a broad boulevard on the opposite of which there seemed to be many shops and restaurants. His rumbling empty stomach told him that it needed food, but he was also concerned about his empty backpack. Within two hundred metres he had bought dried fruit and chocolate bars, two shirts, a thin sweater, some socks, a razor and toothbrush and a lightweight jacket. If anyone investigated the contents of the pack, it now looked as if he was a bona fide traveller.

When he returned to the station, he found a Rumanian-English phrase book which he thought might save his bacon even though he was now supposed to be French. That itself was a worry because although he had a genuine French passport, it didn't have a Rumanian visa in it or a Rumanian entry stamp.

The Constanta train departed on time, pulled by an identical bright blue loco to the previous train, but this was soon up to speed and rattled along. They passed several stations but didn't stop. The countryside was absolutely flat and had the same monotonous regular field pattern; David wondered if Rumania had always been like this or whether it was a pattern imposed by collective agriculture. He had gone through the phase of worrying about all the things that could go wrong, but had given up because he was flying on guesswork. He couldn't think anymore; he was just too tired and he fell asleep for part of the journey. His plan depended on many assumptions; David thought that the boat from Odessa might arrive today, but it was more likely to do so tomorrow. He knew that it arrived in Burgas very early the day after and his idea was to hide on the boat so that he didn't have to go through Bulgarian passport control, then join the rest of the group from Slunchev once they had boarded, becoming British again for the journey to Istanbul.

By the time they arrived in Constanta, it was going dark and he had to find somewhere to spend the night. Opposite the station entrance there appeared to be a large park and David thought it possible that there might be a shelter there where he could sleep. Once inside the park, he saw a sign that he thought said *St. Stefan Orthodox Church*. Standing in front were two

Orthodox priests who looked as if they had just finished evening service. David thought that they might be able to direct him to a hostel where he could stay. He spoke to them in French which, fortunately, they understood.

After a short discussion between themselves one said, "There is a mission for sailors in the old town, run by the Cathedral of St. Petro and St. Pavel." He pointed. "Cross that road and you will see Strada Vasile Caraneche. Go to the end where it turns left. You will see the towers of the two cathedrals. Walk in that direction across the street; that is Strada Archiepiscopale. Go along that road, and the first Cathedral is the Roman Catholic church. Then, a few hundred metres further on, is the big Orthodox Cathedral. Any of the priests in there will point you to the mission where you can stay the night."

It took him at least twenty-five minutes to reach the cathedral, and he wondered if anyone would still be there as it was now quite dark. However, he needn't have worried because it still seemed quite busy and, when he looked through the big open door, he could see a priest standing just inside. David asked him if he could speak French but he shook his head and then, without a word, caught David's arm and guided him to another priest who said in very good French, "I speak both French and English. How may I help you?"

David thought it safer to stick with the French.

"The priest at St. Stefan's told me that you could give me directions to the Church Mission for Sailors. I need somewhere to stay the night before my boat to Burgas tomorrow."

The priest pointed at one of the pews. "Please wait there. I will be no more than ten minutes and then I will take you to the mission."

The mission was at the back of the cathedral, down a narrow street of old buildings, the priest - who had told David that his name was Father Dmitri - took him into the building and told the caretaker that he needed a bed for the night. When David asked how much it cost he said, "The bed is free but the church would always welcome a donation. If I remember correctly the Odessa boat arrives about midday but you must leave the mission no later than ten a.m."

The caretaker took David to what looked like an army barracks. It had five beds along two walls and a bathroom at the far end. David was the only occupant and he flopped onto the bed, exhausted, hoping it didn't have fleas. The mattress was a straw filled leather palliasse on a crudely sprung base; pillows were not provided so he used his backpack as a pillow. As he lay down, he realised that the palliasse smelled of some form of pine scented disinfectant, which he found reassuring.

David was asleep in minutes and slept the sleep of the dead until seven the following morning. It was bad enough having to shave in ice cold water but he couldn't pick up the courage to have an ice cold shower. He hoped that the boat would have hot water. David found the caretaker and pointed to his mouth and stomach, which the man correctly took to mean, 'Where do I get breakfast?'

The caretaker beckoned David out into the middle of the street and pointed to what was obviously a café with three tables outside on the pavement. David studied his Rumanian phrase book while enjoying a breakfast of ham, cheese and ryebread and extremely strong black coffee. Looking down the street he noticed Father Dmitri talking to the caretaker and, after a few minutes, the caretaker pointed towards David at the café and the priest walked over and sat down at his table.

"Did you sleep well last night? The commotion and shouting didn't wake you up?"

"I didn't hear a thing, and slept until just before seven. What was the commotion about?"

"Oh, two drunks were banging on the door. When Marius told them to go away they kept shouting until the police came and took them away. It was lucky I didn't tell Marius your name, because when the police asked him if anyone was staying it was easier for him to say no. If he'd told them about you they would have woken you up to examine your passport."

David thought that the angels must have been on his side during the night.

Father Dmitri said, "The booking office will open at about ten. I will come with you to make sure they understand what you want. Also, I assume you have some dollars or French francs; you'll get a forty per cent discount on the fare if you pay in hard currency - that is, if I'm with you. Otherwise, you get ten percent and he keeps the difference."

When they were in the ticket office, Father Dmitri did all the talking; in fact, a lot of talking. David wondered why it was so complicated to book a ticket to Burgas but, eventually, the priest turned to him. "Right, that's you booked on the Eforie to Burgas. They don't have any single cabins but you're in a cabin on your own unless a lot of people arrive between now and departure time. He asked if you had a visa for Bulgaria; I told him that you did. He says that she's running two hours late and won't arrive until about three o'clock, will depart at four and that you'll get to Burgas very early tomorrow morning."

David thanked him for all the help he had given. "You're absolutely right; I do have a visa for Bulgaria. Can you tell me how I can make a donation to the mission or the church?"

"We would be very grateful if you put a few dollars in the box just inside the cathedral door. But here is a list of things that were stolen from our church during the war; we would be extremely grateful if you could find replacements when you get back to London and we could get them back via the embassy."

As they had been speaking French all the time, David corrected his mistake.

"I assume you mean when I get back to Paris."

"Of course, I meant Paris, not London." He gave David a wink as he said it.

How had he given himself away? Now he was scared. If Father Dmitri had seen through him, so could others. The sooner he was out of Rumania, the better.

David thanked him again and said goodbye.

****

The Eforie slowly chugged into Constanta and moored alongside Quay Number Two; it looked an old ship by design. Its engines seemed a bit noisy and it puffed black smoke from the funnel. However, it had recently been repainted and looked quite smart for such an old ship. A few passengers disembarked and, within minutes, David and the rest of those waiting were asked to go up the gangway. There were only eight of them, all men, who looked as if they were workmen heading to Burgas. David wondered if they were builders, with all the construction underway on the coastal resorts in Bulgaria they probably needed foreign workers. At the top of the gangway, an officer took a cursory look at their tickets and then pointed to a door which David assumed led to the cabins. His cabin had four bunks, so he bounced on the two bottom bunks and chose the more comfortable.

For his plan to work, he had to ensure that no member of the crew would remember the French passenger when he became English after Burgas. Therefore, David decided to stay in the cabin and live on the chocolate bars that he had bought in Bucarest. He had nothing to read except the Rumanian phrasebook, which was hardly a riveting story. After an hour or so he heard the heavy throb of the engines as they increased power and the Eforie moved away from the quay and turned to leave the harbour.

Once at sea, David could feel the slight swell but it was negligible, just a gentle rocking motion that, together with the vibration from the engine, made him feel very sleepy. He didn't put the cabin light on and, as it went dark, he became more and more drowsy. When he awoke it was pitch black. He couldn't find the light switch so he opened the cabin door to look at his watch; it was nearly 4 a.m. everywhere was totally quiet, with just the rumble of the engine breaking the silence. He needed to find somewhere to hide between their arriving at Burgas and the boarding of the Balkantour party for Istanbul.

David didn't want anyone to see him wandering around in the middle of the night, but he needn't have worried, there was no sign of any of the crew. He guessed that, except for the crew on the bridge, they would all be asleep. At the end of the corridor he found a storeroom which didn't seem to be used, except for a few mops and brushes. He thought that might be a good place to hide when the time came, unless they started cleaning when they arrived at Burgas. He knew that not all the cabins were occupied because he had seen the booking sheet in the ticket office at Constanta. If he could find an unused cabin, it would be unlikely that any crew would enter to clean it. David went back to his own cabin, had a shave and then packed all his gear into the back pack. At the forward end of the corridor the last three cabins were empty so he chose the middle one and sat in the chair.

After a while, it seemed as if they were slowing down and, when he looked out of the porthole, he could see lights which he assumed was Burgas. As they crept into the bay he could see that it was getting lighter. It made sense that they would dock at first light which was around half past five. Once it was light enough to see what he was doing he had a good wash and changed his shirt and put on his new jacket to try and look as different as possible from the Frenchman who had boarded in Constanta. David hid his French passport in the lining of the backpack and put the British passport with the visa into his jacket pocket.

Chapter 11

David's plan worked perfectly. He saw the passengers for Burgas disembark. No-one seemed to count them and they left in ones and twos, so there was no reason to think that he would be missed. In the course of the next hour a few crew went ashore, then a truck arrived with some provisions that were loaded by hand, both by crew and shore porters. David saw the bus from Slunchev arrive with about thirty dock workers on it, and a little later the coach arrived with the Balkan tour party. As they started to board, he walked around the bow to the seaward side of the ship and stood behind a lifeboat where he wasn't too conspicuous. Fifteen minutes after the last passenger had boarded the ship pulled away from the quayside. Once they were underway, he went to find the tour guide, who was somewhat surprised to see him.

"Where have you come from? We thought that you'd missed the coach, and we couldn't find you in the hotel."

"I caught the public bus into Burgas, so that I could have a quick look around the town before we boarded, but I came aboard about half an hour before you arrived. I've been on the far side of the ship, watching the other boats. There's a German boat on the far side unloading cargo."

"How do you know which cabin you're in?"

"I don't, that's why I came to find you. Besides, I assumed that you would want to collect my ticket."

"You're in cabin fourteen with Mr and Mrs Janes and Herr Frankel."

David thought that Nina wasn't going to be happy sharing a cabin with two strange men. He knew cabin fourteen because it was next to the cabin in which he had hidden before they arrived. Don and Nina were unpacking when he opened the door and they looked at him, shocked. "Bloody hell, David, where did you spring from? We searched the hotel for you and they opened your room and we could see that your luggage was still there and the bed hadn't been slept in."

David had to give some explanation and said the first thing that came into his head. "It's a long story but I went to the Zeus Bar - you know the one with the gypsy fiddler? Well, I met a girl there and...well, one thing led to another. I went back to my room and packed my small bag with what I needed for this trip and went home with her. I caught the early bus into Burgas this morning." Luckily, they seemed to accept his story.

David hadn't eaten anything - apart from four chocolate bars - in twenty-four hours. His breakfast in the ship's canteen was sausage, bacon and French fries and two coffees, after which he felt substantially more satisfied with life. After a shower and putting on a clean shirt, he was back to being human and on holiday.

The journey to Istanbul was uneventful, until they sailed down the Bosphorus. It was a continuous spectacle of ancient crusader castles, Byzantine ruins and old mosques. Arriving in Istanbul by sea was amazing, the hills dominated by the three great mosques: the Sulimanya, the Blue Mosque and San Sofia. Before mooring, they came to a standstill right by the Dolmebahce Palace, which was a photo opportunity not to be missed. The boat turned round and moored five hundred metres or so from the Galatea Bridge over the Golden Horn. Everyone was excited. The tour guide told them, "The first thing we will do today is, I will take you on a guided tour of the main sites by bus,

101

just to show you where they are. All are within easy walking distance of the boat."

They boarded a minibus for the tour and the guide pointed out the entrance to the Grand bazaar and, not long after, the entrance to the Spies bazaar. Someone questioned why it was called the 'Spies bazaar' only to be told that it wasn't 'spies' but Spice bazaar.

The one sight that David needed, but couldn't ask for, was the whereabouts of the British Consulate. He wanted to get rid of Todorov's report as soon as possible. After his experience in Sofia he assumed that their luggage would be searched on their return to Bulgaria. He dreaded to think what would happen if he was discovered with Todorov's report. He hoped that the Consulate could get it back to the UK for him. After the guided tour, Don, Nina and he were walking across the Galatea Bridge when he heard a loud English voice. It was a tour guide who was struggling to keep her flock in order.

David excused himself to Don and Nina and told them he would rejoin them later. "Excuse me, Miss, I need to find the British Consulate as soon as possible; can you give me directions please?"

She turned to her group, "Wait here and don't move!"

She took David's arm and they crossed over to a policeman standing by the road. In what sounded like fluent Turkish, she obtained the directions, and then, taking a street map from her bag, marked it for him and told him how to get there. David thanked her.

"Keep the map. I have plenty more in our coach." At that she turned, crossed the road, and rejoined her flock.

With the map it wasn't difficult to find the Consulate. David could see the Union Jack from five hundred metres away. He checked carefully before going in — there didn't seem to be anyone watching the building but, just in case, he waited until he saw two other people nearing the building and walked closely behind them, keeping his head down, but not enough to look suspicious. Inside, it was quite impressive: cool and very quiet. The receptionist asked what he wanted. "I need to speak to the British Consul please, it's very important."

"The Consul will only see you if you make an appointment and tell me why you need to see him."

"Tell him that I am employed by the Foreign Office in London and that I have information for them that is most urgent. Would you please show him this? It's my Foreign Office ID."

She disappeared through a door and when she returned she told him to wait and that someone would come for him in a few minutes. He was collected by a very smartly dressed elderly lady and taken to the Consul's office. Above the desk there was a large oil painting of a view of the Thames. It looked like a Canaletto but David assumed that it wasn't the real thing.

"Now then, Mr Hopkins, what can we do for the Foreign Office this morning?"

"Thank you for seeing me so quickly. I need to get this report to Whitehall as quickly and as securely as possible." David passed the report across to him.

"What is it? Why is it important?"

"I don't know; it's all in Russian. All I can tell you is that the man who gave it to me was shot shortly afterwards, and, for that reason, I want to get it away to London urgently."

The Consul looked at him, stunned. "Where did all this take place?"

"I'm sorry, I don't have time and it's a long story. I would like this to be put in a bag addressed to Mr Giles Morris, Department

14, Foreign Office. Then put that into another bag with whatever address you use to get mail to London."

"Yes, of course that can be done. I wish I knew what it is all about."

David said, "That makes two of us. I wish I knew what it was all about as well."

He then had a further thought: it wouldn't be a good idea to be found in Bulgaria with a French passport as well as his British one. He couldn't see why he would need it again.

"One more thing, could you please put this into an envelope and mail it to my home address."

The Consul took it and looked at it then gave him a quizzical look, "What are you doing with someone else's French passport?"

"Just take a look at the photograph."

The Consul looked at him and smiled. "Ah, I see. Always glad to be of service. Where are you off to now? Or shouldn't I ask?"

"That's why I'm in a rush. I need to rejoin the Balkantours group that I'm with, before they miss me. Do you think the opposition keep a watch on the Consulate? I don't want to be seen leaving if possible, is there a back way out?"

"That's always possible. Where is your group going to next?"

"It's just an informal group. This morning we were heading up to the Blue Mosque."

The Consul picked up the phone. "John, I'm sending someone down to the basement garage. Could you meet him there, put him in the back of the van and drop him off in one of those quiet streets near to the Blue Mosque?"

They walked across the hallway to a flight of stairs that went down to the basement and shook hands again. "Thanks for all the help this morning, please ensure that the package gets to London safely."

"Don't worry, it will, I'm always delighted to serve head office. Good luck, whoever you really are."

David hoped that he wouldn't need any good luck now that the dodgy part of the trip was over and he could just enjoy his holiday.

Chapter 12

The rest of the time in Istanbul was great. There were so many things to see and the highlights for David had to be San Sofia and the Topkapi palace; he couldn't believe that there could be so much Ming and Tang porcelain in one place. It was also interesting to cross the Bosphorus and to visit Florence Nightingale's hospital in Scutari, which hadn't been changed since the time of the Crimean War.

They were given an early dinner and then departed Istanbul as the sun was setting. They were all shattered after the hectic tours around the sights and, after a quick drink at the bar, they turned in before ten o'clock. David was getting to be fond of the Eforie as it chugged slowly but steadily northwards, its bows gently rising and falling with the swell. They were soothed to sleep and when they awoke the ship had docked in Burgas. Their instructions were to leave the boat as soon as possible, in order that it could be cleaned before it left for Odessa and they were to be given breakfast in a restaurant in the town. It was a bit chaotic; everyone was dishevelled, some - including David - hadn't had time to shave, but at least they were getting fed. While they were eating the tour guide came up behind him. "Mr Hopkins, these two gentlemen would like to ask you some questions."

David saw two goons - obviously the police heavy brigade - and stood up to face them. In good English one said, "Please finish your breakfast Mr Hopkins. It's nothing urgent that we need to talk about."

After breakfast he was taken to their car and they drove into Burgas. When they stopped in front of the police station, he asked if they were police officers. They took him inside and led him to a small, dreary room, motioning him to sit at one side of a battered table. Only then did they answer his question. "We are not exactly police officers; we're mainly concerned with border security. We would like to know when you came on holiday to Bulgaria, why did you fly to Sofia?"

"I came as a guest of your Ministry of Food in Sofia. I have letters from them, and a copy of my report for them is in my room at the hotel in Slunchev."

"Yes, we've seen those. When we were told that you were missing, we thought it wise to search your room."

"Missing?"

"We would like to know where you disappeared to for three days, and what you were doing."

David wondered what the most plausible response would be, but didn't want to hesitate for too long. "I didn't disappear for three days. Before we left for Istanbul, I had an upset stomach so I stayed in my room, took some pills and didn't eat for a day. Then, the day after, I was feeling better so that afternoon I decided to catch the bus to Burgas and explore the town before joining the boat the next morning."

"Why did you want to explore Burgas?"

"When I arrived in Sofia, I was met at the airport and the guide took me to my hotel. The next morning I was escorted to the Ministry before being put on a plane to Varna, where I was met and taken to Slunchev. I've been in Bulgaria for over two weeks and have seen very little of the country or its people. I wanted to see what ordinary Bulgaria was like, away from the tourist resorts."

"We don't like foreigners wandering around unescorted. They might cause trouble."

"Then I think that's a great shame because, from what I've seen, Bulgaria is a lovely country with lovely people. You should encourage foreigners to wander around, to see for themselves what a great place it is."

The goons said nothing. The door opened and his backpack was brought in. After a short discussion in Bulgarian, it was handed to him.

"I find it interesting that your passport has a Rumanian visa and your case was made in Rumania. Why is that?"

David was expecting a question like this as soon as he saw the backpack. "My Rumanian visa is necessary because I've been asked three times to visit the Ministry of Food in Bucarest and each time the meeting has been cancelled. I have no idea where the backpack was made; it was given to me by a colleague who used to handle the business in Rumania before me, so he could have bought it there."

The simple questions continued for another twenty minutes or so and then David was told that a car would take him back to his hotel in Slunchev.

David waited until he was back in his hotel room to breathe a huge sigh of relief.

Chapter 13

The rest of the holiday was most enjoyable and stress-free: an early morning swim followed by breakfast at the beach bar, sunbathing and sitting chatting to Don and Nina, a leisurely lunch and sitting in the shade in the afternoon. The evenings were, essentially, a long drawn-out dinner with a cabaret at one of the restaurants, or a folk band and singers at another, then too much to drink and fall into bed.

David returned to London with the others of the Balkantours party. Unfortunately, this involved a four hour flight on an Ilyushin 18, which like the IL14 was falling to bits and, having twice the number of engines, was twice as noisy. All of the passengers were thankful when they eventually landed at Heathrow. David had hardly time to unpack or do any jobs at the flat before crashing out in bed, exhausted.

The next morning David was in the office with everyone admiring his suntan and asking if he had had a great holiday. Little did they know what had really happened and, even if he could tell them, they wouldn't believe him. He was getting his thoughts together to write the report of the meeting in Sofia when Mary called. "Your friend Giles is on the phone, do you want to talk to him?"

"Put him through... Giles, good morning."

Giles sounded tense. "David – thank goodness you're back safely. We surmise that everything did not go to plan. We haven't heard a thing from Todorov since you went, and when the package arrived from the Consulate in Istanbul, we at least knew that you had met but that something must have gone wrong. Could you join us for dinner tonight and give us a report?"

"Todorov's dead. I saw him shot in Varna and if you want a report you'll have to take me to an extremely expensive restaurant."

"Don't worry. You'll get your expensive restaurant but not tonight. Colonel Collis would like us to have dinner with him at home. I can promise you an excellent dinner and the Colonel will open a bottle of 1945 claret, which is usually excellent. Can you come to Bentinck Mansions a little earlier than usual, say about six thirty?"

The evening at Bentinck started as usual with Giles pouring two large gin and tonics. Colonel Collis came in, walked over and shook David's hand. "I understand that you've had quite an adventurous holiday; I'm looking forward to hearing all about it."

A lady David had not seen before came in and told them that dinner was ready.

As they sat down at table David asked, "Is that Doris?"

"No, Doris is our housekeeper; she occasionally cooks dinner if I'm in alone. Tonight's cook is a professional chef."

When the starter had been served and the dining room door shut, Colonel Collis said, "You told Giles that Todorov had been shot. Did you see it happen?"

"No, I'd turned to leave the building where we met, when I heard the shots. I looked back through the window and saw him lying on the ground."

"So you don't know for sure that he was dead?"

"No. I didn't stop to find out. I got away as quickly as possible."

"Did you see him arrive? Was he being followed? When you met him did he seem to be scared or nervous?"

"I'd arrived a little early and was waiting on the sixth floor. At the arranged time I walked down to the fourth floor and he was waiting there. I wouldn't say he was scared, but he was being careful. He told me to wait ten minutes after he had left the building before I left. I was watching him leave when he was arrested by three men. I didn't see the shooting but I think he may have tried to escape."

Colonel Collis said, "We'll wait for the main course and then I'd like to hear how you got out unscathed and how our package got to Istanbul."

David's story lasted over the main course and over the cheese course as well. Neither Giles nor the Colonel said very much; David hoped they were impressed. He returned to Ealing to recuperate from his holiday, made himself a cup of tea and sat down to write his weekly letter to Nicole.

Chapter 14

The next food safety problems arose in Switzerland, the food safety authority in Berne rejoicing in the title of Eidgenosische Gesundheitsamt. Apparently, one of the big Swiss food companies - Migros - was concerned about the quality of certain imported packaged foodstuffs. This had spurred the EG to look at the safety of packaged foods both imported and those produced in Switzerland. The questions raised were almost identical to those raised in Poland and the CSSR, so David's reports only needed minor alterations before they were submitted to Berne.

When it came time for him to visit Berne, the D&A Swiss sales manager suggested that they also visited Migros' technical people in Zurich. To David this seemed the opportunity of a lifetime. Nicole and he were in frequent contact by telephone; they usually had a long chat every Friday night and, of course, they had the weekly exchange of intimate love letters. Nicole had been over to London twice to spend the weekend with him in Ealing and now David had the chance to spend some time with her in Basle. As soon as he knew the dates of the two meetings he called her to see if they could spend some time together.

"When is your first meeting?"

"Tuesday morning, in Berne. I propose to fly to Zurich on Monday afternoon. The next meeting is with Migros on Wednesday, and I'll fly back to London the following day. That would give is a bit of time together."

"I'll meet you at the airport, then you can come back to Basle, you can stay with me at my flat. I think that will work well." That seemed a great arrangement, but the next morning she called him at work.

"I've spent some time with the flight time tables; I assume that you get full fare tickets?"

"Yes, why?"

"Well, that means you can reschedule the flights without needing new tickets. There's a Swissair flight to Zurich leaving Heathrow at half seven on the Friday night; and, if you book the next Thursday and Friday off as holiday, you could get the BEA flight home at half three on Sunday afternoon."

"That sounds like a great plan. It will give us ten days together to make up for lost time."

"Oh, before I forget, I suggest that we drive to the Oberland on Saturday morning. I know a lovely inn between Reichenbach and Frutigen where we can stay Saturday to Tuesday morning and then I'll drive you to your meeting in Berne. After your meeting we'll come back to Basle."

What could he say? It was a great advantage him having an executive girlfriend; David thought that Nicole was quite likely to end up as the Managing Director of the company.

They counted the days to their reunion. Every time they spoke on the phone they were becoming more excited. Fortunately for David, the world of food laws was relatively quiet and, apart from a very quick trip to Warsaw to give Messrs Wozniak and Kazmarek the results on the extraction tests and to pop an envelope into the post box in the boulders at Herr Wohl's tomb, he had no more East European adventures.

When the great day arrived - the day he was to fly to his beloved Nicole - David fidgeted all day. He couldn't concentrate and was clock-watching the minutes tick slowly by. A couple of colleagues asked him if he was OK and told him he looked flushed and hot and bothered.

Soon, he was on the Swissair Caravelle looking at France, then over the Vosges and then they were landing at Zurich.

Nicole - looking lovelier than ever - was waiting for him at Arrivals. This wasn't just any beautiful girl, it was his Nicole. Neither of them had eaten dinner so they stopped at a restaurant just a few miles before they reached Basle. Holding hands through dinner created problems; the truth was, they couldn't keep their hands off each other. When they reached Nicole's flat they dumped his case, jumped in to bed, made love, fell asleep and didn't awaken until seven the next morning. David would have been happy to stay in bed all morning, but Nicole wouldn't hear of it. She had their Oberland trip planned in the finest detail. They had to leave by ten o'clock to get to their lunch venue, which was on the shore of Lake Thun.

The holiday passed in a blur. They toured the Oberland and did all the sights. The most memorable times were when Nicole and he sat together in an Alpine meadow with his arm around her, while they looked at the amazing scenery.

David sighed contentedly. "There's a lot to be said for living in Switzerland; views like this only forty minutes' drive from home."

"You've only seen it when the sun's shining. When it's raining and foggy it's not much fun."

"Nowhere's nice when it's raining."

"That's not true; Paris is lovely when it's sunny *and* when it's raining. The streets shine and the pollution goes and you can smell the trees." Nicole breathed in, as if she could smell the Parisian trees right then.

"Do you miss living in Paris?"

"To an extent. I think one problem I have here is living in Basle. I think I'd be happier in Geneva."

"Because of the language?"

"No. It's the people here. They're dull; they don't socialise with anyone but the locals, the 'Schweizerdeutsch'."

David kissed her gently. "I'd be happy anywhere if I was with you."

"Me too, but I don't think you'd settle in Basle. They're very different from the British."

"You're probably right. I'd like to settle down in one of England's old colonies. One where they have beautiful girls and make great wine."

Nicole laughed and punched him on the arm. "Oh, yes? And where's that?"

"Bordeaux. Ouch! What did you do that for?"

"Bordeaux was never an English colony."

"Yes it was. In the fifteenth century. Ouch...If there's one thing I love, it's violent women. Ouch."

****

David's meetings went very much to plan, without any of the East European frustrations. When Nicole dropped him at the front entrance of the EG, David noticed that the building opposite was the Swiss patent office. Just before the meeting started David pointed out of the window, "That's the building where Einstein developed his Theory of Relativity." Their host stood up and asked him to come to the window, "See the end office on the first floor. That is the actual office where Einstein worked. When you come to Berne next, we will arrange for you to visit Einstein's office; it has been preserved just as it was when he worked there."

When Sunday morning arrived, neither David nor Nicole had much to say. Ten days of paradise were coming to an end. David thought both of them knew that they were meant for each other and would spend the rest of their lives together. The problem was that for both of them it would mean a big wrench from their present lives. David couldn't leave his work in London and he didn't think he could settle in Basle even if he could find a job. For Nicole a move to London would mean she would have to give up her great job in pharmaceuticals. David was sure that with her abilities she would get a job in London, but would she be happy there? At their parting by the Departure gate, they were both in tears. David could just about say 'I love you' without breaking down completely.

****

The next few months passed relatively uneventfully with no great excitement. David relished the challenge and the adrenaline surge of the trips to Eastern Europe but the Bulgarian escapade had been a bit *too* exciting. Nicole came over for a few days holiday and he took her to Cheshire to meet his parents.

His father fell in love with her. "All that young lady has to do is to smile and the whole world is a more beautiful place." David never knew his father could be such a romantic.

Then he took her to North Wales. "I know this isn't anything special for someone who's used to that beautiful Swiss scenery, but it's a favourite spot of mine."

Nicole laughed. "Nonsense. Besides, it's good seeing the cliffs where you used to go rock climbing." Her face turned sombre. "Although I must admit that I don't like the idea of you continuing to rock climb."

After that it was another painful separation.

116

Chapter 15

David hadn't heard from Giles for a few weeks, until he called one night to see if they could meet up for dinner at the weekend and then go on to a party that one of his friends from the office was giving. As usual, they met up at Bentinck Mansions first. When David arrived it was Colonel Collis who let him in, telling him that Giles was running late and was still in the shower.

He poured a couple of glasses of whisky, pointed David to a chair by the fireplace and sat opposite him. After a few minutes he said, "The jobs you do with Giles are incredibly important, you know. I don't know how much he tells you about the whys and wherefores, but I think you deserve to know. That Russian report that you got out via Istanbul was military gold dust; we haven't had anything as good as that in years. The problem we have is that you not being a proper employee of Her Majesty makes it difficult for us to show our appreciation. Quite a few people have commented about that operation. We admire your initiative and planning, but we're thinking it would help you if we put you through one of our training schools."

David couldn't comment; he hadn't a clue what training Colonel Collis was talking about. "When you say training school, is that something organised by the bank? What's involved and how long does the course last?"

"No, the bank is a very specialised business. The training courses are run by the Ministry of Defence but funded by the Foreign Office. They last anything from four to six months; it depends on the individual. The courses are designed for each individual."

"But there's no way I could get that much time off work. It would mean resigning from the company and then working full time in the Foreign Office job."

"Would that be such a bad move? It would be a very interesting career."

Just then Giles walked in looking especially smart and asked if David was ready.

Colonel Collis said to Giles, "Don't forget your appointment at half past nine; it might be better to get there a little early. I think you should take David with you."

Giles nodded. "Yes, Sir, I will be there on time."

David had never before heard Giles address the Colonel as 'Sir'. He was also glad that he hadn't had to answer Colonel Collis' question about the potential career change. He needed time to think that one over.

He and Giles walked to dinner chit-chatting about nothing in particular, and David forgot all about Giles' appointment once they were in their favourite Italian restaurant with a bottle of Chianti on the table.

They had finished dinner and were sitting having coffee and a brandy when Giles looked at his watch. "It's time we were leaving; are you going to come with me?"

David looked at Giles in puzzlement. "So where exactly are we going?"

"We're going to Westminster Hall to pay our last respects to the great man himself."

As they went down in the lift, David turned to Giles, "You know the queue to file past the coffin is over a mile long. We will have to wait for an hour to an hour and a half at least." Giles didn't reply and they walked in silence until they reached the Palace of Westminster. David could see the long queue over to the left but Giles ignored it and led David to a small side door with a security guard on duty. Giles produced some document or pass and gave it to the guard and said, "He's with me," pointing at David.

The guard went inside and a minute later reappeared, saying, "Would you please wait inside, for about ten minutes sir. We have stopped the line; it will take about ten minutes for the chapel to clear."

They waited and then were led inside. Giles walked in and stood by the coffin, David stood about two yards to the side and behind him. He waited in complete silence, not even the noise of traffic outside invaded that space. It was a sombre and very moving experience. After about five minutes he heard Giles sigh and, as he turned, David could see a small tear on his cheek and his eyes were wet. David looked again, straight at Giles. The penny dropped. He now knew why Giles looked so familiar and how Miss Robson could afford to send him to Prep school and Dartmouth Naval College.

Neither of them said a word as they walked back to Victoria. Finally, Giles asked if he would like to go back for a nightcap. The last thing David wanted was a drink and explanations from Giles that might upset him. "I think I would rather go back home and think solemnly about what we have done tonight. Goodnight Giles and thank you very much for taking me with you." David turned and then headed to the Tube station.

As the years went by and their friendship continued, David never asked Giles the obvious question and they never spoke about that night again.

Chapter 16

After some two months of peace and quiet, with no calls from Giles or any of his associates, David received a call from Giles' secretary asking if he could please attend a meeting the following afternoon at two o'clock in the Foreign Office annexe in Barham Street. When he arrived, Giles was with two others, one of whom was Giles' boss - the head of Department 14. After introductions Giles said, "We have a somewhat unusual job for you."

"Unusual? That sounds as if it is going to be dodgy or dangerous or both. Where am I going this time?"

"It's a two week holiday in Bulgaria at Golden Sands, all expenses paid."

Bulgaria. David didn't like the sound of that, not after the last time. "What's the catch? What am I taking in or bringing out? Last time I was lucky; my luck might not hold a second time. Anyway, how do we know they haven't traced me from the previous visit, and can we be sure it isn't a trap?"

"No, it isn't a trap. You'll have a clean passport." Giles took a look at his companions and cleared his throat. "As will your wife."

"My wife? But I'm not married and not likely to be in the near future."

"The package that you will be bringing out is your wife."

"Really, Giles. This plot seems a bit fanciful even for you. Now, tell me what this is *really* about."

Giles laughed. "No, this is definitely the assignment, I can assure you. You can't meet her as yet, but as far as you and I know, she is called Anna Margaret Hopkins. She's an important asset and the Russkis want to make sure that she doesn't get to the West. We, on the other hand, want to make sure that she *does*. And that's where you come in."

David thought for a few minutes. 'If the Russians are that determined and they thought they would lose this woman, there is a strong likelihood was that someone will get hurt. I don't want to be me'. Giles continued. "This is how we're going to do it. You and your... wife... are booked on the Monarch flight at ten o'clock on Monday eighteenth June, from Gatwick to Varna, for a two week holiday at Golden Sands. You will travel by train to Gatwick, but your wife's train from Cambridge will be delayed and she will miss the flight. Thomas Cook will arrange alternative flights for her via Prague to Sofia and then Sofia to Varna, where she will arrive Wednesday afternoon. After that, well, just make sure that you have a good holiday and bring her back safe and sound. "

"You make it all sound very simple, but there's a lot that could go wrong with that plan."

Giles held up a hand. "You'll take your wife's passport with you. It will have in it only the Bulgarian visa and entry stamp. When she arrives, she will have a British passport with Russian, Polish and Czech visas and entry stamps; that passport must be totally destroyed as soon as you meet. And don't forget: make sure you act and look like a married couple."

"As I said, there's a lot that could go wrong with this plan. Apart from anything else, I have a long-standing relationship with my girlfriend; I don't want to spoil that."

"You told me that your girlfriend lives in Basle; she'll never know about this job. You get the woman back to the UK and never see her again."

"Well, do we have to share a room?"

121

"Of course you have to share a bloody room; you're supposed to be married for Christ's sake!"

David sighed. "OK, you have the plan but what about the details? What about sleeping arrangements, passion and sex?"

"Surely you don't need sex lessons. Just be careful you don't get her pregnant. And stop worrying. The difficult bit will be when we make the switch at Prague airport. If that goes wrong, your wife doesn't arrive and you come home a single man."

Chapter 17

That night, David lay awake half the night, thinking of all the things that could go wrong. He came to the conclusion that the biggest problem - one that Giles had not discussed - was that it would be ten days between Miss Superspy disappearing in Prague and their flying back to Gatwick. Even PC Plod, let alone the KGB, would think of looking at every flight leaving Prague within two or three hours of her disappearance. By that time every airport and border crossing in East Europe would be watched.

He wondered if there was another way, a safer way. He thought of his apparently authentic French passport in the name of Alain Meschines. The following morning he called the French Embassy and told them that his fiancée, Nicole Marie Derencourt and he were getting married in a couple of weeks. David asked what they had to do to get either a joint passport or her passport changed to her married name.

The problem, he told them, was that she lived in Basle and he was in London. He gave them the details of his home address and passport number, also Nicole's address in Basle. When they asked for the address in Nicole's passport he guessed it would be her parents' address in Bordeaux and gave them that, hoping he was correct. When David called the embassy the following day, the lady asked him to hold because one of her colleagues wanted to speak to him. Eventually, a man's voice came on the line.

"Monsieur Meschines, your request for your passport to include your wife has aroused some interest in Paris. Why didn't you go through your usual channel at the Foreign Office?"

David thought quickly, "I know that we have only two of the French passport blanks remaining, and one of those is earmarked for someone. Rather than use up the last one - especially one for my wife as she's not a member of the department - I thought it would be simpler if I came to you."

"Why will your wife be with you if she isn't operational in the service?"

"Only because if I ever have to use my French ID in an emergency it would be more believable if I was travelling with my wife. To be truthful, I might not want the department to know that she was with me."

"Ah, yes. I understand. Call at the embassy tomorrow afternoon. Ask for me at reception, I will have the passport ready for you."

****

The days passed quickly and David was soon at Gatwick checking in for the flight to Varna. He explained that he had the tickets for both his wife and himself and that one of the cases belonged to his wife, who was on her way. As the minutes ticked by the lady on the desk became more and more agitated at his wife's non-appearance. Eventually, she told David that he had to board immediately or he, too, would miss the flight. He made a show of being upset about leaving his wife behind. Inside, he was pleased that things were going to plan exactly as he had anticipated.

When he reached the hotel, some four or so hours later, the local tour guide told him that she had been informed that alternative flight arrangements were being made for his wife and that she was expected to arrive on Wednesday. So far, so good.

Tuesday was a dull and damp day, which made it easy to hang around the hotel and read a book, trying to look like a husband who had mislaid his better half. There were only a few Brits in the hotel; most of the other guests seemed to be from other Eastern bloc countries - some from East Germany and quite a few Poles.

On the Wednesday they had unbroken sunshine and the temperature climbed until it was just nice to sit where there was some air conditioning. Just before lunch the tour guide found David sitting in the shade. "I've just been informed that your wife is due in Varna at half past four. I've arranged for a car to pick her up at the airport."

David found it difficult to work out how he was feeling; a mixture of eager anticipation and butterflies in the gut. He had never had a wife before, let alone one that he had never even *seen* before. It was worse than a blind date; at least with a blind date you can go home afterwards. In this case they had to stay married for ten days or so. After lunch he walked around the bars and along the beach to kill time, but kept a watch on the hotel entrance, looking for the arrival of a car with a single lady in it. He had decided that it would be safer for them to meet first in the privacy of their room, in case they made any mistakes. He didn't want to be watched by some eagle eyed party official, eager to make a name for himself by discovering a wanted spy.

After the car arrived, David waited twenty minutes before going up to their room. He opened the door. Her passport photo didn't do her justice; she was tall and blonde, with a lovely wide smile. She jumped up, threw her arms around him and shouted "I'm so sorry I messed up our arrangements. I've missed you."

She gave him a long passionate kiss. Anyone walking along the corridor would have known instantly just how close they were to each other. David was just glad that Nicole wasn't walking along the corridor at that precise moment.

When David had first arrived he had given the room a thorough search for bugs but, without one of the sophisticated electronic sweeping devices, he couldn't be sure that they had no listeners, or, indeed, that there weren't any hidden cameras planted in the room. They needed to make this look and sound convincing. They couldn't afford to take any risks, but the problem was that Giles had given him no background information on his wife. David assumed that she had been somewhere in Eastern Europe, in a role quite different to the person to whom he was now married.

After the kiss Anna kicked off her shoes and lay on the bed. "Tell me something about this place. Have you found any decent restaurants? I'm starving. All I had for lunch were some revolting aeroplane snacks." As David lay alongside her, she snuggled up to him and put her arm under his head.

David thought that there was something to be said for married life. Before he had left, Giles had given him just two instructions: "For God's sake don't get her pregnant and don't ask any questions." David had responded that the former wouldn't be a problem – they would, of course, be faking it for any secret eyes and ears. He found, however, that it was more difficult not to ask questions. After all, he was now living with the woman, he deserved to know something about her. Her English was perfect but every so often there was a trace of a foreign accent when pronouncing the odd word. David guessed she wasn't natural born English.

As for Anna, she behaved as he assumed a wife would behave; she wasn't shy or modest and was quite happy to wander around their room stark naked. He couldn't take his eyes

126

off her but she didn't seem to mind. David wondered if she was married or had been married before. Anna's passport said she was twenty-seven, though he had no idea if that was correct, but it seemed about right.

That night when they went to bed she jumped into bed naked. When he started to put on his pyjamas she said, "You won't need those."

Every morning they woke early and went to the beach. Although the air was still cool, the sea was warm. After a good swim they showered at the beach and had breakfast at the beach bar. Afterwards, they would walk back to the hotel hand in hand - obviously a lovely, young happily married couple. At the end of the first week there was a fairly wild beach party and they sat with a young couple from Solihull, who at some point asked the obvious question. "How long have you two been married?"

David was clueless. He didn't know what to say but Anna saved the day. "Just under three years. We were married on July fifth." David was impressed by her quick thinking.

As the end of the holiday drew near they stopped acting and found it very easy to be husband and wife. Anna would automatically put one lump of sugar in David's coffee and give it a stir.

On the last night there was an organised dinner dance where they had one dance together and then went and sat by themselves on the beach. David had kept the dinner tickets as a souvenir and, when he put them into his wallet, Anna took it from him and started looking through it. When she found three of his business cards she took one and put it into her bag and a second she put in her bra saying it would stay next to her heart. David had been given strict instructions not to give her his address or telephone number. However, he considered that he had not disobeyed orders as she had taken them without asking. He then had to raise the problem that had been worrying him all week.

"Anna, we're now going into the most risky part of our mission. I'm sure they'll be looking everywhere for you. It would be naïve to think that they won't search holiday flights as well as regular flights, or anticipate you changing your ID, so I suggest that we go along with the original plan but only up to a point."

She sat back and looked at him, all seriousness. David continued. "Tomorrow we take anything essential in our hand luggage and also divide our things between the two suitcases. We may well have to abandon some luggage. In the morning I'll take one case to the lobby to be loaded into the coach for the airport, so that everyone will think that we intend to fly back with them."

"Ah! I see now."

"Then we'll leave by the side door and take the bus into Varna. From there we'll take a cab to the airport. I have an alternative passport for you but in it you have dark hair. Take this bottle and put it in your bag, along with a towel."

"What is it?"

"It's a fast acting hair dye. It will give you dark hair in about five minutes."

Anna took the hair dye. "They do say blondes have more fun, but I quite fancy being a brunette."

"Oh, I forgot; your new ID is French. Do you speak any French?"

"Well, I got good grades at school, but I'm not fluent."

"OK. Let me do all the talking and only speak when you're confident that you won't make any obvious mistakes."

Neither of them slept well that night and they were up and packed by seven. At eight David took one of their cases to the front lobby, thinking that it would be the last time they would see that one.

Upstairs, Anna checked their room for the last time. When David returned he said, "Are you ready? It's time to put my plan into action. With a bit of luck it won't be necessary and we can just fly home as originally planned."

They went down the fire escape and out through the side door. It was only a few hundred metres to a bus stop which couldn't be seen from the hotel. As they mingled with the few workers in the queue they exchanged a couple of words in French but it was pointless really; they both had their guts tied in knots worrying that something would go wrong. On the bus David explained the plan in a soft voice.

"When we get to the airport you go to the entrance for Departures and stand outside as if waiting for someone. I'll go into Arrivals. From there, you can see into the Departure lounge. I'll have a good look around to see if anything looks unusual or suspicious. If it's OK I'll walk to meet you. If not, I'll get the bus into Varna. You follow me but we mustn't sit together. When we get to Varna I know the way to the train station, so, again, just follow me there. As soon as you see a Ladies toilet, get inside and dye your hair, either at the bus terminus or the station. We don't get together again until after you've dyed your hair. And don't forget to dump the bottle of dye and your towel."

At the airport Anna went to the Departures door and stood looking as if she was waiting for someone. David went into Arrivals and pretended to be scanning the Arrivals schedule. After a few minutes he wandered over to where he could see into Departures.

129

Suspicious had been the wrong word. It was blatantly obvious - the whole area was crawling with police, some armed. When the tour had arrived from the UK there hadn't been a single cop on duty in either Arrivals or Departures. David walked nonchalantly from the building and, making sure that Anna had seen him, he made his way to where the Varna bus was waiting. Anna got on and sat three seats behind him.

Chapter 18

It was only a thirty minute ride to the bus station in the centre of Varna. When they arrived, David started walking towards the exit but noticed that, as the place was not busy, neither were the toilets. He slowed down and Anna took the hint and went into the toilets.

David took a book out of his bag and started to read. After what seemed like ages Anna emerged, looking totally different to how she had gone in. Not only was her hair dark brown but she had pinned it up somehow. She also seemed to be wearing a different jacket until he realised that she had turned it inside out. They started walking to the train station but, instead of Anna walking with him, she followed behind - sometimes fifty metres behind, sometimes a hundred metres. Twice, she disappeared altogether and David thought he had lost her, but, after a few moments' panic she reappeared, looking cool and casual. It crossed David's mind that she might have done this before - either following someone or avoiding detection. She looked like a pro, or, at the very least, someone who had a lot of practice.

His research on train times paid off. He knew that they shouldn't take the first train to Sofia because ten minutes later there was a non-stop train that arrived half an hour before the first. David had considered the potential problem of the non-stop express. If it didn't stop, they couldn't easily escape if they had a problem. On the other hand, if they *did* have to get off the train he had no idea where they would go anyway.

As it was, the journey was uneventful. They sat side by side holding hands under the table, saying very little - partly to spare

Anna's French but also because they were both too scared to talk. David realised that, whatever Anna was escaping from, he was also in it up to his neck. The way they had avoided both the tour party and the Monarch flight was proof that they were guilty. If they were caught, David probably would just disappear. He daren't think of what might happen to Anna.

They passed mountains and beautiful rivers, little towns and monasteries on the top of hills; all just slid by in a blur. Four hours later they could see the outskirts of Sofia and soon they were pulling into Sofia station.

They walked to the exit where there were four old cabs waiting in the hot, humid afternoon. David noted that there were two police standing outside the station, but they didn't seem to be very bothered about anything in particular.

He squeezed Anna's hand. "All OK so far."

Anna said nothing, just held his hand very tight. He could tell she was trembling and David knew she was scared. He was, too, and the strain was beginning to tell on both of them. He was aware that both of them were tired and it would be so easy to foul up. He was worried about Anna. He wondered if she regretted trying to escape or whether she was even ready to give up. The trouble was that he had no idea what she was escaping from or why she wanted out. David didn't even know which country she was escaping from. Her original passport was almost certainly as false as her new one and her very slight accent was European somewhere; it might be Slavic, certainly her features could be Slavic or from anywhere in Northern Europe.

He realised that from now on it would be up to luck. There were no alternative plans; all they had to do was not make any silly mistakes. He wondered if this was easier said than done.

Chapter 19

At the airport they saw the check-in desk for Air France and the notice saying that AF 336 to Paris was scheduled to leave on time. David had bought the open tickets as soon as he knew that he was going back to Bulgaria. After what happened the last time, he had grave misgivings about the wisdom of his return. He had developed the fall back plan just in case. It was possible that if the date on the tickets was before Anna had disappeared - wherever she had disappeared from - it might alleviate suspicion, though he had only made the actual reservations four days before. While the call had been made from Varna, David had given their address as 'care of' the French Embassy in Sofia. He hoped to God that no one had checked.

He took a careful look around and couldn't see any obvious sign of a police or security presence as he walked up to the desk. The Air France lady was obviously French. They couldn't risk Anna being drawn into a conversation so David took her passport and presented both of them at the desk while Anna stood behind him.

"Is your wife unwell; she seems rather pale?"

"Thank you, she is well, but is terrified of flying. She's taken a tranquilliser."

The check-in lady asked, "How long have you lived in England? You're starting to pick up an English accent."

David smiled and said nothing, just took back the passports. They went to sit in the area by the gate. David turned to a pale and drawn Anna. "It seems to be working OK. We'll soon be home, sweetheart, and then you can have a long rest."

Less than an hour later they were airborne and heading for Paris. David called the stewardess and asked for a Ricard and water for himself and a brandy and water for Anna. "We've had a somewhat stressful journey."

After a little while David whispered to Anna. "We're over Austria now. We're safe."

Anna turned and gave him a kiss on the cheek and squeezed his hand.

"Now that we are almost home, can you tell me your real name?"

"My name is Anna Magdalena Petrova and I am from a little town in Russia called Chudovo, south of Leningrad."

"Where are you going to live in England?"

"I don't know."

"What are you going to do?"

Anna smiled. "I don't know that, either. All I was told was that if I followed their instructions they would get me out. Then I was told to meet you and you would get me out as your wife."

David shook his head. "If we'd followed their original instructions we would at best be in prison and, at worst, shot. I'll take charge from now on."

As usual, Air France provided a rather good meal together with half a bottle of a decent wine. At Orly they transferred to the next flight to Heathrow. David was pleased that they didn't have to go through passport control and customs; they might have been convincingly French in Bulgaria but they wouldn't pass as such in France.

There were no problems arriving in London, where they took a cab to David's flat in Ealing. They dumped their luggage in the hall. Anna refused food and drink. "Where's the toilet? I'm so tired I just want to go to bed."

They collapsed on to the bed exhausted, and held onto each other for a long time.

Chapter 20

They awoke with the sun shining in through the curtains. David looked at the clock. "Anna, can you believe we've slept for nearly ten hours?" After a shower, they sat with a cup of tea. David thought about what they had been through and let out a sigh of relief. "I don't think I would ever want to repeat yesterday's journey. I don't know how we did it. I'm still shattered."

Anna smiled at him. "I know how we did it. It's because you're a genius. You must be the best spy in England."

All David could say was "I'm not a spy, I'm a chemist."

Anna just looked at him and smiled once again.

Later that morning, David called the office to say that he had returned with a tummy bug and wouldn't be in for another two or three days. He had no intention of giving Anna up to Giles or whoever in the near future. However, after lunch, when they were out shopping in Ealing Broadway, he saw a headline in a newspaper: 'English couple disappear in Bulgaria' and realised that, sooner or later, they would have to admit to being back in the UK. In the meantime, they used up some of the dollar float that they hadn't spent, buying new clothes for Anna. When they had left Bulgaria they had only the clothes they were wearing at the time. This wasn't a problem for David, of course, since he came back to a wardrobe full of clothes. Anna, however, needed a completely new wardrobe. After two more days spent enjoying each other's company it was time for them to return to reality. David called Giles to ask him if he would like to come to dinner the following evening.

"Oh, thank God, David. Where the hell are you calling from? What do you mean come to dinner? Come *where* to dinner?"

"At home, of course. We could go out somewhere but I thought it would be more private here."

"What the hell has been happening? We thought you'd been arrested or shot...or both. The Bulgarians rumbled our little scheme and we found out that they essentially closed down all routes out of the country. We thought they'd got you. And we have no idea what happened to Anna. They must have got her as they've gone very quiet."

"When you say Anna, do you mean my wife?" David looked at Anna and grinned. She was holding a towel over her face so that Giles couldn't hear her laughter.

"Yes, of course, I mean your supposed wife. Who the hell else do you think I mean?"

"Well, my wife is where any wife should be. She's here by my side. Oh, and less of the 'supposed'. We got married at the registry office yesterday. Sorry we didn't invite you. We just wanted a quiet wedding."

Anna had to dash into the kitchen so that she didn't explode with laughter.

There was silence on the other end of the phone. Then Giles let out a splutter. "You did *what*? I'm coming over there right now!"

"Oh no, you don't! You'll wait until tomorrow night when you and one other are invited to dinner. If you come with your fake Special Branch friends, we won't be here. If we can give the whole of the Bulgarian state police the slip, you and your dozy friends in Department 14 don't stand a chance." And, with that, David put the phone down on a still spluttering Giles. He looked at Anna, who was sitting looking at him wide eyed.

137

"You shouldn't speak to your boss like that, you'll get arrested."

He put his arms around her. "He's not my boss and he needs me a lot more than I need him."

"Well, I hope you're going to tell him tomorrow that we're not *really* married."

David hugged her close. "Maybe, maybe not. It just depends how much he annoys me."

Chapter 21

They put the TV on to get the lunchtime news, but there was nothing said about the couple missing in Bulgaria. David smiled at Anna. "Typical; famous for one day." He switched off the television. Knowing that, for now, they didn't have much more time together he decided to take Anna into town; he wanted to show her some of London's famous places before all she would see would be the inside of stuffy offices and an interminable parade of nameless men asking her questions.

"Where would you like to go?"

Anna thought for a moment. "Westminster Abbey and... where the Queen lives." So they walked from Westminster to Whitehall down the Mall to the Palace and finally rested their feet, watching the ducks in St. James' Park and eating ice-creams.

"Why did you come to England? Are you escaping from something? Why do our intelligence people want you so badly?"

Anna said nothing, deep in thought and staring at the ducks. David was about to start asking more questions, when Anna eventually spoke. Her voice was sad. "It's a long story. One day, when we've known each other for a long time I'll tell you." David nodded slowly as she continued, saying exactly what was in his own mind, but which he had not wanted to raise. "You know that I have to go away for a while; I want you to know that I've never loved anyone else like I love you. I will think of you all the time I'm away and will come back to you as soon as I can."

He could see the tears running down her cheeks and his own eyes started to water as well. He threw his ice-cream down on the ground and took her into his arms, feeling his shirt getting wet from her tears.

After a while, they got up and continued walking around the lake holding hands but saying nothing. David was sure they were thinking the same thoughts but couldn't find any words. Later that evening he asked Anna if she would do something for him. "It's a secret that I want to keep from everybody." When Anna nodded he said, "I don't want anyone to know how we got out of Bulgaria and that I have French passports for my wife and I."

"Why?"

He looked at her with a half smile. "There may come a time when we need to use them again."

Anna walked up to him and gave him a long kiss. "Let's go to bed."

The next day they spent chatting and reminiscing about their adventure. They both agreed that they had seen nothing of the scenery on the journey or, at least, they couldn't remember anything of what they had seen.

David made her a promise. "One day, we'll go back to Bulgaria as tourists and see everything that we missed."

Anna scowled. "No, that's one country I will *never* go back to. I just want to forget it as quickly as I can."

"What about our famous honeymoon? Do you want to forget that?"

Anna smiled. "Don't be silly. I'll only forget that after we've been on our *real* honeymoon."

Later that afternoon, Anna reminded him that she had to prepare a dinner for four.

"I'm not a very good cook, even in Russia. I have no idea what to cook in England."

"Don't worry, there's a fabulous Chinese takeaway just around the corner in Acton. I'll phone an order in at about six o'clock and collect it just before seven. All we have to do is get the oven hot and the plates in the warming drawer."

When Giles arrived he had to take a close look at Anna before he recognised her. She still had her hair done up and it would take weeks before the dye wore off. His partner was introduced as Jenny, with no surname given. This told David that she was MI personnel.

Giles shook David by the hand. "We couldn't believe it when we found that you were both out. We didn't give up hope, because we knew something was going on. When the Monarch flight eventually arrived - two hours late - we learned that every passenger had been interrogated by the security police, who wanted to know where you were. You had a lucky break with your luggage being put on to the flight and two of the people from your hotel said that they had seen you on the beach just before the coach left for the airport."

David didn't consider it lucky; he had put a lot of thought into his plan before he had left England. However, he said nothing to Giles.

Giles sat back in his chair and looked at David appraisingly. "Just how *did* you get out, anyway?"

"That's *our* secret. Your cockeyed scheme nearly got the two of us killed. It's a good job that one of us has some brains."

Giles dismissed that with a wave of the hand. "It's not important, we'll find out soon enough."

Anna called from the kitchen, "Not from me, you won't."

****

After dinner Giles said, "It's time we were leaving." He turned to Anna, "Have you got all your things packed?"

"No. I haven't packed and I'm not leaving David until tomorrow. You can send a car at half past ten in the morning."

David smiled at Anna's spirit. It was one of the many things he loved about her. Giles, however, looked rather taken aback.

****

The next morning they had said their goodbyes and were waiting for Anna's car. A chauffeur driven Ministry car arrived, with Giles in the back looking important. As he got out Anna went to fetch her luggage.

Giles repeated his words of the previous day, "David I don't know how you did it, but it was a brilliant achievement. Well done."

All David could say in reply was. "I don't know what you want from Anna, but take my advice; you have a tiger by the tail. If you attempt to pull it, you'll get hurt."

Anna returned with her new suitcase and hand luggage all bought from Bentalls, in Ealing.

Giles said, "I'm sorry that you two have to part. Say your farewells. It's unlikely that you'll meet again." His voice was cold and matter of fact.

Anna gave David a big kiss, a loud thank you and whispered in his ear, "That's what *he* thinks, you'll see me sooner than you realise."

As they drove away Anna turned round and gave him a final wave.

Chapter 22

David spent the next two days moping around the flat and ignoring the phone. Eventually, he couldn't stand it any longer and decided it was time to go back to work. He had only been in for an hour or so when his boss called. "Jock wants to see the two of us at four o'clock in his office."

"Did he say what he wants to talk about?"

"No. Managing Directors don't have to give explanations."

When they arrived in his office, David guessed that it was nothing serious by the grin on the MD's face. After waiting a couple of minutes while his secretary served tea, Jock said, "Yesterday afternoon I had a rather strange phone call from a senior official in the Foreign Office. He told me that they had received reports from our embassies in Warsaw and Prague that one of our employees...," he pointed his finger at David "...you, David...is very highly regarded in the Ministry of Food in both Poland and CSSR. Our Commercial Attaché in Prague has been informed that our business would flourish if you were more involved."

David knew that this was just a ruse by the devious bastards in the FO to get him going into East Europe more often. He wondered if now was the right time to tell his boss that he was a spy as well as a chemist. However, before he could say anything Jock Johnston went on. "This fits in with a plan that we've been thinking about for some time. We're going to make Willi Marketing Director for all of East Europe, including Russia and East Germany. Giuseppe Lombardo will continue to work with the Russians but report to Willi. And you, David, will be responsible for Poland, CSSR, Hungary and Rumania. As for

Bulgaria, Guiseppe will continue with sales and you'll cover any technical support that's required. The Hamburg office will continue looking after East Germany but they've been told that they must keep you informed."

David wondered if he should tell them that they were being manipulated by the FO, just so that they could get him behind the Iron Curtain more often. However, Jock's next words made him think again.

"This is a big jump in responsibility; you'll get a fifty per cent increase in salary as from today." Fifty per cent? With David's new responsibilities and home situation, this was not to be sniffed at. For that, David could work with the FO's manipulation and sneakiness for a while longer. After all, at least he now knew what to expect from them. What was that old adage about keeping your enemies close? David thanked Jock for the vote of confidence in his abilities.

David's boss turned to him. "Well, you seem to have developed a fan club in far off places."

When he returned to his office there was a note on his desk telling him that Giles had called asking if David would like to join him for dinner that night and to call him after six if he could make it.

****

After a rather long day at the office trying to catch up on three week's work, David was back in the flat feeling rather depressed after losing Anna, thinking about his new role and wondering if he could be bothered going to dinner with Giles. The telephone rang. He ignored it, not feeling in the mood to speak to anyone and it eventually stopped. It would no doubt be Giles, wondering if he was coming over. Ten minutes later it rang again. Somewhat reluctantly, he picked up the receiver.

144

A French voice screamed down the phone *"Mais, Bon Dieu, où étais-tu?"*

Where was he? What did this woman mean? Her shriek meant that he could hardly make out the voice. "Sorry, I don't understand."

"Mais qu'est-ce que tu foutais?"

"Nicole is that you? I don't understand."

"Well, if you want it in English, where the fuck have you been? For nearly two years I have dreamed of the day when you would ask me to marry you. You then get the French Embassy to call and tell me that we're getting married. They said you'd spoken to them about our getting married and asked if it was true and when it is."

"Nicole...I... There must have been some mistake."

"Don't interrupt! I told them the tenth of June. They then asked where we were going for our honeymoon and I said Martinique. It was the first place that came into my head. I've been trying to call you for two weeks to ask what the hell is going on."

David couldn't think of anything to say, he was confused and speechless.

Nicole continued, calming down slightly at last. "If you wanted to surprise me, this was the wrong way to go about it! I wanted a romantic proposal – not an official call from the French Embassy. Really, David."

"It's all some huge mistake. I've got no idea how all that happened. I've been overseas for a time and couldn't call you." He needed some time to think about how he was going to explain to Nicole. "I can't get over to Basle at the moment. I've got so much work piled up because I've been away. I'll get over as soon as I can, I promise."

"That's no excuse. Look, what's happened has happened. It was only a matter of time before we were married. It's all organised. I'm coming to see you next weekend and you *will* be taking me to Martinique for our honeymoon or it's the guillotine for you."

With that, the phone was slammed down. David's head was spinning. He didn't really feel like going out, especially after his conversation with Nicole, but he wanted to hear Giles' version of the afternoon's news. He called Giles, who suggested that they meet at the Spaghetti House in Knightsbridge. As they looked at the menu Giles said, "After all the excitement, have you settled down to normal life? You know that last mission in Bulgaria was incredibly important for us."

Normal life? David's life wouldn't be normal until he got Anna back. He couldn't believe how callous Giles was. "So you say, but what about Anna?"

"It was more important for Anna. It's ensured her future safety and happiness. She's extremely grateful to us for getting her out."

David snorted. "Who's this 'us' that got her out? Your plan was crap."

Giles took a mouthful of food before responding. "She's made it very clear that she regards you as the hero; she told me that without you she would be dead. It gave me no pleasure at all, when I found out just how close the two of you had become, I can assure you. I was extremely glad that you were only kidding when you said you'd got married."

"Surely you're not surprised? You put two young people together and they have to convince the world that they're on honeymoon. They're either going to end up either hating each other or falling in love. And, really, would it have been so bad if we *had* got married?"

Giles looked down at his plate. "I'm really sorry about this, but my advice to both of you is to think of it as a holiday romance and nothing more."

David decided to change the subject before he exploded with anger. He taxed Giles on the events of the afternoon, telling him that he thought the FO was being unethical. Giles laughed. "The FO aren't bright enough to be unethical. For a start, no one there knows where you work. I suspect that it's a genuine report coming via the embassy. I could get my contact in the embassy to find out for you if it's important?"

David muttered. "It doesn't matter." He didn't say what he was thinking: that he didn't believe anything that Giles told him anyway.

Giles then told him that they had been trying to find out how David and Anna had returned to the UK. Since both Anna and he had refused to tell them, they had started their own investigation.

"It's interesting. According to the Bulgarians you and your wife are officially missing in Bulgaria. They're keeping the Consulate informed on the results of their enquiries; they say they know that you haven't left the country. Of course, they say nothing about Anna. We don't even know if they've linked you to her disappearance."

David silently waited for Giles to continue.

"The fact that Anna is out, and that you did it, has been discussed in high places. Both the Minister and C think that you should come and work for us full time. In the Minister's words, 'He's too good to be running around doing mail errands like a postman.' What do you think of that proposal?"

147

David continued eating his Spaghetti Carbonara and said nothing. His mind was reeling. Two job offers in the same day. Giles prompted him. "So, what do you say?"

"I don't know what to say, I need time to think about it. I've got a great job at present that I enjoy very much, and I've just received a huge promotion. I'm not sure I want to become a civil servant."

Giles then expounded on the benefits, salary and pension merits of working for the Foreign Office. "Look, this isn't something which lands on everyone's plate, you know."

"Giles you must consider that my success in the two Bulgarian missions was due to me *not* being a member of your department. Your plans were too rigid. They didn't cater for the unexpected. As a civil servant you're a chess player. All your moves are defined and covered by rules and conventions. I, on the other hand, am a Chinese GO player. I follow no rules. My moves can be irrational and unpredictable; I move a piece and it might be an hour before my opponent realises why I made that move."

"What on earth is GO? I've never heard of it, surely it's not harder than chess?"

"The difference between them sums up this last mission. You don't know *how* I did it and the opposition doesn't know *if* I did it, or even if anything has been done at all."

"Look, there's no need to rush the decision, just think about it, that's all."

"I'll think it over. We can discuss it again in a few weeks' time."

His far greater problem was Nicole; she was due to arrive the day after tomorrow. He hadn't a clue what he was going to say and even less of a clue what *she* was going to say.

148

Chapter 23

On the Friday morning David asked Marian, his landlady, to show Nicole up to his flat if she arrived before he returned from the office.

When he arrived home, Nicole appeared to have settled in. A pink nightdress was folded on one of the pillows on his bed and some of her clothes were hanging in the closet among his shirts and jackets.

Nicole appeared from the kitchen and gave him a big hug and kiss and then another. He noticed that there were tears in her eyes. "You silly man, why didn't you ask me before? I've been in love with you since that first week at Berlitz. I knew that one day you would call and I dreamed of the day when you would ask me to marry you."

David took his handkerchief and wiped her eyes, unsure of quite what to say.

"Why did you have to get the embassy to ask me? Why were you so timid? You must have known that I would say yes."

"Nicole, this is a long story and difficult for me to tell you. I didn't arrange or expect the embassy to call you."

Nicole gazed at him for a long moment, her brow furrowed. "So... you *didn't* want to ask me to marry you?"

"No. I mean...yes. Look, let me explain. But before I do you should know that your new passport saved both my life and that of another person."

Nicole's expression said this had better be a good story or else. He could see she was close to tears.

He took her hand and gently led her to the sofa. "What I'm telling you is a secret. My job - that is, the one you know about -

is only half the story. The other half is that when I'm in East Europe I'm a spy."

"But, David, that's--"

David put his hand up to silence her. "Some weeks ago I was given the difficult and potentially dangerous job of getting a Russian lady - who was wanted by the KGB - out of Russia. I was given two fake British passports - for my wife and I - and a plan of how we were to get out. I was scared that if anything went wrong I was likely to get shot, so I came up with an alternative plan – one that I was much happier with. Several years ago I acquired a French passport in my mother's French maiden name, Meschines. So I persuaded the embassy to give me one for my fiancée, in her married name, for our impending honeymoon."

Nicole said very quietly, "I remembered you telling me that your mother's name had been Meschines; that's how I knew it was you."

"Well, the MI6 plan was useless and the only reason Anna and I managed to get back to England was because of your passport."

"And where is this Russian woman now?" Nicole's voice was small and scared.

"I don't know." He shrugged. "I was only part of the plan. I never knew why she had to get out of Russia or where she went to after we got back to England."

"How long did it take to get out?"

"We were husband and wife on holiday for ten days and two days travelling."

"Did you...? "

"Did I what?"

Nicole bit her lip. "Did you...make love to her?"

David stood up and began to pace the room. "What has that to do with anything?"

"I just want to know if you did or if you didn't"

"Oh, for God's sake, Nicole."

She started to cry. "So you never wanted to marry me at all." It wasn't a question, simply a quiet statement.

David sat down again and took her hands. "Nicole, that's not true. I wanted to marry you from the time we were together at Berlitz. You said you felt that way, and I did, too. I've never met anyone who I want to be as close to as you. I dreamed of our getting together, but you had your new job in Basle and I was in my new job in London. One of us would have had to give up our job and I couldn't see that happening."

"We could have done something about it. You never gave me a chance to make that choice!"

David shrugged. "I'm sorry; I just thought it would be too difficult."

"But you never said anything! You just let me carry on thinking that everything was OK between us. You let me *hope*."

"It was OK."

"Was?"

"*Is* OK. It's just..."

"Well, I've been told that I can move from Basle to the London office. When you asked me...when I *thought* you had asked me...to marry you, I told my boss that I would be leaving to live in London. He fixed the transfer." She looked at him with a mixture of worry and defiance.

David sat dumbstruck. The whole world was going mad. This changed everything, not only with Nicole but also about his decision on the FO job.

Nicole looked at him. "You've gone very quiet, David. Obviously this news isn't as happy for you as I thought it would be." She stood up and walked over to the window. "If you want, I'll leave tomorrow, but I've nowhere to stay tonight. Can I stay here?"

"Of *course* you can stay here." David tried a feeble joke. "After all, your nightie seems to have claimed residency rights. And I don't want you to go tomorrow."

She came and sat down next to him again, tears streaming down her face. He held her for a while, neither of them saying anything, both of them miserable.

Eventually, she lifted her head and looked at him out of red-rimmed eyes. "Are you angry?"

"I'm not angry. Confused, perhaps, but mainly concerned. It appears that I have tricked you into believing that I wanted to marry you, and I'm truly sorry for that. And now, it seems there's no other way. I feel as though I've been pressured into getting married; that's what I'm unhappy about. It seems that we have tricked each other and I don't think that's a good way to start a marriage."

They sat there, saying nothing, at either end of the sofa, lost for words. Then David said, "I think we should back pedal a bit. When do you have to get back to Basle?"

"I don't, except to pick up some more of my things; if I'm staying, I start work at the London office at the beginning of next month."

David nodded and, after a long pause, came to a decision. He gently took her chin in his hand and turned her face to his. "OK, this is what I think we should do. We'll live together as flatmates for a few months. If it turns out that we're as close as ever, then I shall ask you to marry me properly. You'll take me to Bordeaux to meet your parents and, after we've been engaged for a while, we'll get married and have lots of children. Does that sound like a good idea to you?"

Her eyes regained some of their sparkle. She sniffed and wiped her nose inelegantly on the back of her hand, looking for all the world like a small child who had found her favourite toy. "That's a very English plan, completely lacking in Gallic passion and flair, but, nevertheless, it's a good plan."

David held his arms open wide and Nicole closed the gap on the sofa and sat on his knee. Soon, she started to laugh at the funny noises coming from his stomach. David then remembered that he hadn't had anything to eat since breakfast and suggested a visit to the local Chinese restaurant.

Chapter 24

The following Monday, Nicole started her new job and they worked out a daily routine. They left together, David dropping Nicole off at Ealing Common tube station before heading up the North Circular to Park Royal. In the evening they made their way home separately because of their differing business commitments. Like all young couples in love and sharing their lives, they developed a lifestyle and routine that worked. Apart from another very quick trip to Budapest, David was not needed in Eastern Europe. His FDA work was now more to do with proposed legislation in the UK and, to a lesser extent, in France. However, as she settled into her London job, Nicole was required to travel quite frequently in the UK and Scandinavia. When she was away David missed her and spent his evenings aimlessly watching TV or going to the pub if he could find someone to go with.

As he drove back one evening, to a flat that he knew would be empty, he was preoccupied with the choice between an Indian and a Chinese takeaway. He opened the front door and Marian, his landlady shouted from the kitchen. "Dave? Is that you? Can you spare a min?"

He pushed open the kitchen door. He could see that Marian was ironing with one hand and cooking tea with the other. "I had a telephone call for you about half an hour ago. She wouldn't give a name but I think it was that Russian woman."

David's heart leapt. "Do you mean Anna?"

"How many Russian women do you know? Anyway, she said she would call back at six. I started to give her your own phone number but she said that she couldn't use that number for some

154

reason. His lordship isn't back until seven. Why don't you make a pot of tea and wait here until she rings again?"

As the clock struck six, the phone rang; Marian said nothing and just pointed at it.

Dave picked up the receiver. "Anna, is that you? Why are you ringing Marian's number?"

"David! I need to be quick." Her voice was rushed and full of emotion. "I can't ring your number because I've been forbidden to contact you; they said I would be sent back if I tried. Calls from my number are intercepted and I bet they have a phone tap on your line, so I'm calling from a friend's office at work. I promised that I would call you, so here I am. I miss you lots and think of you every day."

"I miss you, too. Where are you working? What are you doing?"

"I'm teaching Russian to undergraduates but I can't tell you where. I just wanted to tell you that I love you lots, miss you terribly and wanted to make sure that you didn't forget me."

"I'm not likely to forget you, but it sounds like you are being kept a prisoner."

"No, no, I'm fine. I have my own flat and I can go anywhere in the city and wander around the shops. I have a bicycle and go for rides exploring the countryside. It's just that I have been forbidden to talk to, or meet with, you and anyone from Russia. If I do they say my safety can't be guaranteed."

"Who says so? Giles?"

"No, I haven't seen Giles for months but I think the people work for him."

David started to say something else but she interrupted him, "I have to go. I think someone's coming into the department. I'll call Marian in a week or so."

As David put the phone down, Marian asked, "Was it Anna? Why did she call here?"

David just nodded a 'yes' and dialled 0.

When the operator answered he said, "Operator, I was supposed to make a note of the number that just called me, but they said goodbye, and forgot to tell me. Could you please tell me their number so that I can return their call."

The operator called back a few minutes later saying, "I can't give you the precise number, because it came from an internal exchange, but I can tell you that they were calling from a Cambridge number."

David thanked her and put the phone down, satisfied. It would be relatively simple to find out the name of the new member of the Russian department at Cambridge.

****

As soon as he was in the office the next day, he called Cambridge University and asked to be connected to the Russian department. Once through, he asked if he could speak to the new lecturer who had just started, "She called me yesterday but I didn't write down her name and I've forgotten what she said she was called."

"That would be Magda Sakharova. I'll put you through."

After a wait of several minutes, the woman came back. "I'm sorry, she hasn't arrived yet. I'll tell her that you called. What name is it and can she call you back?"

David thought that it might not be a good idea if there was a record of him trying to call Anna. "My name is Dr Mike Thompson at University College London. I'll be out for the next hour or so. I'll try again later." When he tried later he was put straight through.

"Magdalena Sakharova speaking."

"Anna, is that you? It's David. I needed to know where you are and that you are safe. I want to see you again."

There was a gasp of surprise from Anna, "How did you find out where I was?"

"That was easy. You forget, I'm a spy! I miss you so much. Where can we meet up? There's so much to talk about and I want to give you a big hug and lots of kisses."

Anna sounded nervous. Her voice was low and breathy. "I can't get away until Saturday. I'd love to see you again, but I don't think it's a good idea for you to come to Cambridge. If I was seen with a man, someone might comment at the department." She was silent for a moment. "I know; I've seen a bus labelled St. Neots, can we meet there? I've not been there so can you find someplace where we can meet and call me back? Call 4224. It's the phone in our office; I share it with just two others. It will save you having to go through the switchboard every time. I'll save up all my love until we meet."

David looked up St. Neots in the AA book and found the Bridge Inn in the list of hotels, with an address in the Market Square. He called Anna and they arranged to meet at eleven at the Bridge Inn. David could hardly concentrate at work with the anticipation. He was just glad Nicole was away. She would surely have noticed his jumpiness and excitement. He felt guilty thinking about Nicole and tried to put her out of his mind. Soon, he would see Anna again.

Chapter 25

David had been waiting since ten o'clock. At eleven o'clock he felt his pulse rate go up as his eyes met Anna's. Nothing had changed. He was as much in love with her as ever. As they embraced, Anna closed her eyes and David felt her relax in his arms.

Suddenly, he noticed her hand resting gently on his chest. He took it and asked, "Why are you wearing a wedding ring?"

Anna looked at him and squeezed his hand, "That's the wedding ring that I wore when we were in Bulgaria. It has never left my finger and it never will, unless you marry someone else."

David felt his throat constrict. He couldn't speak. He knew, however, that - no matter what it took or whatever trouble it caused - he and Anna were destined to be together for the rest of their lives.

After lunch they walked around the town and, eventually, sat looking at the boats on the river. David asked, "Why does there have to be so much secrecy about where you live, and why can't you and I be together?"

"You asked that question when we were escaping from Bulgaria. I told you then that I will explain but not yet."

There was nothing more to be said. They sat holding hands and cuddling; just being together again was all they wanted. When it came time for Anna to get the bus back to Cambridge, they walked back to the square holding hands. Anna asked, "Do you ever see Giles and talk about me?"

David replied, "I haven't seen or heard from Giles for nearly two months, not since he asked if I would join his business full time."

"Do you mean, become a full time spy, like him? I'm not sure that would be a good idea, you want to avoid him and his sort. All they do is cause trouble."

David wondered why Anna would make a comment like that and if she was paranoid about being watched. "If you haven't seen Giles, how do you know that you're being watched? You aren't in Russia now."

"I know I'm not in Russia, but if you had lived in Russia, you would know that we become expert in detecting watchers. One of the people in the Russian department is watching me on behalf of Giles, and my landlady also is in his pay. As for the telephone, I *know* it's tapped. I tried to call you a couple of times but all I heard was a click and the line went dead. Two days later I got a call from Giles reminding me that I am not allowed to contact you under any circumstances. I'm sure that either your phone or mine - most likely both - are being monitored."

David felt a surge of anger towards Giles. "Don't worry, Anna. They won't keep us apart, I promise you."

They agreed that the Bridge Inn would be a nice place to stay away from prying eyes and settled on a weekend together at the end of the month. As he drove back to London he wondered what was going to happen to him and Nicole. She was arranging a holiday for them in Bordeaux when he would be able to meet her parents.

When he arrived back at the flat there was a note from Marian saying that Nicole had called to tell him that she was flying back from Bordeaux in the morning and would go straight into the office. That would give him a day to sort himself out and decide what he was going to do about Nicole and Anna.

However, having spent the day tossing thoughts back and forth in his head, he was no further forward. Nicole was lovely, intelligent, always amusing and they were always on the same wavelength. Together they made a great partnership and would have a great life together. Under normal circumstances, he would be the happiest man on earth to have such a wonderful woman in his life. The problem was Anna. Whenever he saw her, or even thought about her, he was on another planet. He was hopelessly in love with her. He couldn't explain it, but he was. Nicole was the sensible, realistic choice. Anna was the dangerous, improbable choice. He loved Nicole, but he couldn't live without Anna.

That night, when Nicole came home, he decided he had to tell her.

Their reunion was not as warm as usual and Nicole seemed a little stressed. David assumed that she was tired after a hectic few days in Bordeaux.

"Have you been looking after yourself while I've been away?" she asked him.

"Of course I have. I'm not *completely* useless."

"Did you do anything interesting?"

David felt bad about lying to her. "Not really. I had to go up to Cambridge to check that Anna - the Russian woman - was settling in OK."

To David's surprise Nicole didn't say anything.

"Any special news from Bordeaux?"

"Not really, only family problems. It's always family problems." She seemed very down.

"When are you going to take me to meet your folks?"

"Not at present. Not for a while; it isn't the right time."

David wondered what that meant. He knew that he couldn't force Nicole to say anything. It was obvious that she had a problem but he couldn't help if she didn't tell him what it was.

Later that week he gently raised the subject again.

"I'm sorry David, you can't help. It's all to do with the vineyard. My father has to take early retirement and they want me to go back to run it. It's the family business; it's been in the family for nearly three hundred years."

"So I *could* help. I'm a scientist and a businessman; I must be able to help somehow."

"Not really. The problem is that we have to merge two vineyards. I'm taking a week's holiday to see what can be done about it. They're trying to create a dynasty. You can't imagine what it's like being an old family in Bordeaux."

"Well, I'll help if I can. I don't like to see you looking so stressed."

"Don't worry about me. You go and see if Anna's OK and we'll sort it out when I get back."

****

While she was away, David made his decision. The problem was that he didn't know whether he had the strength to keep to that decision once he saw Nicole once more. He knew he was being a coward but he had to do the right thing and tell her when she came back.

When Nicole returned, David was shocked. This family situation was really stressing her out and she looked pale and ill.

"Are you OK? You don't look well at all."

"I don't *feel* well. I was sick on the plane."

"You sit there. I'll make a cup of tea and get you two paracetamol."

"Thanks, but no pills. I don't need any. I think I'll go for a lie down."

"I'll sleep in the spare room, so I don't disturb you."

The next morning, David heard her being sick again. He dressed hurriedly and had a mug of tea waiting for her.

"That damned airline food has really upset my stomach."

As the morning progressed she brightened up and there was more colour in her cheeks. Eventually, she looked at David, her big brown eyes full of sorrow. "I'm sorry, my love, but I've made the decision to return to Bordeaux full time. There's a lot to do in the business. I don't think it would work out for either of us if you and I were together there."

David was shocked. "Do you have another man over there? Someone special?"

"No. I've never had a serious boyfriend in Bordeaux. I did in Paris, but the only one I had in Bordeaux was my childhood sweetheart, from when we were five years old. His family have the vineyard next to ours."

David didn't know what to say and didn't know how he was feeling. He had hated deceiving Nicole but never imagined that she might leave his life in this way. So he said nothing and just sat there thinking.

Four days later he drove her to Heathrow. When they parted both were in tears. A relationship with a great future had just withered and died.

Chapter 26

Anna and David's weekends together at the Bridge Inn became more frequent, with the result that they were accepted as a married couple whose jobs kept them apart during the week. After dinner one Friday night, Anna reached across the table and took David's hand. "Will you marry me?"

David was stunned and couldn't get his words out to say anything for some time. "I'd love to marry you; it's what I've wanted to do for months. But... will they *let* us get married? If they don't even want us to see each other, they'll definitely stop us from getting married."

"I've checked. My passport is a normal British passport, and my National Insurance number and Income Tax number are the same as anyone else's. So I don't see what there is to *stop* us getting married."

"I think you have to have a birth certificate before you can get a licence."

"I've sorted that. I was born during the war and they lost about twenty-five thousand birth registrations due to bombing. All I had to do was give them my date and place of birth, together with my parent's names and they issued me with a replacement certificate."

David knew that he would have many more questions later, but right now his mind was blank, apart from one major headache. "How do we get over the problem of Department 14, Giles and his gang?"

Anna smiled at him. "Simple. We don't tell them." She sat back in her chair, grinning mischievously. "And, in months to come when they *do* find out, it will be too late for them to do anything about it."

David laughed at her innocence and the simple solution she had come up with. "And you think that they won't *try*?"

"To be honest I think they've lost interest in me. They don't check anymore, where I am or where I've been. I don't think they're monitoring me or following me as much. It's only you and I that they are concerned about."

It all sounded very simple. David was sure that, in reality, things wouldn't work out quite as easily.

Chapter 27

Three months later, David and Anna were married in Bedford registry office. That night, after dinner, Anna said, "Now we're married we can't have any secrets from each other and I promised that I would tell you why I had to leave Russia. My father works for the KGB; he was an economist at the University, then he joined the KGB and became head of the Sixth Directorate, which is responsible for economic intelligence."

"Good grief, Anna, I never realised."

"Wait, just let me tell you the rest. This is difficult enough as it is. Anyway, after some time he was promoted to be deputy head of the Second Directorate; they're responsible for internal security and counter intelligence." She took a sip of her wine. Her hand shook. "Now he's number two in the First Directorate. They do all the spying and overseas intelligence, as you know."

David topped up her wine. "Go on."

"However, my mother was killed twelve years ago."

"Oh, Anna. I'm so sorry."

She shook her head, sadly, and pressed a finger to his lips. "Later. I'll tell you that part later. Since then, my father has been spying for the British. He wanted me out of Russia in case he was ever discovered - somewhere I would be safe. Your MI6 guaranteed my safety and *you* got me out."

"My God, Anna, that's one hell of a story." David thought for a moment. "But why don't they want us to be together? I'm part of the department and have clearance for security matters."

"It's not that they don't trust you. It's because you travel behind the Iron Curtain. If you were arrested and interrogated you might disclose the secret. They can't afford to take the risk."

David could now understand what had happened and realised the enormity of the information and the paramount need for secrecy. All he could think of to say was, "How was your mother killed?"

"My mother's parents were taken in one of the purges and sent to a gulag in the East. She was raised by her grandparents and an aunt. When Papa became senior in the KGB he tried to find out what had happened to them and he discovered that they had been sent to one of two camps near to Tomsk. He arranged for the necessary permits and papers for his wife - my mother - to travel to Tomsk. She wanted to find out what had happened to them, and if she could find out where they were buried. She wanted to arrange for a proper grave for them." Her voice trembled and David squeezed her hand. "Some mad junior party official accused her of spying and shot her. As you can imagine, my father was furious and arranged that the man be suitably punished."

David asked, "What happened. Was he shot?"

"No. Worse than that. He was allowed to keep his job. They shot his wife and child in front of his eyes and then sent him back to work."

David said nothing. He was just starting to realise the sort of people he might be up against, when he was doing his errands in the East. The more he thought about it, he wondered if they were that safe in the UK. There were many Soviet sympathisers in the UK and quite a few in Cambridge. *He* had found Anna without too much trouble; surely the opposition could do the same. The problem was that he couldn't raise the issue with

166

Giles and MI14, since he wasn't supposed to know where Anna was. Anna's watchers: were they guardians or there just to ensure she conformed? Or, worse, were they working for the Russians?

David didn't discuss his worries with Anna; she was paranoid enough without him making things worse. Then Anna started to share her own worries.

"You know I told you about Giles' spy in our department? Well, I saw him in The Backs talking to someone. When they saw me the man turned his back, so I couldn't see his face."

"So, what's the problem? We've known for ages that you're being watched."

"Not like this. This new watcher follows me everywhere. I don't think I could lose him between Cambridge and St. Neots."

"Don't worry, we'll work out a way of losing him."

"It's not losing him that's the problem. I'm scared that if their watching method has changed, then it must be for a good reason. But I can't think what."

Chapter 28

As soon as he saw Anna, David knew that something was wrong. The smile was there, but not as big and bright as usual. "It's my father. He's very ill in hospital in Moscow. I've had a letter from him asking me to go back to Moscow to see him."

"Really?"

"I know – he was so worried about me, and keen for me to leave Russia because of the danger. All I can think is that he must be really ill."

"What are you going to do?"

"Well, I want to go to Moscow to see him, but I'm not sure it will be safe for me to go back. It's not just because of Papa but they will want to know why I ran from Russia and how I got out. I can't tell them the truth and if I lie they'll discover that I'm lying, which will make things worse. I've written to my father asking if it will be safe for me to return and I've asked Giles if he can check if I can go back."

"What have they said?"

"I haven't had a reply from my father as yet, but Giles called to say that he thinks it will be safe because over the last twelve months there has been a great thaw and we have much warmer relations with Russia these days. However, he's asked the embassy in Moscow if they can get an assurance from the authorities in Moscow that I will be allowed to return to the UK. What do you think I should do?"

David thought about it. Something didn't seem right. If her father was still a British agent then the logic of getting Anna out of Russia still applied. So why would they let her go back?

"What did your father say in the letter telling you he was in hospital?" Anna handed it to him and he studied it, even though he couldn't read it. It was difficult enough reading printed Russian but handwritten Russian was impossible. "Does he say what's wrong with him and how long he's been in hospital?"

"No, he doesn't say what's wrong with him. He says he has been in the Bolitsa Vikhino for two weeks. That's all he says, apart from that he wants to see me soon. I'm afraid that means there's something seriously wrong. I don't think he would ask unless he was dying."

"Do you know this hospital? Where is it?"

"He is in the Mikhalkov ward at Bolitsa Vykhino at Veshnyakovskya 23."

"What's your father's home address? Maybe we could get some flowers sent to him from you and I. Did you ever tell your father that we were married?"

Anna shook her head.

David wondered if everything was as simple as it appeared. "I will make some enquiries to see what I can find out." He then stressed, "Don't say anything or agree anything with Giles, or anybody, until we find out more about what's going on."

After that, they tried to have a normal relaxing afternoon but Anna was tense and it didn't help that David was too preoccupied trying to work out what might be going on.

As soon as he got home he phoned Guiseppe Lombardo in Milan, forgetting that they were an hour ahead of the UK. Guiseppe answered the phone from his bedroom, just as he was getting into bed.

"Giuseppe, do you know when you'll be in Moscow next?"

"I'm flying to Moscow next Tuesday. Why?"

"I need you to do me a huge favour."

"Well, if I possibly can, I will. I'll be in Moscow for two days. Then I'm visiting the big canning factory in Voronezh, then back to Moscow Friday night and flying home on Sunday, I hope."

"Guiseppe, this is a big ask, but my wife's father is ill in the Bolitsa Vykhino at Veshnyaskaya 23, in the Mikhalkov ward. Could you please visit him and find out what's wrong with him and say that his daughter will come to see him as soon as possible. Just in case he's been released from hospital, he lives at Apartment four D on the fourth floor of three hundred and two Solyanka St, Kitai Gorod."

"He must be important, that's a rather up market area reserved for top officials. If I can fit it in I will, then I'll call you and let you know how he is doing. Ciao! I am now going back to sleep."

"Thank you, Giuseppe. I really appreciate it. I wouldn't ask unless it was urgent."

****

Although the following week followed its usual path - hectic on Monday and relaxing as the week went by - David couldn't relax into the week because he had heard nothing from Guiseppe.

When he got home on Thursday, he was ambushed by Marian as soon as was through the door. "Your Russian lady is on the phone. She wants to speak to you urgently. She's been holding on for twenty minutes."

David dived for the phone, "Anna what's wrong? Are you all right?"

"No, I'm scared! Giles has been on the phone, he says that I have to go back to Moscow as soon as possible. He says he's coming to see me tomorrow to explain and make the necessary arrangements. I told him that I can't leave until the end of term because I have a busy teaching schedule and tutorials. He just said that they'll have to make alternative schedules and he would see me tomorrow morning."

David had had experience of Giles' duplicity before; he was not a man to be trusted.

He spoke very calmly. "Anna, this is what I want you to do. Pack your bag for the weekend but put a few extra things in as you may be away for a bit longer, then get the bus to St. Neots. If there isn't one, get a cab. I'll meet you at the Bridge Inn; ask Mrs Shipley if you can wait in a private room until I arrive. I'll leave as soon as possible. I should be there in under two hours."

Marian stood there with an amazed look on her face and her mouth open. Before she could ask, David said "I'll be back later, explanations can wait until then."

As usual, the North Circular was a pain; not as bad as a Friday night, but still a pain. However, once through Hendon and Apex Corner the A1 was clear and the Riley opened both carburettors and flew up the A1 to St. Neots.

As David entered the Bridge, Mrs Shipley said, "She's in our sitting room at the back," and opened the counter door in the bar to let him through.

Anna looked just as she had when they were fleeing from Bulgaria – petrified, shaking and totally vulnerable. All she said was, "Am I glad to see you." David picked up her bag and thanked Mrs Shipley and apologised for their having to rush.

As they drove down the A1 on their way back to Ealing, he explained. "I think we should avoid Giles for a few days, until we know what's going on. I'm expecting a phone call tonight that might throw some light on the situation."

When they arrived in Ealing, Marian appeared to be waiting for their return. "Is everything OK? I've been worried about you,

171

having to rush off like that. I thought something serious must have happened."

Anna smiled weakly. "I'm sorry, I have a bad headache." David took her into the flat, gave her a couple of aspirin and a cup of tea and told her to lie down for a rest. He closed the curtains and hoped that she might fall asleep. Eventually, she drifted off. Once Anna was asleep, David took an A4 notepad and started jotting down all his thoughts but nothing made much sense, so he gave up and started doodling.

He realised how hungry he was but he was anticipating the call from Giuseppe, so, not wanting to risk being out when he called, David raided the cupboards for something that he could throw together.

At nine o'clock Moscow time the phone rang. Before he had chance to say anything a voice said, "Hi, this is Joe. I have some news for you, but it's a funny line, so I'll call you on Sunday night. I can't talk now, must rush."

David managed to get a word in just before Giuseppe rang off. "Joe, I won't be here on Sunday. I'll ring you."

"I've no idea what time I'll be home."

"Don't worry. I'll call you every half hour until I get you."

Anna, who had been awakened by the phone, asked, "Who was that on the phone?"

"That was about the information I was expecting from Moscow. It must be important, because Giuseppe wasn't prepared to give it to me over the phone from Moscow. If it's that important I don't want him to call here, just in case you're right and this phone is bugged. Our other major problem is that when Giles finds you're not in Cambridge, he'll start looking for you and one of the first places he'll look will be here."

"Oh, David, I'm so scared. What are we going to do?"

172

"Look, don't worry, Anna. It's going to be OK, I promise. Right now, I'm going down the street to make a couple of phone calls."

Fifteen minutes later David was back with a smile on his face. "It's great when all one's plans fall into place. Hang on here, while I go and pack a few things, and change into a decent suit. I assume that you have something smart in that case of yours."

Five minutes later a smart David appeared, carrying a small suitcase. He picked up Anna's case and told her they were leaving immediately. Anna seemed to pick up some of David's enthusiasm. "You make me feel more cheerful, although I don't know what there is to be cheerful about."

"Well, my love, we're going to stay in a lovely hotel in Sonning called The French Horn; it's right by the river and has a rather posh restaurant. No one will find us there and, more importantly, it's near to where a very useful friend of mine lives. You'll meet him sometime tomorrow morning. I'm sure that you and George will get on, he's someone we can trust and I think he will help us. I promise you, this will all work out just fine."

Chapter 29

As they sat at breakfast, looking across the lawn, the mist swirled above the river. Anna was mesmerised by it. "It's just like the mist on the lake at home when I was little."

David took a sideways glance at it while he enjoyed his full English breakfast.

Just after breakfast David looked up from reading the Weekend FT and saw George, a tall, middle-aged man in a linen suit, walking into reception. He stood up. "Good morning, George, I'm so grateful you could come. I have a gut feeling that the next few days are going to be mutually beneficial, but, of course I can't be sure of anything as yet. Come and meet Anna. I want you to get the full picture of what's happened in the past and we'll see if the future can be just as exciting."

They walked back to Anna, who was watching them curiously. "This is my wife Anna. Anna, this is George, a very good friend of mine and I hope he will soon become a very good friend of yours as well." George shook Anna's hand and they all sat. "Anna I want you to tell George in your own words how we got you out of Russia and, particularly, what you and I did to get out. We have no secrets from George we trust him implicitly, and I'll explain everything to you soon, but at this stage I just want you to tell him everything. Don't go beyond your arrival at Cambridge and - as he isn't married to you - you don't need to explain why you had to leave Russia." He smiled at them both and stood up. "Now, I'm going up to our room to make a few phone calls. I'll be back in time for coffee."

When David returned it was obvious that George and Anna were getting on well together and the story was being retold with George asking questions. When David sat down they stopped and looked at him. "Now, I think we'll have a pot of coffee, and then, Anna, I want you to go to the chemist's shop and get some of that hair dye. The same colour that you used last time. The same colour that you used last time. It's possible that we may leave the country the same way we came in."

After Anna had left for the chemists, David outlined the problem to George. "As Anna has told you MI6 et al were desperate to get Anna out of Russia and originally desperate that no one should know that she is in the UK. So it's strange that they now want her to go back."

"This really is a bizarre story, David."

"I know. Believe me, I know. Equally, they were very forceful that Anna and I should not continue our relationship or have any contact at all. Anna's thoughts on this is that it's because I travel in the East a lot and therefore would be a security risk if I was interrogated over there."

George nodded slowly. "That seems reasonable enough to me."

"Exactly! So why are they now so keen to get her back to Russia? From my experience they don't play by the Queensbury rules and I suspect that there's some dirty dealing going on. I might know more, tomorrow night; I have to call a colleague in Milan. The problem is, I'm not sure any of our telephones are secure."

George suggested that they went out for dinner and then called from his home office. When David pointed out that because of the time difference he'd need to start trying from five o'clock, George suggested that one of them go out for fish and chips.

****

At 7.30 p.m. Milan time Guiseppe answered the phone. "Hi, David. I heard your earlier call but I desperately needed a shower and something to eat. I've done both in the last thirty minutes so I now have indigestion. Have I got news for you!"

"Hang on, Giuseppe. I'm going to put you on loudspeaker so that my friend George can hear you as well."

"OK. I went to the Bolitsa Vykhino first thing on Wednesday morning. I asked for the Mikhalkov ward and the receptionist looked confused because all their wards have numbers not names. She asked me the name of the patient and searched their database. They had no record of an Alexei Petrov, either as a current patient or a recent out patient. She asked what was wrong with him to see if she could find a Petrov with another initial. When I said I didn't know it became obvious that she thought I was wasting her time. She told me how many beds they have in the hospital. I wasn't sure I heard right because I thought she said two thousand, but I might have misheard. Then I had an idea and asked if they had a doctor called Mikhalkov."

"Good thinking, Giuseppe."

"Well, not so good as it turned out. The answer was that they didn't have a doctor by that name as far as she knew, so I then went to Petrov's home address to see if he was there, or if one of the neighbours knew which hospital he was in."

"Thanks for going to so much trouble, for us; Anna and I really appreciate it."

"Not a problem at all! It gave me a bit of excitement in an otherwise boring business trip. Anyway, when I got there, apartment four D looked unoccupied. I rang the bell a few times and then when no one answered I tried apartment four C. An old lady answered, and, when I explained what I wanted I asked if she knew where Petrov was. She caught my arm, pulled me inside and closed the door. She told me that it wasn't a good idea to be looking for Petrov, because I might get into trouble."

"Did she say why?"

"Well, according to her, apparently Petrov was arrested by the Secret police two months ago; they raided his apartment in the middle of the night and took him away. Did you know that?"

"Nobody told us anything about that. Go on."

"Anyway, they returned the next day and spent two days searching the place and, since then, no one's been back. She's been keeping a look-out because she likes the guy and was worried about him. She also told me that I was lucky not to have asked at apartment four E because the owner is paid by the police to report any visitors, or anyone who comes looking for Petrov."

"Did she know what had happened to him after that?"

"She said rumour has it that he was taken to the Lubyanka and shot."

David looked at George, shocked. "Christ. This is worse than I thought. Could she give you any more information on that rumour?"

"She told me that there was someone who might know, so she would ask him. I asked for his name, but she wouldn't say. She told me to return on Friday but said that I mustn't knock on Petrov's door under any circumstances."

"And what did she say when you went back?"

"Well, she told me that there was someone who had said he hadn't been shot but sent to some camp; her informant said he would try to find out which one. I spoke to her just before I came home, but she hadn't got any further information. Sorry, David."

"Not at all. I'm so grateful to you for doing that for me. I hope I can return the favour one day."

"I bloody hope not, to steal a phrase from you Brits. I hope I never get mixed up in anything like this! Ciao, David, and I hope you get some good news."

David put the phone down and turned to a solemn looking George. "It seems to me that the Reds want Anna back for the very reason she left Russia. If they have Anna they can force Petrov to do or say anything. The question is, why do our lot want to send her over there? Surely she'd blow both Petrov *and* his British handler, who I assume lives in Moscow."

The two men put their heads together and discussed the situation for some time. Finally, David leaned back and sighed. "OK. This is what I suggest we do."

****

After working out a plan of action, David called Giles at Bentinck Mansions. "I understand that you've been asking for me. Any reason in particular, or is it just a social call?"

"Thank God you've called. We have a big panic on. Anna has disappeared."

"What?" David looked at George who grinned and rolled his eyes.

"We wondered if she's tried to contact you. Or if you have any ideas where she might be hiding?"

David said, "I did bump into her in Bedford five months ago and I suppose I could think of one or two places where she might be. I won't go into the office tomorrow, why don't you come over to my place and we can discuss the possibilities."

David put the phone down and George snorted with laughter. "You deserve an Oscar for that performance."

"Well, George, are you still up for it? Tomorrow could be an exciting day. We both might end up in the tower, or under a load of concrete somewhere."

"Up for it? I should say so. This could be big, really big. I don't think I'll get much sleep tonight."

"I don't think any of us will."

Chapter 30

After a very early start the three of them were at Chatsworth Gardens by eight thirty. David knew that Giles would probably turn up early and, at ten o'clock Giles appeared at the front door. David leaned out of the window and yelled, "I said eleven o'clock. I'm not dressed as yet; you'll have to wait there for a few minutes." He turned to the others. "You know what to do. Anna, you come out of the bedroom as a sleepy Mrs Hopkins on your cue. George, you have your recorder set up in the kitchen, I'll call you in for the 'coup de grâce.' Are we all set?" They nodded and took their places.

David went down to let Giles in. "Did you have to get here so early?"

"You have no idea of the panic that Anna's disappearance has caused; it couldn't have come at a worse time."

"Worse for who? You? Or Anna? It has to be you. I don't think you care a shit about anyone else."

"It's very important. Anna has to go back to Russia."

David struggled to keep his temper. "Why? And is she going of her own free will or are you sending her without her agreement? Christ, Giles. Have you even *asked* her?"

"She doesn't have a say in the matter."

"Is that so? Well I can tell you that *I* do! I very much have a say in the matter. And Anna is not going back to Russia, unless she wants to go back, and with my agreement."

Giles sneered, "What do you have to do with it?"

"I told you that I had seen Anna in Bedford five months ago. You didn't ask why or where. We met at the Registry Office in

Bedford, where we were married. Anna and I have been married for five months and she's now a British citizen."

Giles had become very red in the face during this speech. "You were given a specific order that you couldn't see her again. She was told that one condition of her staying was that she may not have any permanent relationships and, specifically, that she should not see *you* again."

"Giles you've got one thing wrong. You do *not* give me orders. If you do, I shall either ignore them or tell you to get stuffed. As for Anna, we have been reassured that she is now a British citizen and protected by the law. If you try any chicanery, it will be debated in court and you might find more being disclosed than you would like."

Giles glared at him with disdain. "You're a damned fool, David. I don't think you realise who you're talking to. We can revoke that citizenship any time we like and any court action will be held *in camera* away from public scrutiny. May I also remind you that you could be tried under the Official Secrets Act."

David tried to take some of the heat out of the discussion. "OK, let's look at this sensibly. Why is it so important that Anna goes back to Russia? Why do the Russians want her back?"

"Her father, Alexei Petrov - a head man in the KGB - has been a British spy for twelve years. The Russians discovered his activities and shot him several months ago."

David hoped that Anna, in the bedroom, couldn't hear this part of the discussion. He moved Giles further away from the bedroom door. "If her father is dead why do the Russians want her back?"

"They do. And that's all we need to know."

"Come on, Giles, there has to be a better reason than that."

"Look, her father has been shot and his handler - one of our best agents - has been arrested. He's been given twenty-five years hard labour for spying but the Russians will do a swap for Anna."

"Bullshit. You're not telling me the full story. And what you are saying is that you would send a British citizen to Russia, in exchange for one of your MI6 friends, who has probably screwed up."

"We--"

"Shut up, Giles. You're not sending my wife to Russia. And, if you try, I will send a tape recording of this discussion to the press."

"Who will be issued with a D notice, the tape recording will be confiscated and you will be prosecuted under the Official Secrets Act." Giles crossed his arms, smugly, no doubt thinking that he had got David exactly where he wanted him.

David smiled. "I don't think it will come to that." He raised his voice slightly, but still looked at Giles. "Did you get all that on the recorder, George? I think you can come out now."

As George walked out of the kitchen, Giles glowered at him, "Who the hell is he?"

"Giles, may I introduce you to George Schulz, an old friend of mine. George is the London correspondent of the Washington Post."

Giles lost the plot completely. His temper and fury evident, he yelled, "By this time tomorrow you'll be kicked out of the UK, all your recording gear confiscated and I will personally call your editor and tell him that you and anyone else from your paper will be *persona non grata* if any of this is published."

David shook his head and laughed. "Look, Giles, I know you really are a bastard but do you have to act like one?"

Giles clenched his fists. David squared up to him. "Go on, hit me, I've witnesses who will say I acted in self-defence. But when I've finished with you, your friends might not like your looks quite as much."

Giles stormed out of the room and slammed the door behind him. His parting shot was "You'll regret crossing me. You're finished."

Anna came out of the bedroom, "You never told me to come out, so I didn't."

"There wasn't any point, Anna; that was a man to man fight. Now we put the plan into action."

Anna asked, "Has my father really been shot?"

"I'm sorry, Anna. I was hoping you didn't hear that bit. But, in truth, we don't know for sure. Tell me, have you ever spied against Russia or betrayed anyone, or taken any secrets from Russia?"

"You know I haven't."

"Exactly. So why do the KGB, or whoever, want you back if your father is dead? It just doesn't make sense unless your father's alive and they want to use you to put pressure on him. Also we have information, as yet unchecked, that he's alive."

Anna let out a sigh of relief. She wasn't far from tears. David kissed her. "Plan A now starts. We'd better hurry. Giles will be back, I'm sure of it. And this time he'll bring reinforcements. Anna, grab your bag and make sure that you have that hair dye. We'll leave my car where it is." The three of them gathered together their belongings. "We're going to George's on the way to the ferry, you can dye your hair there."

"Which ferry? Where are we going, David?"

"The three of us are booked on the Newhaven to Dieppe ferry. George is travelling by himself in the car." He looked at

George, who nodded. "He'll drop Mr and Mrs Alain Meschines at a bus stop near to the ferry. They're travelling on foot."

Anna shook her head, confused. "But...they'll be looking for us, won't they? They'll have the airports and ferries covered."

David took her by the shoulder. "They'll be looking for Mr and Mrs David Hopkins. Who just happen to be booked on the five o'clock BEA flight from Heathrow to Dublin. I'll call the airport from Newhaven to say that we'll miss the five o'clock flight, but will definitely be on the one that leaves at seven. That should keep them busy for a short while."

Chapter 31

Everything went according to plan. Mrs Meschines looked identical to the one who had left Bulgaria almost a year ago. George kept himself to himself on the boat, so that no one would see them together. It wasn't until they were in Dieppe - when George picked them up at the bus terminal - that they were together again.

In the car Anna asked, "Where are we going?"

"Over to you George," said David.

"I'm not absolutely sure what's happening, to be honest. The Paris office has made the necessary arrangements. They were instructed to arrange accommodation for two 'Post' guests but they were not to reveal any names. As for me, I'll stay in the paper's Paris flat, which is a dirty dive but very discreet."

Anna asked, "What does that mean?"

George laughed, "What it means is that, because it's situated in a dirty back alley, no one with any sense goes there, and so it's very private. Anyway, we'll go to the office first to receive our instructions."

By the time they had eaten and reached the office it was nearly ten o'clock, Paris time. They were told that the paper had taken a furnished flat for one month, with the option to renew. George saw them installed and left them to sort out their accommodation, while he went to his 'dirty dive.'

Anna flopped down onto the bed, exhausted. Her face looked pinched and pale. "Do you really think we'll be here for a month?"

David smoothed her newly darkened hair away from her face. "I don't know, because I don't know what is going to develop over the coming weeks. We'll try to find out what has happened to your father. If he's alive, we'll see if we can find out where he is. That could be the riskiest bit, because we'll have to ask lots of questions. If the authorities find out, it could be risky for us and even riskier for your father; if we cause too much of a stir, they might think it's simpler to shoot him after all. Now, come on, let's try and relax. It's time for bed and I'm knackered."

The next morning David lay in bed, thinking. Something had been bothering him. As Anna started to stir, he nudged her until she was properly awake. "Anna, that letter you had from your father. Are you sure it was his writing?"

Anna thought for a moment, "You know, I can't say. I don't think I've seen anything written by him in ten years." She moved towards the bathroom.

David said, almost to himself, "I wonder how we can get that checked." Before they could discuss it further, there was a knock at the door.

It was George, looking dishevelled, David asked, "Where have you been?"

"I haven't been anywhere. I am not stopping in that rat infested hole another night. I'm moving out."

"Did the rats keep you awake, or what?"

"I don't mind the rats, it's the drunks in the alley singing, fighting and shouting all night that kept me awake. Let's have breakfast and then get over to the office. It should be an interesting day."

David was about to ask him why, when Anna came back in. She took one look at George and said, "What's happened to you?" David laughed. "Don't worry, George, you don't need to repeat everything. Let's go out and get some breakfast

186

someplace and find the nearest boulangerie. There's no food in the flat, just three bottles of cheap white in the fridge."

Over coffee and crêpes George told them that Ghenadie Brusilov was expected in the office later in the morning. Before David could ask who he was, George enlightened them.

"He's the Washington Post in Moscow. He has a special relationship with the authorities and the censors because his policy is that he never reports propaganda, never reports rumours, only facts that he can establish as accurate. And, most importantly, he never writes anything critical of the USSR. The Reds accept this and the Washington Post gets the facts and reports from the authorities that other papers don't get. It also means that Ghenadie is allowed to visit parts of Russia where other correspondents are not permitted."

"Sounds great. Let me see if I can persuade Giuseppe to come to Paris to meet him." He called Giuseppe who, surprisingly, was in his office. David told him of the latest developments and asked if he thought that he could get more information on the whereabouts of Petrov.

"I have only the one contact - this Madam Dhorokina in the neighbouring apartment - but I'm not going to Moscow on my next trip. I'm planning to visit the can manufacturing plants in the south."

"Ah, well, it was just a thought. Thanks anyway, Giuseppe."

That afternoon they went to the newspaper office to meet Ghenadie Brusilov. He seemed to be the sort of person who is instantly likeable. His face had a permanent smile and his eyes twinkled, as if he was up to mischief.

George and David briefed him on what had happened so far. Ghenadie said nothing, but listened intently. After a while he said, "I agree with your assessment that he hasn't been shot;

187

he'll be tucked away someplace, from where he can't defect. Providing his handler doesn't crack, he'll be presumed innocent and just kept safe somewhere. That's why they wanted Anna; she's the key for them. They know that Petrov would crack and admit anything if he thought that Anna's life was at risk."

George said, "We must make sure that, whatever happens, they don't get hold of Anna."

Ghenadie told them that he would fly back to Moscow the following day and start making enquiries. "We have to be very discreet because if the authorities hear of anyone asking about Petrov they'll become suspicious and put him in a locked cell. Probably put me in one too."

"How do we go about this, then?" David asked.

Ghenadie thought for a moment. "I have a few Kremlin contacts and I'll visit Madam Dorokhina. It might be useful for me to have something that links me to Giuseppe Lombardo or Anna so that she trusts me."

David considered this and then snapped his fingers. "If you take the letter that Petrov sent to Anna that will prove you know Anna and, at the same time, you could ask Dorokhina if she thinks that it was written by Petrov. Plus, I've got one of Giuseppe's business cards. I've scribbled on the back, but that won't matter."

Ghenadie excused himself to make some phone calls. George was tapping a pen against his teeth, his feet up on a chair. "David, what's your main motive for finding Petrov? And, if we do find him, what next?"

"Well, he's Anna's dad and she obviously wants to know that he's safe. My motive for doing all this, is that we remove the threat to Anna; remove the reason why she should be sent back to Russia. Why do you ask?"

"Well, I was just thinking." He leaned forward, a look of excitement on his face. "If we could get him out to the West...well...what a story that would make. We get him - a senior KGB man - out and safe to his handlers in the West. What a coup that would be for the Post."

"Do you mean publish the story in order to sell lots of newspapers?"

"Not as such. If the details of our involvement came out we'd be thrown out of Russia. Worse still kept *in* Russia for twenty years in gaol and *then* thrown out. No, my motive is that the Post would become the preferred intelligence news outlet for NATO and every major member of NATO would know about our involvement. If we're successful NATO will love us."

David was not convinced. "It seems like a wild idea. It's never crossed my mind that we could get Petrov out; finding him is proving difficult enough."

George shrugged. "Worth a try?"

"But do you really think it's feasible? I don't want to build up Anna's hopes only for them to come crashing down around her later."

"Until we find him we won't know if it's feasible or not. There's nothing wrong with having that as our goal, is there?"

David agreed, "OK, let's start thinking about how we would do it. There's no point in putting that off until we find him."

Anna walked in, "What are you two plotting? You look very serious."

David told her to sit down. "We're looking at possible ways your father might escape from the USSR if we manage to find him."

Anna gasped. "Oh my God! Really? That would be wonderful."

189

"Look, Anna, this is just pie in the sky right now. Don't get your hopes up. There are lots of things we need to think about."

George fetched a pad. "Right; fire away. Let's get them down."

"Well, for a start, we have to decide which border we would use. The normal European borders are too militarised and too well guarded. From what I've heard the Turkish border is a no-no, the militarized zone extends to thirty miles each side of the border."

George pulled a map out of one of the drawers in the desk. "Well, if we go any further East we're into deserts and the chances are we would be spotted. Those regions are so sparsely populated that strangers stick out like a sore thumb."

Anna went around, to join him, looking at the map. "Possibly, but the indigenous peoples there aren't very keen on the Soviets. I think we would get help from the locals, especially in the Muslim areas." She pointed at the map.

David had been thinking. "What about the Russian-Iranian border? Do we know anything about that one?"

George and Anna shook their heads.

"Can we get any information on it? Do you have any contacts in the region, George?"

George shrugged. "We have a Post correspondent in Teheran but I wouldn't trust him an inch. He's on the take from everybody and anybody. I bet he's in with the Russians."

David said, "I'm going to call our international office in New York. They deal with all the enquiries from the places where we don't have a sales office and they appoint and look after agents and distributors."

By now it was almost time for lunch; they looked for Ghenadie but he was busy on the phone. He was working to Moscow time and missed his lunch.

The three of them sat in the nearest brasserie eating a light lunch. It was a very quiet meal with no idle chatter; each kept their thoughts to themselves. David was worried about Anna, who appeared to have lost her appetite. When they returned to the office, it was clear that Ghenadie had news for them. He was pacing up and down between the desks with an even bigger smile than usual. One contact had been able to tell him that Petrov was suspected of something - he didn't know what - but he hadn't been put on trial for anything. Another said there was a rumour that he had been sent to the salt mines.

George asked, "Surely they don't still do that, I thought that went out with the Tsars."

"No, the Bolsheviks do it as well. However, I haven't heard of anyone being sent there since 1945. I'll make more enquiries when I get back to Moscow and we will see what Madam Dhorokina has to say."

Chapter 32

Two days later, David sat in the office reading a book. Anna couldn't sit still so she had gone to sit by the river and watch the boats. The Post's Paris office wasn't a hive of activity; every ten minutes or so the teleprinter would spring into action and then go back to sleep. One of the office clerks suddenly yelled, "Telex for Schulz."

When he read it, George looked perplexed. "I don't understand this; it's from Ghenadie in Moscow. He proposes that he and I write an article on the economy of the southern states - Georgia, Armenia and Azerbaijan. In particular, how they're developing from primitive rural economies to modern industrial states. Apparently, the report will be sponsored by the Ministry of Development. We'll have authorisation to go anywhere other than two restricted military areas. Also, we're not permitted to travel within fifty kilometres of the Saratov secret zone, where they carry out aeroplane and weapon development."

David took the telex from him and scanned it. "That's funny. He never said anything about it before he left, did he?"

"That's exactly what's interesting about this message. It's what it *doesn't* say that's important. My guess is that he has found something about Petrov. It could be that he's being held in southern Russia and maybe in the Saratov secret zone, otherwise why mention it specifically?"

"OK, so he's found something. But if he can't tell us by phone or by telex, it's not going to be much use to us here."

"That's the point, David. One of us will have to meet him somewhere in the East. Is there any chance that one of your food meetings could be arranged someplace where you and Ghenadie could meet?"

David thought for a while. He needed to talk to Giuseppe but if D&A Milan knew he was calling from Paris then the news would soon get back to D&A London. He was considering the possibility that Giles and Co would be in contact with the D&A London office. In which case, they would soon find out where he and Anna were hiding. Unless... he turned to George, scribbling a number down. "Would you please ring this number in Milan and ask to speak to Guiseppe Lombardo. I don't want his office to know it's me calling. When he answers put him through to me."

George did so and handed the phone over to David when Lombardo came on the line.

"Hi. Guiseppe. It's David..."

"David! Where are you? We've all been worried."

"Never mind where I'm calling from. When are you next in Moscow?"

"Well, I'm due to be there next week, but--"

"Next week; that's great! Can you request that I come to Moscow to meet someone?"

"You mean a customer? Who?"

"It doesn't matter who I meet, as long as I have a good reason for being there. You're always asking if I can visit some of your customers. Maybe I'm coming to meet you in Moscow next week to discuss a trip to see a number of your customers?"

"Hang on a min, while I look in my diary."

The phone went quiet. David assumed that Giuseppe couldn't find his diary, but after a few minutes Giuseppe came back to the phone. "What about Wednesday? If you fly in on Tuesday night we can meet and I'll take you to the airport for the quarter to six flight to London on Wednesday afternoon. That fits with

193

me getting the five o'clock flight to Kharkov. I'll fix the hotel and send you a telex to confirm details."

"Giuseppe, do me a favour. Don't tell the London office until after I get back next week."

Giuseppe paused a moment. "Oh, OK. If that's what you want."

David didn't see any point in confusing him by telling him that he wouldn't be flying back to London and said goodbye before Giuseppe could ask him anything more. Turning to George he said, "OK, George, you tell Ghenadie that I'll meet him in Moscow next Wednesday. Perhaps it's better not to mention my name; it might be a good idea if no one in Moscow knows about the link between The Post and tin cans."

After saying goodbye to Anna, followed by a quick trip to the Russian Embassy to collect his visa - arranged by Giuseppe in Moscow - David returned to the apartment to pick up his bag and then left for Orly.

****

When they landed in Moscow, David had a serious attack of butterflies. It was his first visit to Russia and, although he had visited most of the East European capitals, he wasn't quite sure what to expect. However, when he arrived at his hotel he found it to be a substantial improvement on those that he was used to in Prague and Warsaw. There was a message waiting for him saying that Mr Brusilov would meet him for dinner at seven.

As soon as Ghenadie arrived, David knew he had something to tell him. His broad smile was bigger than ever. As they shook hands David asked, "Do you have any news?"

"News! No, we don't have any news. Moscow is very quiet at this time of year. It's very good of you to meet me when you have such a busy schedule."

194

Ghenadie put his arm round David's shoulder and steered him to the door. Once outside he whispered, "We don't talk in the hotel, in the taxi or in the restaurant. We'll walk to the restaurant and I'll bring you up to date on the way."

At the end of the block they turned the corner and Ghenadie said, "We've found Petrov. Or, at least, I *think* we have. I went to see Dorokhina and introduced myself as a friend of Lombardo. She was very suspicious at first. To be honest, I can't say that I blame her. I was invited in and, at first, all I got were very non-committal replies to my questions. It wasn't until I showed her the letter from Petrov to Anna that she started to thaw. She asked if I had met Anna. I told her I had and, when I told her that I met her in England, she asked me to describe her."

"She sounds like a very shrewd woman."

"Indeed she is. After that she opened up. I asked if she thought the letter was genuine, but she had never had reason to see Petrov's handwriting, so she couldn't comment."

"Damn. That's a shame."

"What she *did* tell me, was that she'd had two visitors. The first told her that he was a friend of Petrov and he'd heard that he was in an open prison, called Camp 385. He asked if anyone else had been looking for Petrov."

"Did she think he was genuine? Did she tell him about Lombardo's visit?"

"No, she didn't tell him anything about that. A few days later, a postcard was pushed through her letterbox. It said that they had a message from Petrov and would call back later. That evening someone called."

"Who was it? The same man that had visited her before?"

Ghenadie shook his head. "Dorokhina didn't know him. She said that he wouldn't give his name. Whoever he was, he said he'd been released from Camp 385 and allowed to return to Moscow. He told her that Petrov was under investigation and was being held at Camp 385."

"Investigation for what?"

"Again, he didn't tell her. When she asked where the camp was, she was told that it was a thousand kilometres or so from Moscow. Apparently, he's under 'town arrest'."

"Town arrest?"

"Yes. He's free to leave the camp but may not leave the town. She was told that he's not in prison and that he's alive and well; however, he can never return to Moscow. She pestered the man to tell her where Camp 385 was, but all he would say was that it was near to Orenburg, at the foot of the Urals."

By now they had walked nearly two miles. Ghenadie saw a cab approaching and waved it down. When Ghenadie told him the address of the restaurant, the cab driver turned around and headed back the way they had walked. The restaurant was only four hundred yards from their hotel.

Over dinner Ghenadie said, "I've been making enquiries about the location that we talked about." He looked at David as though warning him not to say too much. "We think it's a place called Sterlitamak, halfway between Ufa and Orenburg. George may have told you that The Post has been given permission to write an article on the economic development of the Southern States. I propose to pay a visit to the region next week, to have a quick look at what's involved. Tell George that I'll call him when I get back to work out a detailed itinerary and an outline of what we should cover in the report."

David asked the question which had been on his mind since the telex had arrived. "Why on earth do readers in Washington want such details of the economies of remote bits of Russia?"

196

"George and I will put together a factual report of what we find. Here in Moscow they will welcome an independent report; they know that most reports from the regions are modified by party speak and rarely give facts or bad news. After they've censored it we can send it to the USA. Our people in Washington will be happy to get the report as it enhances their knowledge of the region and the readers of the newspaper will only see a synopsis, maybe half a page at most."

"So, what's the plan?"

"Good lord, David; there is no plan - not as yet. I'm going to fly to Orenburg and, if I can hire a car, I'll spend a day or so there, then drive up to Ufa and have a good look around Sterlitamak on the way. I'll then have to go back to Orenburg to return the car. Once I've found something worthwhile we can meet in Paris to discuss what we do next."

After dinner David went back to his hotel and thought through everything he had heard. What could be done, if anything, to rescue Anna's father? He was due to meet Giuseppe at eleven the following morning, but hadn't a clue what he should or shouldn't say to him about the problem of Petrov. After tossing and turning on an uncomfortable bed until two o'clock, when he eventually fell asleep.

It was a somewhat bleary-eyed David that waited for Giuseppe to arrive. As soon as he saw him, David walked to meet him by the door. "I've a bit of a thick head this morning and I need some fresh air. Would you mind if we went for a walk somewhere?"

"Not at all; that's a good idea. Let's take the tram to Lefortovo Park - it's lovely at this time of year."

As they walked through the gate they saw a small crowd, mainly children, gathered around a trainer and his performing bear. To their right a somewhat smaller crowd was watching an outdoor game of chess. Giuseppe pointed towards a pathway through the birch trees. "Down there. We can sit in peace by the lake and no one will disturb us there."

As they sat by the lake David explained some of the problem to Giuseppe.

"My wife, Anna, was born in Russia and grew up here. She only moved to the West some years ago to get a job in the tourism business. Her father is the only close relative she has. He's getting older and is now retired and Anna would like him to move to the UK so that she can look after him." David had thought that it was not a good idea to tell Guiseppe of Petrov's KGB background and had concocted a story that he hoped came across as believable.

"I see," said Giuseppe. "So what's the problem?"

This was where David had to tread a fine line. "Well, the Russians won't let him leave. He's semi-retired and lives in a place called Sterlitamak, near to Orenburg. He's free to move around, but the police won't give him the necessary papers to come to Moscow, let alone leave the country."

"Why? What did he do before he retired? Was he in one of the restricted zones working on weapons?"

"No, I don't think so. He's an economist and had some minor government job." David waved his hand as if to reassure Giuseppe that this was just some minor inconvenience. "We think he's upset someone in the Communist Party, so they're just being bitchy to him." Giuseppe didn't look totally convinced, so David hurried on. "Anyway, I'm looking at ways we might get him out without the necessary paperwork. What I was hoping, was that you could justify a visit to that part of Russia so that I might get to meet him and see what can be done."

Giuseppe said nothing, deep in thought, then pulled a notebook from his pocket. In it was a folded map of Eastern Russia as far as the Urals. "We have a number of plants that we could visit in that region," he said, pointing to places on the map.

"What and where are they?" David asked.

Giuseppe tapped a finger on the map. "There's a tinplate works and a large can-making plant at Ufa and there's a pail-making factory just outside of Sterlitamak. Because there's a big chemicals industry there, they make the pails and drums for the chemical works. And here..." he moved his finger down the map, "further south, at Orenburg, there's a big cannery where they pack fruit and vegetables grown in that region. And further south still, near Atyrau, there's a food processing plant of some sort. Over to the west, here, is a huge fish cannery near Krasnodar. Oh, and also over there is a beer can factory for the big brewery." He passed the map across to David. "So there's no problem in justifying a visit to the region. We just have to see if the bureaucrats will agree to it."

"How long would it take to get the necessary permits?"

"It depends what you're doing this afternoon. I have a meeting with ImproChem at three o'clock. It would be a good idea if you came along. You could tell them what you are doing in the UK and I'm sure they'd be very interested to hear about your work in CSSR, Poland and Bulgaria."

David thought that they most certainly *would* be very interested in his 'work' behind the Iron Curtain, but he wasn't about to tell them.

Giuseppe continued. "You should stress your knowledge of developments in the food packaging industry. They'll fall for that."

Just as Giuseppe had said, the Russians were very keen to get the latest on food packaging in the West, particularly if it was free, and they thought that his proposed visit to the southern canneries was an excellent idea. When David took a chance and asked if he could have a week's holiday touring in Armenia and Azerbaijan they said that they thought this could be arranged, but they would need details of where and when so that they could organise the paperwork.

****

Thirty minutes after landing at Orly, David walked out of Arrivals, straight into the arms of Anna who, with George, was waiting to meet him. After a big hug and kiss she asked him "Did Ghenadie have any news? Has he found my father?"

"Yes, is the answer to both questions, but can we please wait until we're somewhere quieter so we can talk undisturbed by aeroplanes or traffic."

Once they were in the car heading back into Paris, David gave them all the news from Ghenadie. "Of course, we don't know for sure that Petrov *is* in Camp 385 and free to move about. However, Ghenadie is planning to drive to Sterlitamak next Tuesday to see what he can find out about the place. Plus, I had a very interesting meeting with Giuseppe at the offices of ImproChem. They would like – heavily prompted by me - Giuseppe and I to take a tour of the can-making plants and the canneries at Ufa and Orenburg. I chanced my arm and asked if I could take a week's holiday down there while I was in the region. They couldn't say yes immediately but asked for the places that I would like to visit, so fingers crossed. All in all it was a very useful few days."

****

Once he had the necessary paperwork, Ghenadie started to organise his visit to Orenburg and Sterlitamak. His first problem was that he soon found it impossible to hire a car in that part of Russia. In theory, there was a car hire place in Orenburg but when he called them the response was, "We haven't been allocated a car for hire in the last three years."

He then called his contact at the Ministry who were sponsoring the report, putting the man on speakerphone. "I can't find any transport down there; what do you suggest?"

"Hmm, let me see what I can do. I tell you what, get the train to Rostov and ask for Zvelindovsky at the Economic area office. He'll find something for you."

"That's great; I really appreciate it. I'll be there tomorrow. Thank you."

"I wouldn't thank me yet. I'm not promising anything luxurious. In fact, it might be rather basic."

Ghenadie put the phone down. "I'm not sure I like the sound of 'basic'."

Chapter

All David, Anna and George could do was to wait impatiently for Ghenadie's return. He had told them that he wouldn't be able to phone and that they should just expect him when they saw him, so George carried on working as normal and David and Anna spent most of the time being tourists and enjoying each other's company. They walked in the Bois de Boulogne and, one afternoon, they hired a boat on the lake. David rowed across to the restaurant on the island in the middle of the lake. There they had coffee and crêpes while discussing their great love for each other. Another day they wandered around the Père Lachaise cemetery until David found the grave of Frédéric Chopin. "If only I could play half as well as he."

Just when they thought they couldn't stand the suspense any more, Ghenadie arrived back. He looked exhausted, but very pleased with himself. He told them what had happened. "They were right about the damn car being basic," he said. "Zvelindovsky had a spare Lada that he said I could use. He said it was only a year old so it should be reliable...more or less. He gave me the keys and told me I would find it in the car park." He paused and looked at each of them in turn, obviously enjoying their rapt attention as he told his story. "Do you know how difficult it is to find one Lada in a whole car park full of them? It took me ages. He should have told me it was the only clean one there; I would have found it more quickly."

After a two day drive Ghenadie had arrived in Orenburg. It had been suggested that he contacted the managers at the soda ash plant and the Rayon works in Sterlitamak. When he had asked where he could find a hotel, the manager of the Rayon works had invited him to stay at the corporate hostel at the factory. He had arrived just after lunch and started to wander around the town. Not far from the factory gate he'd found a bar, full of workers who had just finished the early shift. "I asked the barman if any of our comrades from Camp 385 ever came in for a drink. He told me that they sometimes had a couple of them in on a Thursday, as that was their afternoon off, and they got the bus from Ufa. He said they would just come and get drunk and that if they caused trouble or started pestering the women, they would be in trouble. They then lose their privileges and are not allowed out of the camp for three months. I couldn't believe my luck. I'd been planning to return to Moscow on the Thursday, but thought it would be useful to talk to some of the camp inmates. Anyway, he told me where they caught the bus from Ufa, so I thought I'd go up there and take a look, to see if I could find anyone around to talk to." His eyes twinkled as he looked at David, Anna and George, hanging on every word. "Are you sure I'm not boring you?"

"Just get on with it," said David.

On Thursday Ghenadie had taken an early lunch and had then driven out to find the bus stop. He had parked the Lada off-road, walked back and waited at the bus stop. The camp inmates had started to arrive in twos and threes. When there were about twelve of them there he had asked if Alexei Petrov was coming as he hadn't seen him. He wasn't that sure he would recognise Petrov from the one poor photograph that he had seen.

An elderly man with a big bushy white beard came and looked at him, "What do you want here? We don't like strangers."

"I'm waiting for Alexei Petrov." One of the inmates overheard him, "Petrov doesn't mix with any of us. He always waits until the last minute to arrive, Petrov is antisocial." The others murmured in agreement. They seemed to be put out by Petrov's behaviour, but Ghenadie thought that if they knew he was ex-KGB they wouldn't *want* to associate with him.

"Just before the bus was due, I spotted a solitary figure striding along the track towards the bus stop. I guessed it must be Petrov so I started walking towards him, to meet him on the track. I didn't want any curious ears listening to our conversation. We met about three hundred metres from the end of the track. Petrov had stopped and stared at him, saying nothing." Ghenadie relayed his conversation with Petrov.

"Alexei Petrov you don't know me; my name is Ghenadie Brusilov. I come as a friend and would like to talk to you."

"I'll miss my bus."

"It doesn't matter. I have a car and will take you to Sterlitamak."

"Why?"

"I'd like to ask you some questions."

"I don't answer questions, particularly from people who say they are my friend."

"OK. I won't ask any questions; I'll make statements. Your daughter, Anna, thinks about you a lot and wants to know that you are safe and well."

Ghenadie paused dramatically in his re-telling.

Anna was practically bouncing in her seat. "What did he say?"

Ghenadie shook his head. "Nothing." He continued with his story. He said that Petrov had looked at him, a flinty glare in his eyes, and Ghenadie had been almost reluctant to continue; so he had made his next statement a big one.

"Anna would like you to join her in the West."

No response.

204

"Anna is safe and well in Paris."

"Not true. She's in England."

"No. She's left England for her safety. Her husband is a friend of mine and he found out that they were planning to send her back to Russia in exchange for one of their people who has been arrested in Moscow."

Petrov had looked at Ghenadie questioningly. His lips moved but no question came.

Ghenadie had continued. "I was born in Russia but I'm now an American citizen and work for a Washington newspaper here in Russia. We want the story of your escape from Russia; that's why we're helping Anna and her husband to get you out."

Petrov had thought for a while, then said, "I didn't know she was married. An Englishman? You'll make a lot of money from my story. How much do *I* get?"

Ghenadie had been rather taken aback by that. "Yes, we'll make money from the story, but not as much as we'd like because it will be expensive to get you out. You get nothing except a comfortable safe life in the West. I think that's worth a lot, don't you?"

Petrov had just continued to glare at him. "We should keep walking. If someone sees us talking for too long they'll ask questions."

"I'll drive you to Sterlitamak and we should have a drink in a bar and talk to the barman. I want the barman to say if anyone asks that you were talking to a Russian, not a Westerner. If asked, you could say I was just a nosey Russian asking about life in the camp."

Petrov said, "That wouldn't convince *me* if I were asking the questions."

"Well, do you want to get out or not?"

There had been a long silence before Petrov spoke next. "Yes. If it can be done safely and no one gets hurt."

"We haven't worked out the details as yet so it will be a few weeks before anything happens. We'll pick you up here on a Thursday but you must be on your own. Either get here early or miss the bus and it will either be me or an Italian friend called Giuseppe Lombardo who comes to meet you."

As they entered Sterlitamak, Petrov had pointed at a road saying, "Turn left here. There's a bar on this road which sells great but expensive vodka. Nobody from the camp uses it. I suggest that you buy the most expensive vodka. That way, the barman will remember us. He'll probably think that you're a senior party member, if you can afford expensive vodka."

As they pulled up outside the bar Ghenadie had put his hand on Petrov's shoulder. "Remember, set up a pattern of solitary waiting over the next few weeks; we won't be ready for at least four weeks. We may speak to you again before the real pick up but we may not."

As they had turned to go into the bar, Ghenadie had said, "Turn and face the sun, smile slightly and don't move. I'll take a couple of photos, in case we need passport photos for something."

Ghenadie sat back in his chair, a self-satisfied look on his face. "So, after a couple of vodkas we left the bar. I called out "See you again" - in Russian, of course. Then I drove up to Ufa, arranged for the car to be kept secure – no doubt we'll need it again - and took the train to Moscow. And here I am."

"So when can we get my father out?"

"All in good time, Anna," Ghenadie said. "He's safe and well where he is and we have lots of arrangements to make. We need to do this carefully if we're going to do it. There's no point going in all guns blazing like a bunch of cowboys."

"So, what *is* next?" David said.

Ghenadie thought for a moment. "I think the first thing we need to do is get Giuseppe to join us. We need to fill him in on the details."

"Yes," David said. "He doesn't know the full story. If he's going to help us further he deserves to know everything."

****

The following Tuesday, with the exception of Anna, they were all gathered around the table in the diminutive meeting room at the Post's Paris office. It was hot and the air conditioning wasn't working.

Giuseppe said, "If this is the best they can do they don't deserve a big story."

George agreed, "For the next meeting we'll hire a room."

For the benefit of Giuseppi, Ghenadie gave them a detailed report of his travels in southern USSR, summarising it at the end by saying, "Petrov is well and he's happy for us to try to get him out. The condition is, that he doesn't want to get shot and, touchingly, he doesn't want any of us get hurt trying to help him."

"I'll second that." said Giuseppe. "I knew there was something else going on besides what you were telling me, David."

"Sorry Giuseppe. I felt bad about not telling you everything, but I couldn't jeopardise things at that stage."

Giuseppe continued, checking his notes. "I have the agreement and the permits are on the way for David and I to take an extended trip round the can factories and canneries in that part of the world. They want us to visit the big can factory in

Ufa and have also invited us to see the new tinplate plant there. I can't see the point of that but we may have to show our face. Then we're to visit either or both of the drum and pail plants in Sterlitamak. Further south, we're scheduled to meet the technical people at the cannery in Orenburg." He looked up at David. "They've requested that you give a presentation on the latest developments in the West."

David nodded. "No problem."

"Then they'd like us to drive to Krasnodar where they have a huge fish cannery and also a brewery which cans beer. Apparently, it's a new line and the only one of its kind in Russia and they're very proud of it. There's also a speciality can plant in Rostov we might visit."

David raised his eyes. "God, at this rate we're going to spend all our time visiting factories and none actually on the job in hand."

"Yep. The problem is that all these plants and others want to be the best in Russia and they want to hear about the latest technology. We'd be down there for six months if we visited them all. The only bad news is that we have to provide our own transport and buy our own gas."

David picked up his own report. "At our last meeting we agreed that the Russo-Iranian border might be promising and so I said I'd look at it. I asked our export office if we ever had any enquiries from Iran for canning or bottling technology. It appears that they have no indigenous food packaging industry; a surprising amount of food is processed and stored by home bottling. Professor Moyuddin - who's the professor of agriculture at Teheran University - has been pushing to develop a food packaging industry, so that food production in Iran can be increased. He contacts us sporadically, asking for information and advice. I called him and introduced myself as D&A's technical expert in Europe. He's begging me to go to Iran to give a series of lectures and presentations to government, agricultural producers and potential investors."

Ghenadie asked, "So how does all that help us to get Petrov out of Russia?"

"Well, I told him that in a few weeks I would be in South Russia and asked if he knew any way I could cross the border when my Russian visa stipulated that I must leave via Sheremetyevo airport in Moscow. He said he'd make enquiries."

"Ah, I see. And?"

"He came back to me two days ago. There are two possible ways out - one from Armenia to Tabriz and one from the Khanates to Mashad. He advised against the latter route; it's very remote on the Uzbekistan side of the border and would involve crossing a desert, usually only crossed by camel caravans. It would be very slow and the Reds don't like foreigners travelling in that part of the USSR, in case they stir up trouble with the locals. The preferred route - and he sounded very optimistic - would be from Armenia into Iran. The Iranians never persecuted the Armenians like the Turks, so there are friendly relations across the border. Also, the Armenians aren't keen on Moscow because they try to close the Armenian churches. Apparently, the communist philosophy is that all churches are bad news but if there *has* to be one, it must be Russian Orthodox. He reckons that, for a price, he could get me across the border quite safely."

George asked, "And how much would that cost?"

"How much? The first class airfare from Sheremetyevo to London and from London to Teheran. The guide is a very sharp business man."

"Is he Russian or Iranian? What's his name?" Ghenadie said.

"I don't know, he didn't say. He goes by the nickname of 'The Mule'."

"Probably because he carries things across the border."

George said, "Unless anyone has a better suggestion I propose that we go with Professor Moyuddin's idea." He looked around at the group. All of them nodded. "David you get back to him and work out the details. I suggest that you don't give him a name. I'll try to work out how we can get the cash to him without our man in Teheran knowing about it."

At this point the room got even hotter and they decided to continue in the nearest bar. All had ideas as to how they should proceed but this was George's area of expertise and he took command. After listening to everyone's comments he said, "Tomorrow's Thursday. We'll aim for three weeks from tomorrow. That means that you, Giuseppe and David, need to be in the Orenburg area by then. I suggest that should be the middle of your schedule."

"OK, but why do you think that?" Giuseppe asked.

"Well, if Petrov were to disappear just after you've arrived, it might cause suspicion, and we don't want that. The same goes for Ghenadie and me. We need to be in the Ufa/Orenburg/Astrakhan area at the same time."

Ghenadie said, "I don't think it's feasible in the time. I need to set up a base and meetings around Tbilisi and Yerevan before then. That's the way out. Surely it's less important for us to be established in Orenburg before the pickup?"

"Good point," George said. "OK, if you all feel easier we will go for four weeks from tomorrow."

As they walked back to the office David asked George, "Have you ever come across anyone from the DSTE?"

"The French spooks? Why would you want to know them? They're the most devious, untrustworthy bunch I've ever come across."

"They can't be any worse than that bunch we've left behind in London. Anyway, I met two at a meeting once in London. They seemed good guys. I was going to sound them out about Iran, theoretically speaking."

"Well, theoretically speaking the head guy is Jean-Pierre Lefaivre. He's a recluse, never gets seen in public. Don't know any of his minions. I've got a number for the front desk if it's any use?"

****

David met up with Anna and they returned to the flat where David filled her in on the meeting. He then called the number that George had given to him and asked to speak to Monsieur Lefaivre.

"Monsieur Lefaivre does not take external calls."

David said, "Please ensure that this call is recorded and is passed to M. Lefaivre as soon as possible. I've been told to contact him by the French correspondent of the Washington Post. My name is Alain Meschines and my passport number is 701157. Please check the validity of that number, but please don't contact London. That will establish my credentials. Tell M. Lefaivre that I have some important information for him and he can contact me on this number. And, again, it is vital that you don't contact London."

Just as the TV news was finishing, the telephone rang. David answered. The voice on the other end barked out a series of questions. "Monsieur Meschines? This is Jean-Pierre Lefaivre. I hope you're not wasting my time. What is a British citizen doing using a French passport in France? What do you want from me?"

211

"I'm not wasting your time, I promise. I need thirty minutes to explain how I'm going to give you a priceless piece of intelligence, if you want it."

"Report to reception at half past ten tomorrow morning and you've got thirty minutes." The phone went down before David could reply.

Chapter 34

David reported to reception as instructed and was taken to the head of DTSE via the private lift that only went to the seventh floor.

"You have half an hour. Not a moment longer," Lefaivre said.

At exactly half past ten, David started his presentation. The telephone rang at twenty five past eleven. "Monsieur Lefaivre they are waiting for you in the meeting."

"Yes, I know. Please tell them I will be another ten minutes."

David continued with his story. At midday Lefaivre called his secretary on the intercom. "Cancel all meetings for today and ask the four heads to await my call. I don't want any interruptions." After switching off the intercom he turned to David. "Now, David, is there anything else that we can do?"

"No, I don't think so. If you could be responsible for Petrov's safety after we cross into Turkey and work out the best way of getting him to Paris that would be ideal. I don't think there's anything we need while we're getting out." David shrugged. "Either it works or it doesn't."

Lefaivre said, "I can give you a piece of relevant information that came in from London a few days ago. They've informed the security people of all NATO members that they're looking for a woman who has gone missing in the UK with vital military intelligence. Her name is Anna Magdalena Petrova, travelling under an alias of Magda Sakharova." He sat back and looked at David appraisingly. "I don't suppose you know where she is?"

David's concern was obvious. He opened his mouth to speak, but Lefaivre held up a hand to stop him. "I thought as much. Don't worry. I'll inform them there is no one of that name in

France and that we are being vigilant." He gave David a smile and a wink.

"Thank you."

Lefaivre waved away David's thanks. "Now, there's someone I want you to meet."

He called his secretary, "Would you ask Michel Charnay to come to my office."

"Michel is one of our stars on the Middle East, fluent in Arabic and..."

A well-tanned man with dark curly hair walked in, "Good Morning chief."

"Ah, Michel, sorry to keep you waiting all morning, but something interesting has arisen. Let me introduce you to Alain Meschines." David and Michel shook hands, taking the measure of each other. Lefaivre continued. "Michel, three weeks from now you will be based at our embassy in Ankara. You'll be there for two or three weeks, on twenty-four hour call from either Alain or I and will report to me every day. I'll ensure that you can call me wherever I am." Michel nodded impassively, as though this was an everyday occurrence and Lefaivre turned to David. "As we agreed, Alain, no one here will know anything about you or your, er, uncle until it's all over. The documents for your uncle will be delivered before the end of the week." He stood up and shook David's hand, "We won't let you down. I want to be sure that the next time you two meet you both have a happy face."

Turning to Charnay he said, "You wait here, I have a very interesting operation for you."

****

When David returned to the office, George was waiting for him. "Where have you been? I asked Anna and she seemed very

214

evasive, just said something about an interesting telephone call last night."

"It's no big secret. I've been talking to Immigration. I've been trying to set up Petrov's paperwork for him to get into France. We don't think he'd be that safe in the UK and he doesn't want to go to the United States, so the obvious place to settle him would be here in France. There's a large Russian émigré community here in Paris where they would make him welcome and feel at home."

"Not if they knew he was ex-KGB." called Anna from the other office.

David indicated to George that he wanted to speak to him where Anna couldn't overhear them, so George shut his office door. "What's wrong?"

"I learned this morning that London has asked all NATO security services to look out for Anna. We must be careful to keep to our new identities."

George's phone rang. He answered and looked at David. "There's a Michel Charnay on the phone for 'Alain'. He wants to talk about Jacobin."

"Bonjour, Michel. What's Jacobin?"

"Jacobin is the codeword for this operation. Can you come over to my office Thursday afternoon around half three to pick up your uncle's passport? Don't forget to bring the photograph of him. Also bring your French passport."

****

That evening David sat worrying about how he could keep Anna safe. In a flash of inspiration he realised that there was one place that neither NATO nor the USSR would look for her. He put the idea to Anna who just grinned and said, "You bet."

First thing the following morning he called Michel Charnay and outlined his plan.

Michel thought for a minute or so and then laughed. "*Mon Dieu, audacieux*. Bring her passport as well."

As Anna had nothing to do she went with David to the DSTE office. Michel met them and took them into a private meeting room by reception.

"Here's the passport for your uncle. You will note that it contains a valid Russian visa and an entry stamp dated next Friday. It also has an entry stamp at Teheran airport; you'll have to scribble a date on it if required. If you leave your passports with me we'll get Russian visas and entry stamps put into them. We'll leave the port of departure blank. You may have to think of a reason why you couldn't give them a port of departure."

While he was telling them this, he thumbed through Mme Meschines' passport. He stopped and looked at the photograph of Nicole. "This is no good. You need a new passport with a proper likeness in it. We'll get it sorted while you're here." He picked up the telephone, "I need six passport photographs immediately. Bring your camera to my office. Yes, take them in my office." He put the phone down and looked at Anna. "Anna please come back to collect your new passport tomorrow morning."

That evening David told Anna that tomorrow he was going to slip back to London as Alain Meschines. "You don't need me with you when you collect your passport and I need to see a pal of mine in the Ministry of Aviation."

Chapter 35

David and Giuseppe left the Orenburg cannery to head north to Sterlitamak; Giuseppe was leading in his car and David and Anna following in the Lada provided courtesy of the Washington Post, as Ghenadie described it. When they reached the outskirts of Sterlitamak David and Anna turned left, as arranged, and took the road that bypassed the town, while Giuseppe continued on the main road through the centre of Sterlitamak. As Giuseppe approached the rendezvous he checked the time; it was just before two o'clock. He didn't know if Petrov would be alone before the others arrived for the bus or whether he would deliberately miss the bus, as he had when Ghenadie had met him. By quarter past two there were some twenty people waiting for the bus. As it arrived, Giuseppe could see a solitary figure striding along the dirt track but too late for the bus.

Giuseppe started the car and drove so that he reached the road end just as Petrov arrived. He pulled up beside him and wound down the window. "Mr Petrov?"

Petrov bent forward and peered into the car, "Your name?"

"I'm Giuseppe Lombardo. Please get in, Mr Petrov."

"Where are we going?"

"I'm going to Ufa, but you're only with me for a few kilometres until I hand you over to the people who will get you out."

****

Giuseppe saw David's Lada parked at the roadside and pulled up nearby.

"This is the next stage of your journey. Good luck, Mr Petrov. The next time we meet, you'll be in the West."

Petrov got out and slung his rucksack over his shoulder and walked across to the Lada. As soon as he recognised Anna in the car, he exploded with a string of swear words. David opened the door to the back seat. "Please get in, Mr Petrov. We can continue the discussion as we drive."

Before Petrov could say anything, David accelerated away and turned right on to the road that bypassed the town. In his mirror he saw Guiseppe's car disappear into the distance. The whole incident was over within a minute and was seen by nobody.

After ten minutes of soothing words from Anna, Petrov began to calm down. Anna said, "Please, Papa, be quiet. We have to keep to a strict schedule for our plan to work."

"Oh, you do have a plan then; I'm glad to hear it. I can't believe you're endangering yourself by being here. Or that others have put you in danger."

David tried to calm things down. "Everything's fine, Mr Petrov. We'll explain it all to you when we have more time."

He could feel Petrov's glare as it bored into the back of his head. "Is this your husband? Not very bright is he? I hope this isn't *his* plan."

David didn't rise to the bait and, with no response, Petrov lapsed into silence.

Chapter 36

Giuseppe

Guiseppe wished them well, gave them a farewell wave and continued his journey north to Ufa. The road ran as straight as a railway line through the flat, boring countryside. Occasionally, there would be a field with a crop but it was mainly grass steppe and he thought how easy it would be easy to fall asleep at the wheel. Every few miles one could see a ruined farm and the infrequent ruined dacha. But there were few people around and no variation in the scenery. The Germans in the Great War had not penetrated so far east; the buildings' previous inhabitants were probably victims of the Revolution.

He saw few cars. The sparse traffic was mainly tankers carrying salt and soda from the chemical plant in Sterlitamak. The boredom was only relieved by the horses and carts, most of which were not under control when being passed by a large truck. By teatime he was entering Ufa and decided to go to his hotel and have a nap.

Checking in was the usual bureaucratic nightmare. They wanted to examine his passport and some other form of identification, his permit to travel to Bashkortostan, and the invitations to the can plant in Ufa. When that part of checking in was completed they wanted to see his driving licence, permit to drive in the USSR and proof that he was the owner of the car that was now sitting in their car park. It was an exhausting business, but he was composed and confident. Everything had gone to plan so far. He went up to his room, collapsed on the bed and promptly fell asleep.

There was a loud banging on the door; Giuseppe staggered out of bed and opened the door to be faced with two large policemen.

David and Anna

Two hours after waving goodbye to Giuseppe, David, Anna and her father were nearing the outskirts of Orenburg. They stopped for a short break at the abandoned monastery at Mayorskya. It looked sad, all closed up and surrounded by barbed wire. Nevertheless, its magnificent golden cupolas were still gleaming in the bright sunlight.

Petrov suddenly announced that he didn't like the idea of driving through Orenburg, "If they've missed me, they'll have road blocks this side of Orenburg."

"That's why we're going to take the next turn on the right. We'll enter Orenburg from the west on the P234, just in case. We can't avoid it; we have to cross the Ural at the Orenburg Bridge. If they have a road block at the bridge we're stuffed, but we can stop a few hundred metres before, and have a look."

Petrov didn't look happy, "I hope you know what you're doing. And I still can't believe that you brought Anna here."

David sighed. They had been through this several times since they had picked up Petrov. "I brought Anna because the bastards in England wanted to use her as an exchange for Smithson or whatever your friend, their agent, is called. They'll never guess that she's in Russia."

"You're an idiot."

"Maybe, but I'm the only son-in-law you've got."

"God help us all."

"Father, be quiet and lie down on the back seat under that blanket. As far as any casual watcher can see, there's only a man and woman in this car."

David smiled gratefully at Anna. Perhaps that would keep her father quiet for a while.

Giuseppe

One of the policemen was right up in Giuseppe's face. "You have arrived in Ufa today from Orenburg?"

"Yes, I checked in at five o'clock. Look, what's all this--"

"What time did you leave Orenburg?"

"I'm not sure. I worked at the hotel - in the bar - writing my report. I guess it would be just before lunch. The hotel would know, if you need the exact time. What *is* this?"

"Please get dressed and come with us; we need to talk to you at the office."

"What office?" But there was no response. They simply motioned to Giuseppe to go with them.

Giuseppe followed them out to their car. It was only a short drive to the police station but they didn't stop there. They pulled up just around the corner in front of a large grey building next to the town hall. He assumed it was some annexe to the police station. On the first floor he was shown into an office, where there was a hatchet-faced woman sitting looking at him.

After five minutes she spoke. "I am Commissar Zhukova. I wish to check your papers with our people in Moscow." Giuseppe took his passport and travel permits from his jacket pocket and passed them across the desk. He felt a sense of relief - he knew that his papers were fine. This was obviously just some routine check. The Commissar took a cursory look at them and pressed a bell on her desk. An assistant entered.

"Get these checked in Moscow as soon as possible."

The assistant scurried out.

David and Anna

They passed through Orenburg and crossed over the River Ural. Just as they were leaving the city they turned right on to the road, sign posted Uralsk.

Petrov came to life. "If we're going to Uralsk you've taken the wrong road. The Uralsk road was just before the bridge."

David explained patiently. "That was the main road and it goes through Uralsk, if we'd taken that we would have to cross the river in Uralsk."

"So?"

"In three hours, every bridge in Russia might have a road block on it."

"Idiot." Petrov settled back under the blanket without a further word. Anna rolled her eyes at David.

Giuseppe

"Now, Mr Lombardo, I'm sure that your papers are in order. What really interests me is why you are wandering around the Bashkortostan province of the USSR."

"The company that I work for supplies chemicals and plastics, which are used for food packaging in Russia. I visit regularly and ImproChem and State Can Manufacturing Org in Moscow are always asking me to visit the factories that use our products. I agreed to make a tour, visiting the can factories in Rostov and Ufa and the canneries in Orenburg and Krasnodar. I can give you the names of the people in Moscow who I meet and you'll also find their names on the travel permits."

"What do you do on these visits?"

222

"I tell them about the best practices in the industry in Europe and the USA. I bring reports on new developments, make suggestions on how the plants can run more efficiently."

Commissar Zhukova didn't smile, just stared at him.

"Yes, yes. I know that's what you're *supposed* to do, though I can't imagine how you can make our plants more efficient. Why are you here at this particular time?"

The questions went on and on, round and round, most seemingly irrelevant. After two hours she asked, "Which way did you come from Orenburg?"

Giuseppe knew he needed to be careful with this line of questioning. "I drove up the P314 past Kumartau, Salavat, Sterlitamak to Ufa."

"Did you stop on the road?"

David and Anna
At first they were driving through miles and miles of sunflowers but this slowly changed to miles of birch forest and scrub. David had heard of the Russian steppe but he had never imagined that anywhere could be so flat. To their right there was woodland alongside the river, but to the south the steppe stretched to infinity.

Anna pointed to a sign. "Ilek, 5 kilometres."

"If we see a gas station, I'll fill up. We're going on some remote roads and I'd like to keep the tank full."

"Anyone with half a brain would have a reserve can," Petrov said from the back seat.

David counted to five under his breath. "Then your son-in-law has *two* half brains. That's why we have two five litre cans in the boot. I *still* want to keep the tank full, just in case."

223

They turned off the P335 and found a gas station just before the town. David and Anna walked into the shop and David smiled at the man behind the counter. "Please could you fill the tank."

"*Nyet*. I don't serve petit bourgeoisie from the West."

"Then I'll fill it myself."

"No gas for Westerners." sneered the man."

But then his face went pale; he was paralysed with fear and shaking like a leaf. What had scared him so much? David spun round.

Giuseppe

Commissar Zhukova leaned forward over her desk. "I asked you if you stopped on the road."

"No."

"Not even once?"

"I stopped twice to go to the toilet."

"You said you didn't stop."

"I meant, I didn't stop for food."

"You must have eaten something."

"No. I didn't eat anything between breakfast and having a snack here at the hotel."

The inane questions went on until, at eight p.m., she stood up. "That's enough for tonight. We will be keeping your passport. You may not leave Ufa. Tomorrow we will send a car for you at eight in the morning."

David and Anna

Petrov had walked into the garage behind them.

"Yes sir. I will do it immediately," said the garage man. All four went out to the car.

224

Anna looked at David, who shrugged his shoulders. Petrov had not said a word.

After paying for the petrol they climbed back into the car. As they did so, Petrov said, "Wait for me, I'll only be a minute." He then walked back into the garage.

"Did he recognise your father? What the hell happened in there?"

Anna looked perplexed, "I don't know. Something happened. I saw Papa fiddle with the lapel of his jacket."

Petrov got into the back of the car. "We were never here. No one has filled up with petrol since last night, and here is a can of oil as an apology for being rude."

David and Anna stared at him, open mouthed.

Petrov stared back at them. "What? For God's sake don't look at me like a pair of salmon. We haven't got all day. Go!"

David gave a long-suffering sigh. "Uralsk next stop."

Shortly after leaving Ilek, David turned right from the main road on to an unmarked gravel road.

Petrov asked, "Do you know what you are doing?"

David didn't reply. The track was a very smooth gravel road running west in a dead straight line. Even so, he didn't want to risk a puncture. He kept the speed down to no more than forty mph.

After an hour they could see the town of Borilli to the north. At least, David assumed it was Borilli, as their road map marked the town, but not the road they were travelling on.

Petrov couldn't contain his curiosity any longer, "OK, exceptionally talented son-in-law, how the hell did you know this road was here and where it goes?"

David glanced at him in the rear view mirror. "I'll tell you how I knew about this road, when you tell me how you scared that man at the garage in Ilek."

Petrov didn't reply, which suited David down to the ground. He had no intention of telling anyone, that RAF photo reconnaissance Canberras had overflown most of southern Russia from bases in Turkey and Iran. In the Ministry of Aviation he had used his contacts to take a good look at all the aerial photographs of the area through which they would be travelling. They had spotted small cars using the gravel road, so he'd made the assumption that they could use it. He was just glad that assumption was correct.

He said, casually, "I thought it was worth a try. No one would think of putting a checkpoint on it and, if anyone sees our dust trail, they'll assume that we're locals. It also has the advantage that we can travel south without going through Uralsk."

Anna was looking at the map. "Why, on some signs, is it called Uralsk but on this map it's called Oral Uralsk?"

The voice in the rear said, "Uralsk is the Russian name. Here we are in Kazakhstan, Oral is the Kazakh name for it."

"Well we're nearly there."

When they rejoined the main road, they were back on a good tarmac surface. Anna said, "We turn right to join the A28 going south."

David was not so sure. "Maybe, but that means we go through Uralsk and cross the bridge over the Ural. We should turn south at the next left turn and go south on the opposite bank to the A28."

"Well, we've only two hours or so of daylight, where do we spend the night?"

David wondered if Petrov ever had anything positive to say, but tried to keep from snapping as he answered. "I'm not sure as yet; it will be a few hours before I know."

"Do you mean my son-in-law hasn't thought that we need to sleep some time?"

"Alexei do you have to keep calling me 'son-in-law'? My name's David."

Petrov was silent a moment. "Well, David it is. But you don't call me Alexei, you call me Papa."

"Fine. That's agreed, then. I will call you Alyosha."

There was a loud snort from the back seat and Petrov lapsed into silence.

Anna laughed. Alyosha was the baby name for Alexei. "How do you know the name Alyosha?"

"Alyosha was the youngest of the 'Brothers Karamazov'. You'd know if you had read Dostoevsky; it's one of my favourite books."

As they drove on in silence the wilderness became oppressive. On their right there were trees along the banks of the Ural but, where they could see across the river, the wilderness extended as far as one could see to the West. On their side of the river, billiard-table flat scrub grassland stretched out of sight to the East.

As it started to go dark David put on their lights. They weren't very bright and he didn't dare to drive quickly. Anna suddenly stared into the distance. "There's a car parked at the side of the road."

The parked car turned on both its headlights when they came closer and David slowed right down. As they drove past they could see two cars - one a Mercedes with its lights on and the other a Russian four wheel drive jeep. They drove past, staring ahead, not daring to look inside the parked cars. After a few hundred metres, David slowed and switched off the lights and they pulled in to the side of the road.

He jumped out, "Wait here and don't put the lights on. I'm just going to have a look at who's parked back there."

Giuseppe

Back at the hotel and safely in his room, Giuseppe discovered that he was shaking all over. He knew that there would be more questions tomorrow, and he was worried about the turn they would take. His instinct was to pack up and leave immediately. If he set off now, he could take his car and be in Moscow and on a plane home before they came to get him at eight o'clock. He would need to leave via the fire escape to make sure that the hotel staff didn't see him, just in case they had been told to keep an eye on him. He glanced out of the window to where his car was parked. In the darkness of the car park everything looked quiet. As he was about to turn away from the window and make his escape he spotted a red glow in the car parked next to his. The window was rolled down and a curl of cigarette smoke lazily dissipated in the breeze.

David and Anna

David kept off the road, and, staying low, he approached the parked cars. He was only about two hundred metres away when there were suddenly a lot of shouted goodbyes and the truck took off, straight across the steppe to the East.

David found George and Ghenadie waiting for him by the Mercedes.

George shook him warmly by the hand. "Hi David. Sorry about that. It was a couple of Kazakh herdsmen; they saw us camped here and were curious. They'd been to Uralsk for supplies and wanted to chat."

"Wanted some free vodka, is more like it," Ghenadie said. "They wouldn't clear off until I gave them a bottle and told them we wanted to turn in for the night. They have to cross twenty miles of steppe until they get to their herd."

"I'll run back to Anna and turn the car around to join you."

"And we'll start on supper."

When David reached the car, he briefly explained that they were staying the night there, and that George and Ghenadie were preparing a meal and making camp.

When they returned, George and Ghenadie were introduced to Petrov and a brief explanation was given as to how they were involved. They sat down to the meal that had been pre-prepared and coffee made on a gas stove.

Petrov didn't speak until after the meal. "Those two who were here, were they Russian or Kazakh?"

"Kazhakh herdsmen. Why?"

"Could they speak Russian?"

George realised why Petrov was being cautious. "I couldn't understand a word they said but Ghenadie could."

"Well, that's not quite true, they spoke Russian but with such a strong Kazakh dialect that I couldn't understand much of what they said either. The only word that's common to Russian and Kazakh is vodka."

Petrov relaxed slightly.

As soon as they had finished eating Anna and David retreated to the sleeping bag that George had brought for them. Both were absolutely shattered after such a long day, but sleep evaded them for a while as they gazed at the limitless sky, full of stars. The only noise in the otherwise total silence, was a hissing sound that came whenever a slight breath of air blew through the grasses on the steppe.

Petrov had become aware of Ghenadie's efforts on his behalf in Moscow and of his visits to Madame Dorokhina. He wanted to hear all the details of what she had said, and what had happened to his apartment. They were still talking after David and Anna had finally fallen asleep.

Giuseppe

As might be expected, Giuseppe did not sleep well. It felt as though he had just gone to sleep when the receptionist called, telling him that his breakfast would be at seven a.m. and that the police were coming at eight.

He was once again shown into Zhukova's office. This time she was not alone. Before he could ask, the man introduced himself, "My name is Kabalevsky. I am also interested in your visit to Bashkortostan. I am an official of state security and I take an interest in all foreign visitors."

"I'm afraid I don't understand why--"

"Why did you come to Bashkorto province?"

All the questions from the previous day were repeated and Giuseppe's answers, too, were the same. He tried to remain calm and patient.

"Yesterday, did you drive through Sterlitamak?"

"Yes."

"Did you stop in Sterlitamak?"

Oh God. Had someone seen? "No."

"Did you see anyone on the road?"

Giuseppe played for time while he decided what to say to the question he knew was coming. "There was very little traffic on the road."

David and Anna

David awoke to the sound of Petrov's voice, telling Ghenadie that he had had a better night's sleep when he was in the camp.

Ghenadie shut him up, "At least you're with friends and you knew we wouldn't shoot you in the night."

"*I* might be tempted." George said, sounding as though he had had to listen to Petrov moaning all night.

"Now you know what Anna and I have had to put up with, cooped up in that tiny Lada." David asked George if any news or comments had been picked up from Moscow radio.

"No, they'll never say that a senior officer in the KGB has been arrested, nor will they admit that a prisoner has escaped. It helps us because they won't let the general public know that they've lost someone. You can be sure, however, that every office of state security will know."

"The main thing that worries me is our car. Someone will have seen it and noticed three people in it. All it needs is one suspicion and they'll look for that car all over Russia."

George said, "And that's why we're changing cars. You and Anna will take our Merc. It's registered to the Post. You've got your documents that say that you're working for the Post, on the economic survey, so you're the legal driver."

David shook his head. "But that doesn't solve the problem of the Lada being recognised."

"Yes it does. Ghenadie has arranged for us to pick up another car in Atyrau, this one will be spare parts in no time at all."

Petrov had been listening to the conversation carefully. "I'm glad I won't have to sit in the back of that piece of crap anymore. I rather fancy the Mercedes - I'm used to comfort with my status."

George looked at him with a mixture of glee and dismay. "Sorry, Mr. Petrov, you'll be in the crap car as far as Atyrau. You're coming with us, unfortunately. David and Anna are heading for the cannery in Krasnodar as arranged. Hopefully they'll meet up with Giuseppe and find out what happened with his part of the plan."

Petrov asked, "What's *our* part of the plan?"

George smiled at him. "Plan? We don't have a plan. We play it by ear from now on."

"God help us, I'm with the cadets."

"In England we call them Boy Scouts, Papa."

Petrov wandered off, muttering under his breath. "Why do I need a son- in-law?"

Giuseppe

"Did you see anyone walking?"

"No. Well, there was a man standing in the middle of nowhere. He looked as if he was waiting for a bus. I asked if I could give him a lift to Tolbazy."

"So, you *did* stop?"

"Well, I didn't really stop. Just pulled up and left the engine running while I spoke to him. I thought you meant had I stopped the car and got--"

"So you gave him a lift?"

"Yes. Once he was in the car he asked if I could take him as far as Ufa. I told him that I was going to Ufa to the can-making factory."

"Did he tell you his name? What did you talk about?"

"We didn't. I don't think he said more than ten words all the way to Ufa."

Kabalevsky passed a photograph across the desk. "Is that the man?"

Giuseppe looked at it for a minute or so. "I'm sorry, I can't say. When I stopped he was standing and I was looking up at him. Because the sun was behind him, I couldn't see very well. When I was driving I could only see him to the side of me. It could be the same man but I'm not sure. Why do you want him? Has he escaped from gaol?"

Zhukova, who had a face as black as thunder, said, "You're not being very helpful. We can keep you here until you are."

Kabalevsky ignored her and asked, "When you arrived in Ufa where did you drop him?"

"I'm not sure. He pointed at the road ahead and said he would get out there. I think he was going to the railway station because the sign on the corner pointed to the train station. I could show you where we were, if you like."

Zhukova pulled a street map out a drawer and spread it on the desk. "Show me where you dropped him."

Giuseppe turned the map. "I stopped here, on Mingazheva Street. He got out and crossed in front of me towards Ibrazimova; I had to wait a while until two trucks had gone past before I could pull out. The last time I saw him he was walking quickly down Ibrazimova towards the station."

Zhukova turned to Kabalevsky. "The only train due at that time is the Trans-Siberian heading East."

Kabalevsky looked thoughtful. "He might think that we would assume that he would want to get back to Moscow. He could have taken that just to confuse us."

Zhukova said. "That would have got into Omsk this morning. He would get off there because he wouldn't stay on it any longer than necessary. He would know that we would have the train searched as soon as we found out that he went to the station."

Giuseppe cleared his throat and the two turned back to him, as though they had forgotten he was there. Kabalevsky looked at his watch, "I don't think you can help us anymore, Mr Lombardo. I'll get a car to take you back to your hotel. You've missed your meeting at the can factory; I will ask them so see you first thing in the morning. Also, I will arrange for a permit for you to drive through the Saratov prohibited area. That will save you a day's driving to get to Krasnodar. The permit will be at your hotel by tomorrow morning." Giuseppe wondered at this sudden helpfulness, but thanked him profusely and walked out of the room.

Zhukova didn't look at him as he left the office. He heard her say, in Russian, "He's lying. I'll get Moscow to keep a close watch on him."

Giuseppe waited outside the office door to hear Kabalevsky's reply. All he heard was Zhukova say, "I'll have him followed to Krasnodar."

When he got back to the hotel Giuseppe started thinking about the day. It had gone to plan; they had assumed that he would be interrogated by the police at some point. If he could lead them in the wrong direction for just a day it would help. He now thought that it would be great if he could somehow confirm their suspicions that Petrov had gone to Omsk. He assumed that Zhukova had checked his statement with both the Orenburg and Ufa factories. If that *was* the case, neither had said anything about David being with him, otherwise she would have asked him where David was now. He came to the conclusion that he should skip the Krasnodar visit - all it would do would be to bring David back into the picture. However, Zhukova had said she would have him followed to Krasnodar. If he didn't go there, they would be suspicious. He sat there weighing up his options. In the end he decided that it would be safer to avoid Krasnodar, do the two day drive back to Moscow and fly straight home to Milan. Now he just needed to lose his tail.

David and Anna
David and George walked away from the others. "OK, David, you're booked into the hotel in Astrakhan tonight and then you'll head up to Krasnodar tomorrow. It will take you two or three hours to get to Atyrau and you should get to the hotel in time for dinner. Tomorrow will be a long day, but, God willing, you'll make it to the hotel the can people have booked for you, without any trouble. If Giuseppe is there, that's great. If not, and there's no message, wait one more day only. You mustn't wait more than two days or it throws everything else out of synch. I don't want to make any telephone calls about changing arrangements, it's too risky."

"Where are you going and how will we meet up?"

"We're going to take Petrov for a little holiday by the Black Sea."

"Christ. Rather you than me."

George laughed. "He is rather...difficult, isn't he? Anyway, when you're driving south on the M27, it turns into the E97 just after Gagra. We'll pick you up between there and Gudauta. If you get as far as Sukhumit without seeing us, turn round and try again from Gagra and if either of us has a big problem we go alone. If you don't make it, Ghenadie and I will do our economic research and try to get Petrov to the rendezvous. If we get arrested or can't meet you for any reason, then you go out the way we planned. I suppose that you could go out the way you

235

came in. That would be legal, but maybe you would be subjected to closer scrutiny."

"Well, here's hoping that everything goes according to plan and we see you soon." David held out his hand to George. "Good luck. And thanks."

Giuseppe

Giuseppe was feeling very pleased with himself. He had managed to lose his tail somewhere in Samara. Luckily, they had assumed that he was not aware that he was being followed and their procedures had, at best, been shoddy. He didn't like to think of the reception they would have got when Zhukova found out. His final act of mischief after he had checked in at Sheremetyevo airport was to approach a bunch of pressmen who were obviously waiting for someone important to arrive. He grabbed one by the shoulder. "Do you want a good story? I inadvertently gave a lift to an escaped prisoner near Orenburg. The KGB are after him. Apparently, he caught the Trans-Siberian to Omsk and he's hiding there." As the man started to ask a question Giuseppe told him that his flight had been called and he had to rush.

Chapter 37

When David and George returned, Ghenadie and Anna had swapped cars and packed everything, ready for a quick start. They agreed that they shouldn't be seen driving together, so George started first and asked David to wait thirty minutes before following. David spent the time checking the oil, tyre pressures and spare cans of petrol in the boot. He commented how nice it would be not to have Petrov moaning in the back seat. "I know he's your father, but..."

Anna grinned at him. "You didn't have to grow up with him."

They started south and within just a few miles they were driving through what David considered total desert. Although it was flat, in the distance they could see sand dunes and salt pans - some the size of small lakes. "This is more like being in the Middle East than Russia," David said.

Atyrau was like a frontier town in a western movie. The main street was dotted with haphazard buildings, most of which were falling down. There was no incentive to stop. After leaving the town Anna leaned forward and peered through the windscreen. "There's something in the road way up ahead. It's a big lump of something."

"That big lump is a group of camels. Never knew you had camels in Russia."

"Neither did I."

David pulled up at the side of the road and Anna took over the driving. It wasn't until they were almost in Astrakhan when David said, "Pull up by that Nodding Donkey and I'll take over."

"Nodding Donkey?"

"That old oil well. That's what you call that sort of oil well."

They eventually found the hotel and, after a quick meal, were fast asleep even though the bed was as uncomfortable as the steppe the previous night. The following day they soon found the A154 leading West out of Astrakhan. After a hundred miles of desert, followed by another hundred of grass steppe, they started to see something that looked like farmland. There were both cattle and sheep and some signs of irrigation. Unlike Atyrau, these villages looked like places where people lived as opposed to simply surviving. What surprised them both was that one village just north of Astrakhan had Buddhist shrines and another had mosques. It wasn't until they reached Elista that they began to see the traditional Russian Orthodox churches and shrines.

When they reached the Hotel Baikal near to the airport in Krasnodar, there was a message waiting for them from Giuseppe. 'Regret delayed in Ufa. Have now returned to Moscow. Go to cannery if you want, give them my apologies. Everything fine at my end. Have a lovely holiday. See you when you are back in Moscow. Giuseppe.'

"Do you think he wants us to go back to Moscow?"

"No. I think that's Guiseppe being devious."

"What do you think we should do?" said Anna.

"I'll ask the hotel to call either Mr Vasilyev or Mr Rasulov at the cannery to ask if they would like to see me by myself. It depends, I suppose, on whether they or anyone else there speaks English."

The following morning David visited the cannery and was met by Vasilyev and his assistant Georgi Noviks, who spoke very good English. After a short technical meeting he was given a tour of the factory, after which they asked him which factory he was visiting next.

238

"This is the last of my factory visits. My wife and I are taking a week's vacation. We're going to visit Armenia and look at some of the old churches."

"Are you going to stay in Tbilisi? It's a lovely city with fine buildings."

"No, the travel plan that they approved in Moscow specifically states that we must not visit Tbilisi. Our approved route is to the West."

Noviks said, "That's nonsense. The only good road goes through Tbilisi. They haven't a clue in Moscow. Take the A545 through Tbilisi. If anyone stops you they will be Georgian and will take great delight in doing the opposite of what Moscow says. You won't be stopped; in the South we don't worry about Moscow's affairs."

When David returned and climbed into the car, Anna sniffed and pulled a face. David noticed her expression, "If you visit a fish canning plant you don't have many close friends afterwards." He thought it would be several showers before he stopped smelling of fish. Just after lunch they started the drive to the coast.

Chapter 38

In Ufa, Kabalevsky wasn't amused at being summoned so abruptly to Zhukova's office. He was a state official and far senior to any local commissar. He didn't knock as he entered. Zhukova was standing in her office; her face was as red as a bowl of borscht and she looked as if she might explode. "Do we have a problem?" he asked.

"I instructed our security police in Omsk to make enquiries about anyone seen getting off the Trans-Siberian two days ago. They weren't very helpful. All they could say was that lots of people get off the train in Omsk and, unless they're conspicuous, no one will remember them. So I told them to look at all the hotels to see who has checked in and to look for any strangers in the town. The chief in Omsk has just called; apparently the press are there, all looking for an escaped KGB prisoner. They've found the taxi driver who picked him up at the station and took him into the city. The cab driver has given them a description of Petrov; it appears that between Ufa and Omsk he grew a beard."

Kabalevsky sat down and pulled a notebook from his pocket. "There's something else. I checked our Mr Lombardo with State Can and ImProChem. It seems that he was travelling with a colleague from England, a technical expert. Our friends at the can factory omitted to tell us that. After leaving Ufa they were going to Krasnodar. Did you have a man follow Lombardo?"

"Yes. He lost him in Samara."

"Eto piz'dets!"

"Not necessarily. I had someone check when Lombardo arrived at Krasnodar."

"And?"

"He never arrived."

"And you're only telling me this now?"

Zhukova shrugged. " I checked with the hotel. Lombardo called to say that he wasn't well and was on his way to Moscow."

"Did the other man, the Englishman, arrive?"

"I didn't know about any Englishman, so I didn't ask. I'll call back."

"No," said Kabalevsky, "I'll speak to the cannery at Krasnodar and find out what went on from them."

When he eventually got through, he introduced himself and asked to be brought up to date with the visitors from the West. He was told that only one visitor had arrived and he had spent the morning with Noviks and Vasilyev. "Well, put me through to Noviks."

Noviks came on the line. "Hello, this is Noviks. Can I help you?"

"Kabalevsky. State Security. I want to hear about your visitor. And what happened to Lombardo?"

Noviks hesitated slightly. "We received a call from Mr Lombardo to say he wasn't well and that he was returning to Moscow. Mr Hopkins arrived early Wednesday morning. He's the technical expert from our suppliers."

"And *was* he a technical expert?"

"Oh yes, he was very helpful."

"Where was he going after Krasnodar?"

"He'd finished the business part of his trip. He and his wife had Moscow approval to take a sightseeing trip before leaving Russia."

"Where were they going on holiday?"

Noviks hesitated once again; he'd told them to make an unapproved visit to Tbilisi. "They didn't say, exactly, but I think they were planning to take the ferry at Kerch and visit Yalta before going home."

"Thank you Comrade Noviks, you have been most helpful."

Kabalevsky turned to Zhukova and decided to exert his authority, "I want you to organise a watch on the ferry at Kerch. Miss nothing. If I were you, I wouldn't send the imbeciles who lost Lombardo. I want a list of all foreigners using the ferry and your men should ask if any have used it in the last two days. Also, check with all hotels in Yalta to see if anyone from the West is booked in. Only give them the name Hopkins if they have foreigners staying. I'm taking over the investigation in Omsk; we need to know what's going on there. Finally, I'll call the office in Moscow to find out what happened to Lombardo."

Zhukova had been stewing throughout this speech. She was furious. She hated all the Moscow bureaucrats who told her what to do, then went home when things went wrong, usually blaming the locals for their own mistakes.

"We will meet here at five o'clock to continue our investigation." With that, Kabalevsky turned smartly and left the office. After he had gone, Zhukova threw the folder containing her notes of the meeting into the waste paper bin.

Promptly at five, Kabalevsky returned, "Well, Commissar Zhukova, what have you to report?"

"Comrade Kabalevsky, I have wasted a whole day. At Kerch the ferry doesn't have any system for recording the names or car numbers of people using the ferry. The crew working today is a relief crew and they've seen no foreigners. The normal crew return tomorrow, so we won't know about the last two days until then. I then called all the big hotels in Yalta. None have any

Western visitors. I asked the local police to check with the smaller hotels."

"Djirjmo! By the time they have done that our English friends will be back in the UK."

"Well, Comrade Kabalevsky, have you done any better?"

Kabalevsky ignored the sarcasm. "In the first place, I've issued an order to all border security posts to look out for and detain Mr and Mrs David Hopkins and anyone who might be travelling with them. Our friend Lombardo left Sheremetyevo on a Swiss Air flight to Zurich several days ago. What I've found out in Omsk is more interesting. Apparently, the local press there received a call from the Moscow press saying that there was a rumour of an escaped political prisoner on the run in Omsk. Everyone there started chasing their own tails. You would think there were half a dozen escaped prisoners from all the sightings. My colleagues in Omsk interviewed the cab driver. When he was stark naked and about to be thrown into the river, he admitted to making up the story. Every time the press asked him questions they gave him money and some vodka. The interesting bit about the rumour is that it's quite specific, in saying that the man was a KGB prisoner being held at a camp near to Orenburg."

"And how, exactly, is that interesting?"

"There are only two people who know that about Petrov and one is the camp commander." Kabalevsky paused and glared at Zhukova. "The other, Comrade, is you."

Zhukova reared back as if she had been slapped.

Kabalevsky continued. "Only you knew about our suspicion that he caught the train to Omsk. My conclusion is that you were indiscreet when talking to people in Moscow about Lombardo."

Zhukova screamed, "That's a preposterous lie."

"Well, that's what I'm saying in my report. You can refute it at a later date. My conclusion is that Petrov is no longer in Omsk, if he was ever there."

He walked out of the office, leaving Zhukova speechless. She thought that if the KGB were stupid enough to lose a prisoner, then they weren't bright enough to find him. She was certain that Lombardo was the key and returned to her desk, muttering under her breath. "Woe betide him if he ever returns to Ufa."

Chapter 39

"We should be at the coast in one hour; Novik told me that it's a good road all the way down to Sochi. He didn't know the road south of Sochi, but he reckoned on three hours maximum."

Once they had passed through Sochi, Anna took over the driving. She had only been at the wheel for ten minutes when she said, "We're being followed." David turned round. "I don't see anything that looks like a police car."

"It's a pale green Lada."

"There isn't a pale green Lada behind us."

"Maybe not, but there will be soon."

David remembered when he and Anna were in Bulgaria and he had suspected that she'd had professional surveillance training. Now it seemed she also had telepathic powers, or maybe all Russians were scared of their own shadow.

"There he is." Her voice sounded self-satisfied. David turned to look. He could see a pale green Lada some six hundred metres or so behind them. Anna slowed to a halt at the side of the road and the Lada turned off down a side road. Just a few minutes after restarting their journey the Lada reappeared. Soon they saw the sign for Sukhumit, and, as they entered the town, the Lada disappeared once again.

Anna said, "Our instructions were to go back to Gagra and start again if we didn't see them." She turned round and headed towards Gagra. Just before they reached the town, David saw a pale green Lada parked at the side of the road.

"Look at that. Do you think it's the same one?"

As they drove past, the Lada flashed its headlights. As soon as they reached the sign for Gagra, Anna turned the car and started south once more. After a few miles they stopped at traffic lights and the Lada pulled alongside. With the window down they could see it was Ghenadie. He yelled, "Follow me and when I stop and wave you on, pull into the driveway."

Within twenty minutes they entered Gudauta. After a few turns the Lada turned into a leafy avenue of old villas. It came to a stop and Ghenadie waved them to overtake and turn in. Immediately in front of the Lada was a driveway to one of the villas. Anna turned into it rather slowly. It was a tight squeeze for the Merc. As soon as they were in, George appeared and closed the high wooden gate behind them. Ghenadie left the Lada parked on the road and joined them through a side gate.

David asked, "What was all that about? Were you trying to scare us?"

"That was our KGB anti-surveillance training. Petrov insisted that we ensured that you weren't being followed."

"Where is he now?"

"Out there somewhere. He's making sure that *I* wasn't being followed. He'll be with us shortly."

Anna went upstairs, saying that she was going to take a shower.

David looked at George, "Is he behaving himself?"

"Yes, we're getting on well. He's good company."

David snorted.

"No really. He's a bit more relaxed now that we've got this far. Ghenadie has discovered something interesting about him." David looked at Ghenadie, but he indicated to George to carry on. "Two nights ago his jacket had fallen on the floor. When I

246

picked it up I noticed a small blue badge stitched on the inside of the lapel. I told Ghenadie, who had a peep at it last night."

David turned to Ghenadie, "So, what is it?"

"Your father-in-law has a NKVD badge on his jacket. That must mean that he was in the NKVD... or still is."

"I thought the NKVD were disbanded years ago when the KGB were formed?"

Ghenadie nodded. "Yes, in theory they were. Officially, they don't exist, but very few people in Russia believe that. Most think that they still exist but are very secret."

David snapped his fingers. "That explains something. When Anna and I were in Ilek, trying to fill up with petrol, the garage man was being difficult. Petrov walked in and the guy just about wet himself."

As if on cue, Petrov entered through the back door. As George looked at him he said, "All clear. It's very quiet out there. No one followed you and I'm sure this house isn't being watched."

"Thanks Alexei. What do you want to do now?"

"I'm going back to work in my room."

"Work?" David looked at George but Ghenadie answered, "You'll remember that we're supposed to be working on a report on the economy of the states of Southern Russia. Well, we are, and George and I *have* been doing some legwork. But the report is being written by one of the best economists in Russia."

"Certainly one of the best *informed* economists in Russia." added George.

"The best from many perspectives," said Petrov as he left the room.

Anna came downstairs looking very refreshed. "It's your turn now, David. Do I have to remind you that you still stink of fish?"

George looked at Ghenadie with a smile, "So, it's *David* that stinks, I was beginning to think it was you."

David laughed. "OK, OK, I get the message. Before I go, can we have a quick recap of where we are with the plan? As far as I can tell we're still on schedule."

George said, "Actually, we're ahead of schedule. We have three days to go before our first possible meeting with 'The Mule' and he's said that he'll wait. Or, at least, return to the rendezvous for three days. It is possible to do it in one day from here but I think that's too risky, in case of problems on the road. We could go tomorrow, but that might mean that you're hanging around by the rendezvous for a couple of days. No one knows you're here and you can't be seen, so this is the safest place to wait. I suggest we stay here for one more day and then leave the day after tomorrow. Ghenadie and I will come with you to Yerevan, or just south of the city, at least. We have genuine business there, gathering market info for the report. Alexei can travel with us until the final stage and after that you're on your own."

Anna said, "What do we do if the Mule doesn't turn up?"

George looked at her and then back at David. "Yes, I'm sure you've thought about the possibility, but you've said very little. What *will* you do?"

David said nothing for a moment. There were parts of his plan that he didn't want to discuss too soon. "I can tell you, but you're not to say anything to Alexei as yet. That's my job. The trouble is that he might not like it."

He had the attention of all three of them now. "Do you remember before we left Paris and I had a meeting at the DSTE?

Well, I explained to them my concerns that Petrov and Anna weren't safe in England because there are people in London who would send them to their death in Russia if they could exchange them for Smithson, if that's his real name. The French gave me a guarantee that Anna's father will get a French ID and citizenship, plus French protection from any dodgy deals, if he shares his information with them. They've also assured me verbally that they'll honour the commitments that I've made to the Post about the escape story."

George looked impressed. "Do you have this in writing?"

"Unfortunately not. They wouldn't agree to put *anything* in writing. I had no alternative but to trust them. I haven't told Alexei as yet; I'm not sure that he'll like the idea of being French."

"It's better than being shot." Ghenadie walked over to the sofa and made himself comfortable.

"What's all this got to do with an alternative plan to get out?" said George.

"I persuaded them to give me a French passport for my father-in-law. I promised that it would only be used in Russia as a last resort. If he's arrested trying to get out using a genuine French passport, there would be a serious diplomatic row. The problem is that it doesn't have a Russian entry visa in it. The DSTE refused to get involved in forgery. If he uses it to get out, then there is a real risk someone will ask how he got in without a visa."

Chapter 40

Both cars were packed and the house cleared of anything that might indicate that the five of them had been staying there.

Anna asked George, "What happens to this place when we've gone?"

"We're keeping the house for another three weeks. When we've finished the report, we'll find a local steno to type the report, so that we can give it to the Ministry when we return to Moscow."

Ghenadie added, "We can't leave immediately, because once the story is published, someone would put two and two together, once they realised that George and I were here at the same time and left at the same time as Alexei. It's important that the Post remains *persona grata* in Russia. So we hang around here and in Moscow for another few weeks twiddling our thumbs."

David took George to one side, "I've been thinking. Everything has gone well up to now, but a lot of people know that I'm here in Russia and might now be looking for me. I propose that from now on Mr and Mrs Hopkins disappear and that we become M. and Mme. Meschines, working for the Washington Post. We've got our passports and the accreditation that you arranged in Moscow. If we get stopped and searched we'd be in serious trouble if they found two sets of passports. Should we burn the English passports or would you take them back for us? The minute we leave that gate we are the Meschines family from Paris."

"Don't worry. I'll take your passports and keep them till you're back in Paris." He then took out the map and spread it over the bonnet of the Merc. "This is our route; we go down the coast to Sukhumi. Then we turn inland, through Gali to Samtredi on route 97. I'll lead the way but, just in case we get separated, use the map as well. I'll stop for a drink somewhere between Samtredi and Kutaisi."

Ghenadie yelled, "I'm away. I'll see you later. Hopefully."

Anna asked, "Where's Ghenadie going? Isn't he coming with us?"

George shook his head. "He's taking the Lada. He'll be half an hour in front of us. If he sees any roadblocks or checkpoints he'll turn back and warn us. He's also going to talk to the cement factory on the way so that our journey looks official."

"And if the Lada blows up en route?"

"Then, of course, we'll pick him up and he'll come with one of us."

It was a scenic drive along the coast to Sukhumi, followed by miles and miles of pleasant woods and orchards. After an hour or so, the country became hillier and more heavily forested. Eventually, George indicated that he was turning into a small bar and café. As they entered the car park the little green Lada driven by Ghenadie pulled out of the car park and turned on to the road.

Over coffee George said, "Look relaxed; we're on holiday. Take your time, take photographs, don't look suspicious. Ghenadie has to make his business call and see if he can find us a hotel or inn for the night."

Petrov growled, "Don't look suspicious? We *are* suspicious! The four of us should not be seen sitting together and chatting like old friends. At lunch, we eat separately."

George said, "Alexei and I have been thinking. When we get near to Tbilisi, he's going to navigate us around the outskirts, so that if we're stopped you can say you followed instructions and didn't go into Tbilisi. That means we can't be sure of which road we'll use. Stay close so that we don't get separated."

David was confused. "I thought the plan was that you leave us at Tbilisi and we make our own way down to the rendezvous?"

"That's because there's nothing that far south of Yerevan to justify our being there. But Ghenadie's planning to ask at the cement works if there's anyone else we might visit near to Yerevan and, perhaps, do a short sightseeing detour while we're there."

They were approaching the Armenian border when they saw Ghenadie's Lada waiting for them. Ghenadie got out and came over to David. "There's a checkpoint at the border. You keep going and we'll catch up with you later. Don't worry."

As they pulled away, rather slowly, David said, "Don't worry? That's a damned stupid thing to say. Of course we'll worry. I reckon that's your Dad making sure that we're safe."

They drove through the checkpoint with the guards only giving a cursory look at their passports and Intourist travel permits. After a few miles David spotted a layby and pulled in to await the others. Forty five minutes later they saw George's Volga coming towards them.

The Volga pulled into the layby and George came over to their car. David rolled down his window. "What happened? How did you get through?"

"Ghenadie gave us his press permits and travel papers before he left and we bluffed our way through with those. The only problem is that we have to report to them on the way back tomorrow. But hopefully it will be OK because the real Ghenadie will join us later."

"How will he get through the checkpoint?"

"Don't forget he's 'Russian' driving a Ministry of Supply car on 'official' business. That car will be 'stolen' in Yerevan and he'll return with me."

"So, what's next?"

"All we have to do now is find the Marneuli Guesthouse, on the road just before Yerevan. The Meschines family will stay there. Ghenadie and I will find somewhere else to stay and then see you before you leave for the meeting tomorrow."

They were standing outside the guesthouse debating what to do about dinner when the little green Lada pulled up alongside. Ghenadie with his big grin got out and said, "Sorry to have been so long. I waited until the guards at the checkpoint changed shift."

Dinner that night was a very quiet affair. Each in their own way was worried about the outcome the following day. Having come so far, they all realised that there was no going back to disappear into the USSR. They talked about their concerns.

Petrov was worried that he had admitted his guilt and that both he and Anna would end up being shot. Anna just worried. George thought it might all be some fiendish KGB plot. David wondered if the Mule would turn up. What if he kept the half already paid and sold them out to the Reds? He took a piece of paper out of his pocket and stared at it.

"David, what's that scrap of paper that you keep looking at?"

David turned it over and showed it to George. All it had on it was, قاطر "This is what I have to show to the Mule. I have to ask if he reads Farsi and show him the paper."

Chapter 41

Next morning they met for breakfast. George turned up looking as dishevelled as he had when staying at the Paris flat. "Good Lord George what happened to you?"

"I had to sleep in the goddam car that's what happened to me. Ghenadie slept in the field."

After a quick breakfast the team broke up and went their separate ways. George and Ghenadie drove with them for a few miles to make sure they were on the road to the ruined monastery at Novorank. Ghenadie left the Lada where it wouldn't be found for a while then, with much waving and shouts of good luck, the Volga turned north back towards Yerevan.

The Meschines family drove through the mountains to the rendezvous at Novorank. David was apprehensive about staying at the same place for three nights if the Mule didn't show.

They approached Novorank through a deep ravine, then on to open mountainside. They could see the ruined church abandoned on the barren landscape. As they neared, David could see no sign of any other cars. It was only twenty minutes after two. His instructions were to wait until five.

As they pulled into a car parking space at the side of the church, a solitary figure emerged from the dark interior and stood by the door. David took his scrap of paper and walked to meet the man. He held out the piece of paper. The man took a quick look at it and said, in quite good English, "Mr Hopkins, it's good to meet you - typical English; always punctual." He looked over at the car. Petrov was just getting out. "Is that the man I'm taking over? I hope he's fit. We have some walking to do in order to get him over the border safely."

Petrov walked over and examined his guide from head to toe as if he was assessing a prize bull. "Mr Mule. Pleased to meet you, when do we start?"

"Now. While there's no one about." The Mule took Petrov's arm, turned him around, and pointed down the hillside at the back of the monastery.

"Fine. Let's go."

The Mule turned back to David. "Leave that thing parked outside your hotel in Maku and I'll find you in three days, maybe four."

Anna called after them. "Good luck, Dad. I love you."

David thought, 'me too, you miserable old git.'

Anna and David turned to face each other. Both felt a mixture of deflation and relief, thinking it would soon be all over. They held hands as they walked back to the car. David gave Anna a kiss on the cheek and they set off for the border in silence.

****

The border wasn't very busy and Anna wondered if that was a good thing or not. There were only two guards on duty. One sat in a tiny office smoking a cigarette, while the other examined the papers of those crossing the border. Within twenty minutes they were at the head of the queue while the guard perused their passports. "Have you enjoyed your visit to the USSR?"

Anna answered, "We've had a great vacation. Azerbaijan is a beautiful country."

"It's Armenia we've been to," David said.

Anna poked him in the ribs to shut him up.

The guard didn't seem to notice. "Where are you going to in Iran?"

255

"I am taking my wife to Tabriz, she's flying to Teheran to stay with friends. I'll be coming back to Russia in two days. I haven't finished my work here."

"Work? What work?"

David gave him some of the papers from the Ministry in Moscow authorising the report on the economies of the Southern states. The guard took one look at the papers, raised the barriers, and waved them through. "We'll see you the day after tomorrow, have a safe journey."

They looked at each other, amazed at how easy it had been.

"Why did you poke me when I said we were in Armenia?"

If I'd told him that we thought Armenia was lovely and we'd enjoyed our time there, we'd still be there arguing. He probably would have wanted a bribe to let us through."

"Why?"

"He was an Azerbaijani."

David pulled out the road map. He hadn't a clue what the road signs said. When they were approaching Mazargan he said, "I feel like Lawrence of Arabia here, this place is more like the deserts of the Middle East than Iran. Lawrence's camels could go days without water; our camel needs some petrol. If there isn't a gas station in Mazargan, I'll have to use one of the reserve cans."

By late afternoon they reached the dusty hotel in Maku that Moyuddin had booked for them. It was only slightly less dusty inside than out. They went to their room, desperate for a shower but they found that the hot tap didn't work, so they were reconciled to having a cold shower. However, when they turned on the cold tap, the water came out warm. David supposed that the cold water tank being in the roof was the reason for that.

The Mule had not given them any indication as to what time he would arrive. In fact he hadn't even committed to what day he would arrive. They had parked the Merc outside the hotel and waited as instructed.

The following day they waited in vain. All they saw was a never-ending stream of trucks heading for the Turkish border. With nothing to read and no radio, watching the traffic was the only entertainment they had. They had just gone inside for some lunch on the second day when they heard car doors slamming and some rather loud Russian being spoken. David peeped through the grimy window. It was Petrov and the Mule, standing by a fairly new American Jeep, shaking hands and exchanging bear hugs. Anna and David went outside to greet them.

The Mule said, "Mr David, you have to give me a letter for Moyuddin to say that I have delivered your father safely as agreed."

David went inside to write the letter while Anna and her father were celebrating their reunion. David thought that if the Mule could get Petrov across the border in one piece he might be useful to British Intelligence. He went back and gave the Mule the letter. As he did so, he steered him away from Anna and Petrov. "You did a great service for us getting him out. I wondered… would you be interested in working for British Intelligence on a regular basis? We would pay well."

"If I work for the British would I be allowed to continue with my normal business?"

"Which is what?"

"Smuggling, of course! If so I would do it for ten thousand American dollars a year."

"No. that's too much. Five thousand dollars a year, plus a bonus of five thousand; - if you perform as we wish."

"That is agreed." They shook hands and the Mule jumped into his Jeep and was gone.

Chapter 42

Anna asked, "When do we leave for the Turkish border?" Before David could answer, Petrov said, "Not today, not until I've had some sleep. And I need somewhere to lie down where my arse can recover."

Anna and David exchanged a questioning look. David said, "OK, Alexei, just how did you get across?"

"After I left you we walked about eight kilometres - mainly downhill, fortunately - to where he had a battered Gaz four wheel drive, hidden in a barn. We drove about fifteen kilometres on a dirt track to where there was another wooden hut. We left the Gaz there and continued on horseback with two more tethered behind us. I don't know how far we travelled. Then, when it was completely dark, we camped. We slept until lunch time then started again after lunch, up hills, down hills, across a stream and a big river, sometimes on a track, sometimes not. At one point, we had an appointment with a border guard. He and the Mule had a smoke and did some business and then we were on our way again. We travelled, walking and riding, most of the second night and had a rest for two hours or so when it was almost dawn. Then, after another ride we came to the place where he keeps that Jeep. That's it. All very straightforward...if you're the Mule."

"How can he find his way in the dark, if it's not a proper track?"

"That's the interesting bit," said Petrov. "Before 1920 there was a big smuggling racket across the border. Some routes belonged to the Russian smugglers and some to the Iranians. They never argued; each kept to their specific routes. After 1920 the Russian border police closed down all the Russian smuggling routes, but they never knew the Iranian routes, so they're still used. I get the impression that the Mule has an almost exclusive business across that border."

"What does he smuggle across?"

"I didn't ask. As long as he got me across I didn't care but I can guess. Iran does grow an awful lot of poppies."

After something of a sleep they left for the border, the Merc looking incongruous in the long line of trucks.

Ahead, they saw the border at Bazargan, with a large sign reading 'Welcome to Turkey'. At least, they assumed that was what it said. It was bad enough trying to read signs in Iran but Turkish seemed infinitely worse. As they neared the checkpoint they could see the queue of at least fifty large trucks waiting there and David pulled in behind the last truck, "It looks as if we're going to be here for several hours. I hope there's a loo."

Anna snuggled down in her seat, "Wake me up when we get to the other side."

Just as she said that an Iranian official rapped on the car door and pointed to an unused channel at the checkpoint, "Cars."

David gave him a wave and pulled out of the queue to cross to the channel reserved for cars. He handed the three passports to the Iranian border guard who, with only a cursory glance into the car, lifted the barrier and waved them through. "Nearly there," David said.

They stopped at the Turkish barrier. Two border guards sauntered over to their car. They looked bored stiff but examined the passports carefully and then peered into the car, comparing their likeness to the passports. After quite a lot of Turkish discussions, one turned to David and asked in English, "Why are you coming to Turkey? What is your business here?"

"We're French. Do you speak French?"

"No, only English. Why do you wish to come to Turkey?"

"I'm taking my wife and her father to Ankara. They will then fly to Istanbul to stay with friends. I'll then return to Teheran where I work."

The guard lifted the barrier and waved them through, pointing to a parking space outside an office block.

"Why aren't they just letting us through?" said Anna, sounding worried.

David tried to reassure her. "I don't know. Keep calm. Everything will be fine."

They entered the space and a senior police officer came out of the office. "I have information that you are travelling under an assumed name and that your passports are forged and not valid. I have a warrant for your arrest for the murder of three policemen in Russia."

David, Anna and Petrov sat for a moment in stunned silence. Then David spoke. "What? That's nonsense. We haven't murdered anyone. Do we *look* like murderers?"

"This warrant is issued by the senior judge in Erzerum. You will be extradited to Russia to face charges there."

The office door opened and a man and woman came out and stood facing them. The woman screamed, "I was right, Kabalevsky. I *knew* we would catch them here." She pointed at Alexei, "Him. That's Alexei Petrov, the murderer."

Chapter 43

No one had noticed a Turkish Army officer walking over to them. "I am Major Asim Kasalay. What's the problem here?"

The Turkish policeman saluted smartly and said, "They're being arrested for extradition to Russia on a charge of murder."

"They most certainly aren't. Mr and Mrs Meschines and their father are guests of the Turkish government."

The policeman bridled. "I am Inspector Sinan Kucuk. You have no authority here. I am in charge, they are under arrest."

"I think you will find that I *do* have the authority. *That* is my authority," said the Major, and pointed to an armoured car and two armoured personnel carriers that had drawn up facing the office.

Zhukova shouted, "If he's not going back alive, then he will go back dead." As she pulled an automatic out of her bag, a shot rang out. The Major turned to another officer standing behind him and said in a quiet voice, "Thank you, Captain Ilgin. We cannot allow officials of other states to use violence on our territory."

Kabalevsky looked at the Major. "I greatly regret that your action was necessary. Commissar Zhukova had no business to be carrying a gun in Turkey; I certainly didn't know that she had one. I shall report that you were totally justified in shooting her, to prevent what would have been a serious diplomatic incident."

He faced Petrov and, speaking in Russian, said, "Monsieur Meschines, please accept my apology for this unpleasant affair."

The lid opened on one of the APCs and a helmeted head popped out. "Hi, Alain, I hope you didn't think I'd deserted you."

It was Michel Charnay dressed in what looked like an ill-fitting Turkish Army uniform, complete with combat helmet. He gave a stunned David a broad grin. "Haven't had as much excitement in ages."

The Turkish Major ignored the interruption and turned to the police officer who was standing looking pale, still holding the arrest warrant. "You and your crooked judge will be interrogated at the army base tomorrow. We will determine just how much you were paid to stage this charade." He then went up to Kabalevsky and, speaking in a very quiet voice, said, "Mr Kabalevsky, I think it would be a good idea if you returned to Russia as soon as you can. Tomorrow Kucuk and his friend will tell me who paid them; that person will then be charged with the bribery of state officials." He signalled to two of his men and pointed with his foot at the body of Commissar Zhukova. "You two get this moved and buried somewhere." He turned to David. "We're now going back to the barracks at Dogubayazit. Do you want to come in our vehicle or follow us in your car?"

David said, "I'd like to go with Michel, and Anna can come with me."

The Major nodded. Every movement he made was brisk and efficient. "Captain, you will drive the Mercedes back to camp. I will travel with our guests in the carrier behind the armoured car. You follow me and the second APC can bring up the rear."

The convoy set off for the army base. Over the deafening roar of the engine David yelled into Michel's ear. "Were you expecting trouble at the border? It was good so see you arrive, just in time."

"We didn't just arrive, you know. We've been waiting for you for four days. We - or I should say the Turks - have had two observers in Iran watching over you like guardian angels since

263

you arrived in Maku. The reception committee was arranged by the Turkish High Command. They advised that in this part of Turkey there is a high proportion of brigands and bandits, who would do anything for a few thousand dollars. Most of the officials, police, judges and administrators are on the take from somebody. So they anticipated something like this happening."

They hit a rock and bounced a foot in the air. David asked, "How far are we going in this thing?"

Michel laughed. "It's only about another ten kilometres to the army base. We've a short take-off plane waiting to take us to Ankara. Then we've a plane waiting to take Petrov and I back to Paris. Your friends from the Washington Post will be coming to join you in Ankara. I understand they've made the travel arrangements for you and your wife back to Paris. I think the Major has arranged for someone to drive the Mercedes back to Ankara."

They all fell silent. It was just too difficult to talk over the deafening roar of the engine. At last, they came to a standstill and the engine was turned off. Anna said, "Can I get out first? I'm going to be sick."

They all climbed out into the fresh air. A smart suited man walked up to them. "Welcome to Turkey. I'm Ziya Tasciolglu from the Defense Ministry in Ankara. It's my job, together with Monsieur Charnay, to ensure that you have a pleasant stay in Turkey."

David replied, "I'm sure we will, thanks to your Major Kasalay."

Tascioglu asked, "Well, Major, everything went well, I assume?"

"Oh yes, just a minor dispute with two friends from across the border; nothing serious."

Three hours later they touched down at Akinci airforce base outside of Ankara. As they walked across the tarmac they could see George and Ghenadie waiting for them. George, with a big grin on his face, whooped, "We did it!"

Ghenadie with an even bigger grin than usual simply asked, "Did you have any problems at the border?"

David and Alexei both started to answer, "Not at the border. Some mad Russian woman tried to shoot me after we were in Turkey."

"The Turkish officer shot her before she could pull the trigger."

George asked, "Who was she?"

"Zhukova, Commissar Zhukova," said David.

Alexei shrugged. "Don't look at me. I'd never seen her before. I tell you something, that man Kabalevsky was calling the shots, never seen him before either."

Michel, Tasciolglu and another officer came over to them. "The plan is for us to stay here tonight and then we go back to Paris tomorrow. We can have a shower and get changed and we'll all have dinner together tonight."

"I haven't any clean clothes."

"Neither have I," said David.

The officer told them that he would get them some clean uniforms, "But they might not fit very well."

Dinner that evening was a strange occasion, elation mixed with tiredness, comradeship that would end once they were back in Paris. Nevertheless, everyone was enjoying animated chat, when an officer entered and passed a piece of paper to Tasciolglu who said nothing, left the room and came back few minutes later. Shortly after, two senior officers entered and spoke quietly to him.

The others, sensing that something was wrong, looked at him in anticipation.

"Gentlemen - sorry Anna - we have just heard that the Mercedes has been destroyed by a bomb about eighty kilometres West of Dogubayazit. Apparently, it was hidden in a culvert under the road. A press release is being prepared. There were no survivors. Mr and Mrs Meschines and Mr Meschines, senior, were all killed in the explosion. It is thought that the bomb was placed by Kurdish rebels."

Petrov stood up. "Kurdish rebels my arse. It's that bastard Kabalevsky; he was too polite at the border. He'd arranged that without telling the Zhukova woman."

Michel thought for a moment, "This might be a blessing in disguise. David, it means that you and Anna can return to the UK as Mr and Mrs Hopkins and Alexei will become someone else within twenty-four hours of our landing in Paris. As far as we know the Reds never made the link between the 'Meschines' and the Hopkins."

****

The following morning, the French Air Force plane started warming its engines at the far side of the airfield. Michel and Alexei met Anna just after breakfast. "We'll be leaving soon. Say goodbye to your father now. You won't be able to see him for a few weeks. When we get back to Paris we'll ensure that he's safe and comfortable and he'll contact you as soon as he's settled."

Anna gave her father a big hug. "I love you, Dad. I'm glad you're now safe."

"Thanks, Anna, and thank that husband of yours. You've a good man there. Look after him."

Chapter 44

The Washington Post had their big story and, as a result, David, Anna, George and Ghenadie flew back to Paris, First Class, on an Air France flight out of Ankara. They sat drinking champagne but, while they had a great sense of satisfaction, they all felt a great sense of deflation as well.

George summed up the mood. "The truth is, that for the four of us, we will probably do nothing as exciting for the rest of our lives." They realised that, once back in Paris, their team was finished; they had one day remaining. Then Ghenadie had to return to Moscow, David had a pile of work waiting for him at the office, and George had received a cable in Ankara asking him to go to Washington as soon as possible.

Ghenadie said, "There's no doubt, George, you are going to get a big promotion; they haven't had a story as big as this since the McCarthy-Army affair."

"Promotion? I doubt it; in fact, I'll probably get fired. I've overrun my year's expense budget by seven thousand dollars and the Mercedes wasn't insured for being blown up."

"Quit worrying. I never told you how much the Ministry are paying for our economic survey. We'll show a profit at the end of the day, don't you worry."

Anna said, "Don't forget the two Ladas - one destroyed and one stolen."

Ghenadie looked at George, who frowned, "Ladas? I don't remember using any Ladas!"

****

Two days later, they were sitting in the office in Paris eating pastries and drinking coffee when they heard a familiar voice outside. The door opened and Giuseppe breezed in. There were smiles, hugs and handshakes all round. George asked, "How did you know we were back?"

Giuseppe laughed, "Perfume and chocolates." Pointing to the outer office.

As they recounted their story Giuseppe listened with interest. George recounted the story with glee, interrupted often by David and Anna. "David said the only time it looked like going wrong was in Turkey when that mad woman Zhukova tried to shoot Alexei."

Giuseppe jumped up. "Zhukova? Commissar Zhukova? That bitch interrogated me for two days. Her mate Kabalevsky believed me but she didn't. I heard her say she would have me followed to Krasnodar, that's why I didn't go."

George said, "They must have been hot on our heels all the time."

"I'm not so sure. I got my own back on her in Moscow. I leaked it to the press that the KGB had lost a prisoner and he'd caught the train to Omsk."

"We met Kabalevsky in Turkey. He seemed a much nicer guy... though... he *did* try to blow Petrov up with a bomb."

George said, "You know, I'm not sure about that either. The Turks never told us who was in the Merc when it was blown up. They didn't seem upset about losing three army officers. We only *assumed* Kabalevsky was behind it because he was so reasonable at the border."

Anna said, "That nice Turkish officer told me that it was probably Kurdish rebels who'd done it."

George continued, deep in thought, "You don't get to be the head of the DSTE by being a nice guy. Lefaivre has the reputation of being one of the smartest, snakiest guys in the business."

"You mean sneakiest."

"No. I don't. I mean snakiest."

Chapter 45

With a great sense of anti-climax Anna and David returned from Paris, back to their flat in Ealing and the boring - if pleasantly tranquil - everyday life of going to the office and earning a living. David could imagine the pile of unread mail that would be waiting for him. He hoped that there wouldn't be a request for an urgent meeting in Poland, or wherever. He wanted a rest from Eastern Europe and its problems.

Within thirty minutes or so Marian appeared at the door. "I knew you were back. I could hear the clattering and banging from the kitchen. Have you had a good holiday? Where did you get to?"

David had no intention of letting on where they had been, so he settled for a half truth. "We have been staying in Paris with friends. Very quiet – a nice relaxing time."

"I told that friend of yours, Giles somebody, he called twice asking where you were. I told him that you hadn't said where you were going. He asked if I'd had a card or message from you that would give him a clue as to your whereabouts. Apparently, he'd called your office and someone told him that you were away on business and when he asked where, they checked and apologised and told him that you were on vacation. He seemed rather annoyed with you."

"Thanks, Marian, I'm sorry that he's been pestering you. The guy's becoming a pain in the rear."

David couldn't wait any longer, his curiosity getting the better of him. He rang Giles at home then, receiving no reply, tried his number at Department 14. When Giles eventually answered,

David said, "I hear that you've been looking for me. What do you want?"

"Where the hell have you been? We needed you."

"Tough! After your behaviour last time, I owe you nothing. My wife and I have been staying with friends in Paris; we've had two weeks' holiday."

"You've been away for three!"

David was enjoying winding Giles up. "Part of the time I was on business visiting can factories."

"Well, what I said last time still holds. Anna is going back to Russia."

"No need to take that snotty tone with me. And I suggest that you ask your Red friends if they still want her. Did you know that Petrov is neither ill nor dead?" Giles didn't answer. "But you *did* know that they wanted her back to use her against Petrov."

Giles remained silent.

"I don't think they'll want her back, now that Petrov is no longer in Russia." He didn't wait for a response. Slamming the phone down was very satisfying.

****

Two days later David was sitting in his office at Park Royal when the telephone rang,

"Call for you, David, he wouldn't give his name."

The caller introduced himself as Rishton, from the Foreign Office. "I've heard a lot about you and your exploits from colleagues here in the Foreign Office. I would be honoured if you would join me for dinner either at home or at the Foreign Office on Tuesday or Wednesday to talk things over. Not surprisingly you've fallen out with Giles and his friends, so I'm taking over from Giles for the time being. We've had various reports about your adventures and would like to hear your version. Would you like to come to the Foreign Office and we'll have an informal dinner where we can chat uninterrupted?"

"Who else will be there?"

"Only one other, Sir Peter Lupton."

"What does he do? I don't think I've heard of him."

"You will have heard him referred to as 'C'."

David went quiet. "This sounds more like a heavy grilling than a friendly chat. However, if it's the latter I would like to bring someone with me."

"Who would that be?"

"My wife."

Rishton said, "That's a brilliant idea. We would both like to meet you and your wife, very much indeed."

****

When Anna and David arrived at the Foreign Office and showed their passes, they were escorted by a uniformed official to the dining room on the first floor. It was a majestic room with heavy drapes and a gilded ceiling. The long dining table was set for fourteen people but the four of them sat at one end of the table, like four solitary peas in an enormous pod.

They had drinks - rather large G & Ts which David suspected were designed to loosen the tongue of any guests of the FO. Then they sat down to dinner. After two courses, during which there was a pleasant exchange of trivial chat, Sir Peter turned to David.

"You know, we were very intrigued, nay, mystified as to how you two got out of Bulgaria."

"So we've been told a number of times. That's our little secret. Just in case we need to go on... holiday... again."

C looked at Anna. She gave him that winning smile and winked at him. David saw C's reaction; it was the end of the match. C had fallen in love with his wife, he knew they couldn't lose.

C said, "On the subject of holidays, I hear that you have just got back from one. Where did you get to this time?"

"Southern Russia."

"What on earth for? What's the attraction there? I've always thought it a boring place with flat, non-existent scenery, uncivil, uncultured people and all the decent buildings falling down."

"The area was chosen for me. My company asked me to visit the can-making factory in Ufa and the cannery in Orenburg. When a friend of mine heard about the trip he arranged for me to get a freelance job with the Washington Post, to write an article on the economy and the industries of that region."

"Oh yes, we've heard of your relationship with that newspaper. You might be interested to learn that two weeks ago I received a telling-off from the editor of that paper. Apparently, one member of staff here in London had tried to lean on him not to publish anything he heard from his London correspondent on matters of security."

David thought that Giles must be losing his marbles to try that with a newspaper. Most papers would then do just the opposite. He was about to ask the question when C started up again.

"The editor told me that not even the President of the United States can lean on the Washington Post. He said, 'If it's legal, and not against the interests of the USA, then we will publish.' At the time I hadn't a clue what he was on about, so I assured him that no one in our organisation had the authority to make such threats. In the end we finished up having a quite amicable chat."

Rishton, who had said very little during the evening, suddenly chimed in, "We've been told that Petrov is no longer in the USSR."

Anna interrupted him, "By Petrov, do you mean my Dad?"

Sir Peter said, "I'm sorry, Anna, yes of course we mean your father. Is he alive and well?"

"Yes he's very well, thank you."

"Do you know where he is now?"

"Any dutiful daughter who is concerned for his welfare, would know the whereabouts of her father."

"I only have sons, and the only thing they care about is the weekly allowance they get from me." Sir Peter sounded rueful.

Rishton asked, "Do you think that it would be possible for us to talk to your father?"

David put his hand on Anna's. "He won't come to the UK, but he's agreed to answer - truthfully - any questions that you put to him through Anna."

"David, are we correct in assuming that you played some part in getting him out?"

Anna jumped in. "No, he didn't play a part in it. He organised it and masterminded it, just like he did for me."

Having finished the sweet course the cheeseboard was then placed in the middle of the table and Rishton took the stopper from the port decanter and started to pass it around the table. When it came to David he took some port and, to Sir Peter's surprise, he passed the decanter to his right. "You didn't expect that did you? When Anna disappeared because you intended to send her back to Russia, where was the last place you would look?"

Neither of them answered. Then, after a few moments, a look of astonishment appeared on the face of C. "No! I don't believe it. You didn't take her to Russia with you?"

David smiled, "I told you that I was unpredictable." Rishton looked uncomfortable and Anna seemed to be enjoying herself.

"It was a great advantage my having a wife who couldn't speak any Russian but who could understand every word they said."

Rishton asked, "Well, how did you get him across the border?"

"More important, which border?" chipped in C.

"I'm sorry. We're not saying. What we will do, however, is give you an incredible agent in Southern Russia. For ten thousand dollars a year you can have him exclusively, five thousand now and five thousand paid into a UK bank account which is his, provided he stays loyal. He knows that if he's arrested he's on his own, but - if he needs it – you'll provide him with an ID and a British passport and help him get to the West."

"What's his name?"

"He never gave us his real name; he goes by the nickname of 'The Mule'."

Sir Peter said "We can go into the details at another meeting. Another issue that we need to discuss is that there have been some staff changes since you went away."

"Oh?"

"We've decided to close the Collis Bank operation. It's outlived its usefulness and Colonel Collis is well past retiring age. It will be announced formally within a few weeks. All creditors will be paid, the accounts closed and the business wound up. Your friend Giles is being transferred to an operation in South

America. In the immediate future he's based in the Canary Islands."

David didn't know what to say. He assumed that Giles had blotted his copy book with his behaviour to Anna or by upsetting the Washington Post.

"He was a friend of yours, wasn't he?"

"Yes. He was very kind to me when I first came to London and his mother and my mother are good friends. However, he wasn't totally honest with me when he started using me as a courier. His friendship depended on my usefulness to him."

C pushed his chair back from the table and sat looking at David. "Now that business is all cleared up, will you come and work for us full time?"

David didn't wait to answer, "As I told Giles, the advantage that I have is that I can think outside of the box, act like a maverick, do the unexpected. I'm not sure that I'd fit into the Foreign Office hierarchy and discipline."

"Probably not," said C, smiling. "But would you mind if we ask your wife if *she* would like to work for us. We could use another analyst in our Russian section. We have lots of Russian linguists in GCHQ and I'm sure their translations are accurate. What we *really* need is someone who thinks like a Russian, someone who can explain to us what the information really means."

They all looked at Anna expectantly.

****

Two days later, David and Anna sat down to dinner. Anna looked flushed and happy, but as though her mind wasn't really on what she was doing. She had already been back into the kitchen twice for things she'd forgotten. "So, you've decided to take the job then? Is that what you're so excited about?"

276

Anna smiled. "On the contrary, I've decided *not* to take the job."

David put down his fork. "Really? I thought you would jump at the chance. When we were in Paris you said you were looking forward to getting back to work."

"I'm going to be too busy."

"Doing what?"

Anna looked at him and grinned. "Why, looking after the baby, of course."

"The...? I... What...?"

"You'd better sit down before you fall."

Epilogue

David sat in St James' Park on the seat that he and Anna had claimed as their own. He thought about everything that had happened since Anna had announced she was pregnant. Life had settled down to something approaching normality, although David knew that, with a baby on the way, things would never really be 'normal' again.

Anna and he had bought an Edwardian house in Richmond and had an idyllic life there. David, though he still travelled widely in Europe, had given up the world of intelligence and spies. That business was now left to Anna, who worked as an analyst at the Ministry of Defence, until starting maternity leave. Anna's father had kept his new name and seemed to be very settled in Paris. He had developed a close knit group of friends within the Russian émigré community in Paris and attended St. Anthoine, the Russian Orthodox Church in Billancourt. Petrov of the KGB had disappeared and his earlier life never became known. Anna and David visited him in Paris regularly, but he had never visited them in the UK. He and David had become good friends, though their escape from Russia was never discussed. When they first visited him in his new home in St. Cloud he had said to David.

"I will be eternally grateful for what you have done for Anna and I."

Petrov had kept his part of the bargain and a substantial amount of information had been passed to MI6 via Anna. David never asked what it was; he was no longer interested in spying, intelligence and the machinations of the Foreign Office. His exciting years working with Giles in Department 14, had, in hindsight, been rather *too* exciting.

****

David could remember the following nine months very clearly. They were months of great happiness and laughter. They laughed at the size of Anna's tummy. They laughed the first time that Igor had started kicking. He remembered vividly the day that Anna had gone into labour and he had rushed her to the maternity unit, still laughing.

After a wait of six hours the baby had been born. He remembered the nurse bringing Igor for him to see.

"I'm going to take him for a little wash, but I just thought you'd like to see how beautiful he is."

"Can I see Anna now?"

"Not yet; the doctors are with her. The nurse will come to tell you when you can go in to see her."

After a wait of what had seemed like forever, he remembered the look on the doctor's face when he came to see him.

"I'm sorry David. Your wife is seriously ill. We had no idea. We had no warning that it was going to go so wrong,"

David looked at him, "Is she going to be alright?"

He remembered the doctor's face, holding back tears, as he shook his head.

"Go in and sit with her for a while."

Anna was deathly white, but she recognised him and gave him a little smile. David sat and held her hand. It was very cold.

Anna whispered, "Our baby, is he going to be...?"

They hadn't thought too much about names, not knowing if it was going to be a boy or girl. He said the first name coming into his head. "Igor is fine; he is a big healthy boy."

"Igor, Igor..." and Anna passed away.

****

David had come to their bench many times in the weeks and months that had followed, and he still came often. When it had been suggested that he give up Igor for adoption, his reaction to the proposal was somewhat violent.

"I saved Anna's life. I saved Anna's father's life. I'll be damned if I'll give up Igor just because it might be difficult." The social worker who had made the proposal hadn't dared to ask what he had saved them from.

His employers had been totally supportive and his colleagues and the three people who worked for him had been very kind. They had soon noticed that, sometimes, he took a long lunch break. He always returned with very red eyes and had obviously been crying. Lewis, a young man who worked for David, had followed him a few times. It was partly out of curiosity but mainly out of concern for his boss. He enjoyed working for David and respected him. Lewis thought that he had a duty of care. He knew that David would have cared for him in the same way. He'd reported back to the others that David always went to sit on the same bench in the park. He would sit with a blank look on his face, sometimes with tears rolling down his cheeks, sometimes just staring at the ducks. He never ate lunch or had anything to drink when he was there.

Over the years, however, the extended lunchtimes had become less frequent; sometimes two or three months would elapse between visits. He still came, as often as he could, but he didn't cry these days.

Igor, now growing up into a boisterous imp, was the sole reason for David's existence. As David sat on his and Anna's bench, he thought that at Easter he would take Igor to see his grandfather in Paris before he started at nursery. He and Petrov had become good friends and kept in touch. Petrov had only once come to the UK, and that was for Anna's funeral. Although neither David nor Anna had been great churchgoers, David had arranged the funeral in St Peter's, the Russian Orthodox Church in South Kensington.

That day, the church had been full of mourners, half of whom were spies and the other half spycatchers. He remembered his surprise seeing the new C in the congregation. After the service he had introduced Petrov to C.

"Sir John, this is Anna's father."

"I'm delighted to meet you sir, but not in these circumstances."

Petrov said nothing.

C continued. "Are you comfortable in Paris? I hope so, because we are very, very grateful to you for your service over many years."

Petrov shook his hand, "Thank you. She was the sole reason for my existence."

C said, "She was a wonderful woman, adored by all."

Petrov didn't reply, simply nodded in agreement, tears running down his cheeks.

****

As it was a lovely summer day, David had left the office just after midday and walked to St James' Park. Their seat was empty and he sat looking at the ducks. He didn't cry these days. He didn't think about anything really, but he liked watching the planes going into Heathrow and the scurrying of the ducks as another crust was thrown to them.

He became vaguely aware of a young girl, walking towards him. She stopped and extended her hand, holding out a bag of sweets.

"Would you like a sweet, Daddy?"

Instinctively, he held out his hand and took a sweet. "Thank you." Before he put it into his mouth he realised that something wasn't right.

David went hot and cold at the same time. His pulse was racing and he felt faint. His eyes wouldn't focus properly. He thought he was going mad. Standing in front of him was Nicole, aged eight, just as she had looked in the childhood pictures she had showed him. She had those big brown eyes and the long dark hair with slight waves, which he had seen so many times before. He couldn't put words into his mouth; he just continued looking at the young girl. She was beautiful, amazingly so.

"Why did you say that?"

"Mummy told me to say it."

"Where is your Mummy now?"

"She's standing behind you."

David turned to look. Nicole, standing some thirty yards or so behind him, started to walk towards them. He didn't know if it was really happening and he didn't know what to say.

Eventually, he stammered, "How did you know where to find me?"

"I've been trying to pluck up enough courage to come and see you for over a year. I went to Marian's. She told me where you lived and where you worked. This morning we called at your office to see if we might have lunch together. We'd just missed you, but a nice man called Lewis told me exactly where to find you."

"How did he know where I would be?"

"Lewis told me that he wasn't sure, but he thought that this seat had some special memories for you. Is it... you and Anna?"

David nodded a 'yes', still bemused by what had happened.

"A couple of years ago I met an old colleague of yours in Bordeaux, Roland Porter. When I realised that he worked for D&A France I asked about you. He told me that you had left D&A to join an American chemical company and he told me about the tragic death of Anna."

"Why did you wait all this time?"

Nicole shook her head and shrugged.

All the time the little girl stood looking at him, with those big brown eyes that he had loved so many years ago.

"What's your name?"

"Marie-Hélène."

"That's a lovely name. I've never met a Marie-Hélène before."

Turning back to Nicole, he said, "And you, what's happened to you? Are you and your husband still in Bordeaux?"

"Yes, we're still in Bordeaux, but I'm not married. The marriage...well... it didn't last three years."

David didn't ask, but Nicole continued, "André was my childhood sweetheart and I think you know that our families encouraged us to get married. It was a way of amalgamating the two vineyards and ensuring the continuity of the family business in future generations. They didn't want me to have a career in pharmaceuticals in Basle or London. What his family knew, but didn't say, was that he was homosexual. He wasn't interested in girls; only his boyfriends."

David looked at Hélène and raised his eyebrows to ask.

"Marie-Hélène is *our* child, David. I knew I was pregnant when I went back to France but said nothing. I knew of your deep love for Anna. I could only spoil that, but gain nothing. So I pretended that André was the father, and everyone in Bordeaux accepted that, including André, of course, because it meant he could continue to hide his secret. We continued the charade for three years, but he would just disappear with one of his boyfriends for weeks at a time. I was left looking after Marie-Hélène, the house and two vineyards. When the break came it was quick and painless and, in the end, André was relieved to be able to get away from the lies and the responsibility. Both his father and mine helped me to find a good manager for the vineyards. He's now merged the two businesses and taken over all the day-to-day management. "

"Mummy, I'm hungry. Can I have a cake, please?"

Nicole looked at her watch. David stepped close and took her into his arms, kissed her on both cheeks and on the lips and held her very tight. Nicole was startled.

David had suddenly turned into a block of stone and stepped back, looking out over the lake. "What's wrong?" said Nicole.

"She's standing by the lake looking at us."

"Who is?"

"It's Anna. She's by the lake watching us."

Nicole looked but there was no one there. She took David's hand. "Yes I see her, but don't you see she's smiling? She's happy that we're together at last." She turned to Marie-Hélène, "Come along, we have to get Daddy home and look after him, and you have to look after your young brother."

David was worried it was only a dream. "Which hotel are you in? Do you have any luggage to collect?"

"We're not in a hotel; we're staying with Marian and Alistair."

****

As the years went by they became an everyday but wonderfully happy family. Nicole kept control over the vineyard and the 'négociant éleveur'. Every two months they went to Bordeaux so that she would know exactly what was happening in the business. In late September they all went to help with the grape

284

harvest, which the children thought was great fun, particularly being spoiled by grandparents and all the neighbours. At school Marie-Hélène and Igor did well, loving sciences and maths; to them languages were a bore. David had tried to teach Igor to speak Russian since he was a tot, and Grandad Petrov also liked to speak Russian with his grandson. Marie-Hélène was bilingual in French and English and, because of her, Igor also spoke excellent French. However the 'Imp' hadn't changed. Knowing that his French teacher also spoke Russian, if he was asked a question in French he would answer, or at least try to answer, in Russian. Invariably this caused great amusement in class.

Igor was now in his third year at High School, and Marie-Hélène was studying for her 'A' levels. The television was on too loud, as usual, and David was trying to do the Telegraph crossword. Nicole was trying to repair a rip in Igor's school trousers. When the programme finished, Marie-Hélène turned off the TV and she and Igor came over to David and stood in front of him, nudging each other. When David finally looked up, Igor said, "Mum says you used to be a spy, is it true?"

"Was I a spy? I suppose I was."

They asked another question, one that was not answered. Nicole looked at him, and knew that he was a long way away, probably with Anna.